PANTHEON GIRLS

Praise for Jean Copeland

Spellbound—co-authored with Jackie D

"The story is a mixture of history and present day, fantasy and real life, and is really well done. I especially liked the biting humor that pops up occasionally. The characters are vibrant and likable (except the bad guys, who are really nasty). There is a good deal of angst with both romances, but a lot of 'aww' moments as well."
—*Rainbow Reflections*

"*Spellbound* is a very exciting read, fast-paced, thrilling, funny too…The authors mix politics and the fight against patriarchy with time travel and witch fights with brilliant results."—*Jude in the Stars*

"[T]he themes and contextual events in this book were very poignant in relation to the current political climate in the United States. The fashion in which existing prejudices related to race, socioeconomic status, and gender were manipulated to cause discord were staggering, but also a reflection of the current state of things here in the USA. I really enjoyed this aspect of the book and I am so glad that I read it when I did."—*Mermaid Reviews*

The Ashford Place

"[A] charming story that I can recommend to anyone who likes a well-written mystery with a good dose of romance."—*Rainbow Reflections*

"Another enjoyable story from Jean Copeland with a bit of a difference. I think this book is definitely one to enjoy with a glass of wine near the warm fire."—*Les Rêveur*

The Revelation of Beatrice Darby

"*The Revelation of Beatrice Darby* at its epicentre is a story…of discovering oneself and learning to not only live with it but to also love it. This book is definitely worth a read."—*Lesbian Review*

"Debut author Jean Copeland has come out with a novel that is abnormally superb. The pace whirls like a hula-hoop; the plot is as textured as the fabric in a touch-and-feel board book. And, with more dimension than a stereoscopic flick, the girls in 3-D incite much pulp friction as they defy the torrid, florid, horrid outcomes to which they were formerly fated."—*Curve*

"This story of Bea and her struggle to accept her homosexuality and find a place in the world is absolutely wonderful…Bea was such an interesting character and her life was that of many gay people of the time—hiding, shame, rejection. In the end though it was uplifting and an amazing first novel for Jean Copeland."—*Inked Rainbow Reads*

The Second Wave

"This is a must-read for anyone who enjoys romances and for those who like stories with a bit of a nostalgic or historic theme."
—*Lesbian Review*

"Copeland shines a light on characters rarely depicted in romance, or in pop culture in general."—*The Lesbrary*

"The characters felt so real and I just couldn't stop reading. This is one of those books that will stay with me a long time."—*2017 Rainbow Awards Honorable Mention*

Summer Fling

"The love story between Kate and Jordan was one they make movies about, it was complex but you knew from the beginning these women had found their soul mates in each other."—*Les Rêveur*

By the Author

The Revelation of Beatrice Darby

The Second Wave

Summer Fling

The Ashford Place

Spellbound

One Woman's Treasure

Swift Vengeance

Poison Pen

Pantheon Girls

Visit us at www.boldstrokesbooks.com

PANTHEON GIRLS

by

Jean Copeland

2023

Credits
Editor: Shelley Thrasher
Production Design: Stacia Seaman
Cover Design by Jeanine Henning

Acknowledgments

I could not keep doing what I love so much without the support of a legion of amazing women: Sandy, Rad, and all the ladies behind the scenes at Bold Strokes Books, especially my editor, the delightful Shelley Thrasher; my longtime BFF and beta reader, Anne Santello; and the many others who continue to buy, review, and share my books. And a special shoutout to the guys out there who've purchased my novels in support of my joyful craft. Thank you to my pal, former East Haven Mayor April Capone, for sharing her campaign knowledge on this one, and last but not least, thank you to the great CT brew masters Christian, Sean, and Johnny, who've always opened their brewery doors to me for my book launch parties! I thank you all so much and appreciate your loyalty.

This book is for all the women out there who know
how to be authentic, selfless, and supportive friends to other women.
I celebrate you.

CHAPTER ONE

Cassie Burke and her best friend, Maggie, sat across from each other at a sunlit table in New Haven's newest trendy bistro. She volleyed her attention between the entrance and Maggie as she awaited both their other friend Jenn and Maggie's next dubious move. As they both eyed the miniature salt-and-pepper shakers and ridiculously teeny individual bottles of hot sauce, Cassie flashed her the two-finger signal that she had her eyes on her.

"What?" Maggie said defensively.

"Please wait till after brunch before you pocket those shakers."

Maggie sucked in her cheek. "I don't know what you're talking about."

Cassie sighed, half entertained, half annoyed. "Why are you still doing this?"

"It makes me feel alive." Though her face was expressionless, her eyes sparkled with mischief.

"You're not embarrassed? You're fifty years old."

"Almost fifty," Maggie replied. "Now stop. You're ruining it for me. It's not exciting if you know I'm gonna do it."

Maggie liked stealing small things, a pastime she'd acquired a couple of years ago as a sort of reward for being the first one of their trio to complete menopause.

"I feel better knowing when you're gonna do it," Cassie said. "So I won't be caught off guard the day a loss-prevention officer finally escorts you away."

"A place like this doesn't care if you lift their salt shakers. They expect it."

Cassie rolled her eyes. "You need a hobby to make you feel alive, preferably one that won't result in misdemeanor charges. Better yet, how about a girlfriend?"

"I don't need a girlfriend," she replied, caressing the small crystal vase holding a fresh rose. "As you know, I've gone the way of intimate entanglements in the past and came to realize they're not for me."

"You can have a relationship and still be asexual, Mags. You're not the only asexual person in Connecticut."

"I know, but sometimes it feels that way."

Cassie slapped the linen tablecloth with determination. "Well, we're going to change that this year."

Maggie shrank in her seat. "No, we're not."

But Cassie was off and running. "This is our fiftieth year on this planet. Are we really just going to sit back and do the same old things we've always done?"

"Yes, we are."

"We're gonna shake things up for our half-century mark, Mags, and we're starting with you."

"No, we're not."

"Wait till Jenn gets here. She'll be so excited about this."

"No, she won't. Listen, Cass. How about reining it in for a minute? I'm fine with my life as a single woman. I don't want anyone to play matchmaker. If you insist on starting off the second half-century of our lives making major changes, let's start with you. Your relationship track record has left something to be desired, too, you know."

"Wow. I bet you've had that one on standby for a while."

Maggie grinned. "You know what I mean. I'd like to see you settled into a happy, stable relationship, too. But you can't force these things. They'll happen when they're meant to."

"I certainly believed that early on in life, but as you know, I've had reasons to become somewhat of a cynic."

Maggie lowered her voice to a conspiratorial whisper. "I mean, look at Jenn. She's been with Amelia for almost twenty years. I'd never want to be that settled."

Cassie gave a diplomatic shrug. "Well, it seems to work for them."

"Does it? I guess that's the magic recipe when it comes to relationships. It just seems like more work than I'm willing to put in."

Cassie nodded and glanced around the newly opened bistro, searching for signs of familiarity in its upscale modern decor. The renovated former factory building in New Haven had seen many incarnations in its hundred-plus-year existence, but her former nightclub, Pantheon, would live on as the one that had changed Cassie's life forever.

When she returned her gaze to the table, all the tiny hot-sauce bottles were gone. "You better give me one of those when the eggs come."

"Oh, look. Jenn's here," Maggie said excitedly.

Cassie waved.

The blond tips of Jenn's short, sleek hair reached toward the ceiling, unmoving as she rushed over to them. "Sorry I was running late. Oh, I couldn't wait to see you guys," she said as she gave each of them a long, tight hug.

"We *cannot* go months again without getting together," Cassie said as they sat. "I missed the fuck out of both of you."

"No more than a month—two, tops," Jenn said. "I can't believe what they've done to this place. It's just gorgeous, all windows."

"I can't believe this used to be Pantheon." Cassie glanced around nostalgically.

"I know, right?" Jenn said. "So many memories from those Pantheon days."

Cassie shook her head. "Crazy how the best and worst times of my life were centered around this space." She gazed at both of them and squeezed their hands. "Thank God you guys were with me through it all."

"It was all so wonderfully awkward to watch," Maggie said.

Jenn laughed as she spread her napkin in her lap. "Who'd ever have thought that over twenty years after it closed, we'd be sitting in the same place having brunch, planning our fiftieth birthday get-away?"

"For a minute there I wasn't sure you'd make it to fifty," Cassie said. "Not that I want to get all dark this morning."

"Yeah. This is supposed to be a happy, long-overdue reunion," Jenn said, but she appeared to be forcing her smile. She looked at the pitcher of mimosas sitting in front of her.

"I'm sorry," Maggie said. "I ordered a pitcher but didn't even think…"

Jenn waved her off. "Don't be silly. I told you guys that I chose clean living for my health. I don't expect or want anyone to change their habits around me. It's not a big deal."

"We're so impressed," Cassie said. "It was obviously a great decision. You've never looked better."

"Thank you." Jenn beamed. "That's really good to hear, especially now."

"Why? Because we're here planning our fiftieth birthday bash?" Maggie asked. "God. It sounds so weird to say."

Despite how great Jenn looked, the vibe felt off. Cassie exhaled to release the knot forming in her stomach. "Jenn, is everything okay?"

She tried to elude her concern. "Come on. I thought we weren't gonna go dark this morning."

Cassie refused to let it pass. "What's wrong?"

Jenn's hesitation was clearly making Maggie nervous, too. She grabbed Jenn's hand. "Please tell us."

"I just had my annual scan and…" She stopped as her voice began to quiver.

"Jesus," Cassie said involuntarily.

"They found something?" Maggie asked.

Jenn nodded. "My oncologist said not to worry. It could be nothing, but even if it is, they'll just remove my thyroid. She thinks they detected the problem early enough."

"She thinks?" Cassie said.

"Look," Jenn said. "Dr. Guerrera is the best cancer surgeon around." She pointed to her right breast. "Why do you think I'm still sitting here? If she says not to panic, I'm not gonna panic."

Cassie and Maggie exchanged glances as if giving each other permission to believe Jenn. Cassie then downed half of the mimosa left in her glass.

Jenn's eyes twinkled as she sipped from her water glass. "Hey, can we get back to the business at hand? We three old broads have a birthday extravaganza to plan."

"Yes, right." Cassie let out a cautious laugh at the remark as she pulled out a journal-style notebook. When she picked up her pen, her hand shook.

"Want me to be the notetaker?" Maggie asked.

"No. I'm fine." She inhaled deeply to calm herself. This wasn't the first time she'd had to face Jenn's mortality with her. But at this stage in their lives, she'd thought—hoped—they were over all the big challenges.

Jenn grabbed her forearm. "Cass. I'm gonna be okay."

She looked into Jenn's eyes. They were as intoxicating as they were when they were teenagers coming of age and discovering their sexuality together. What a time that was. Their friendship had endured many tests since it began, but none had been as terrifying as her bout with breast cancer a few years ago.

"Cass?" Jenn said.

"I know you're gonna be okay." She displayed the most confident smile she'd ever given. "I have no doubt. Now, what's the first item on our agenda?"

"We need to pick a destination," Maggie said. "I vote for P-Town."

Cassie grimaced. "Really? You don't want something tropical?"

"I was thinking something more exciting, like Vegas or LA," Jenn said.

Maggie shook her head. "I want something gay."

"That doesn't matter anymore," Jenn said. "It's the twenty-first century, not high school in the 80s."

"She has a point, Jenn," Cassie said. "If we leave the country, it does matter, depending on where we go."

Jenn sucked her cheek. "Okay. Then I'm putting a slash mark through any developing nation or one currently under Sharia law."

"This is dumb," Cassie said. "This should be easy."

"On the contrary," Maggie said. "We're marking a huge milestone birthday and over thirty years of friendship. Choosing a location is the most important detail of this whole plan."

Jenn pointed at Maggie and nodded along. "The availability of fine cuisine is paramount."

"With not a lot of access to small objects," Cassie added.

Jenn arched an eyebrow at Maggie. "You're still doing that?"

Maggie raised the menu to shield her face.

Jenn turned to Cassie. "Imagine you're a kid in middle school scrolling your newsfeed one day and come across a story about your school psychologist getting pinched for shoplifting?"

Cassie chuckled. "I keep telling her that."

"Hey, I'm the school psychologist we all needed growing up. The kids would probably love me more if that ever happened. Besides, I stopped doing it in stores. Now it's just symbolic pilfering." She pulled a tiny pepper shaker from her pocket. "Like this."

Cassie plucked it from her hand and returned it to the table.

Jenn looked at her with mock adoration. "Oh, Maggie. Don't ever change, you adorable wacko, you."

"Getting back to business," Cassie said. "So we know our locale should be gay friendly and have excellent cuisine and loss-prevention officers at souvenir shops who hate their jobs."

"This is gonna be epic," Jenn said.

"I'd expect nothing less," Cassie replied.

"Doesn't it sound so weird to say we're turning *fifty*?" Maggie asked.

Cassie nodded. "And that we've been friends for more than half our lives."

Jenn feigned a fond recollection. "Oh my, yes. It seems like only yesterday we were seniors in high school beating some girl's ass for picking on dear Maggie."

Their unison cackling garnered the attention of the surrounding subdued Sunday-brunch crowd.

"Poor Mags," Cassie said.

Maggie's expression dialed down the energy. "It was a horrible experience, but that bully was the best thing that ever happened to me. I can't imagine how my life would've turned out if I hadn't met you guys."

Cassie clutched her hand. "Aww, Maggie."

"She's right," Jenn said. "The end of senior year with you guys was the best time I ever had in high school. I might not have graduated if it weren't for you."

Cassie's eyes pooled as she squeezed their hands again. "Same, guys. Same. I mean, I was about to lose my virginity to Dominic Vitello until you two pulled me away from the jock clique."

They laughed again, this time even louder.

"Too bad Mr. Pike didn't know that. He could've dubbed us the Gold Star Girls instead of Pantheon Girls." Jenn couldn't pronounce her words through her giggling.

Once their laughter died down, Cassie said, "We have way more than just our fiftieth birthdays to celebrate this year." She smiled through the thought of Jenn possibly receiving another cancer diagnosis.

Jenn seemed to sense what she meant as she raised her glass. "Here's to us."

They clinked their glasses together and resumed their planning over brunch.

CHAPTER TWO

Spring 1989

In Greek Mythology, Cassie glanced around the class at the back of everyone's head as the teacher droned at the front of the room. All the talk with her friends over the weekend about the prom had sent her nerves into overdrive. The cheer squad had insisted that she and her boyfriend, Dominic, were coming to the overnight after-party, and they wouldn't take no for an answer, especially since Nicky's father was rich and would foot the bill for the after-prom hotel suite. How was she supposed to get out of having sex with Dominic then? They'd just celebrated their year anniversary, and she was the last virgin in the group.

She glanced to her left at the sketch that burnout girl, Jenn Ferrano, who worshipped Joan Jett, was doodling in her notebook. She might have looked like she was a second away from knifing someone on a city bus, but she was an awesome artist. This time she was drawing some vampire woman with bloody fangs and huge, exposed boobs. If Mr. Pike walked by and saw that, she'd get a referral to guidance for sure.

Her gaze then traveled a desk over to Maggie Lavery, the quiet nerd, who'd ripped a loud fart in the middle of class on Friday—presumably by accident. Surprisingly, she hadn't transferred schools after the incident like Cassie would've if she'd ever done something so mortifying in front of her classmates.

Mr. Pike's nasal voice jolted Cassie back into focus. "Who remembers from Friday what the collection of gods and goddesses of Mount Olympus is called?"

Crickets.

"Come on now, boys and girls." Mr. Pike frowned and pushed up the eyeglasses slipping down his greasy nose. "We just discussed this Friday in class."

"We partied too much this weekend," one of the football players said, and everyone laughed.

Despite once hearing one of the burnouts refer to her as "that blond ass-kisser," Cassie raised her hand.

"Yes, Miss Burke?"

"The pantheon," she said with lukewarm enthusiasm. "You know. Zeus and Hera and all them."

"Well, it's nice to see that someone reserved some brain cells for class today." Mr. Pike was the only one who appreciated the quip.

"A pantheon is also a temple, like the famous one in Rome," Cassie added at great personal risk to her A-list cheerleader reputation.

Mr. Pike's face lit up. "Why yes, it is."

Cassie swore she'd detected Jenn's eyes roll as she was sketching what looked like Satan. Annoyed at the slight, she got up to use the lavatory and made a point to smile pleasantly at Jenn on her way out of the room. But while she was still smiling spitefully at Jenn, her hip hit the back of Maggie's desk, causing her to squeeze her grape Hi-C juice box, which then squirted all over her wrinkled oxford shirt.

"Oh my God. I'm sorry," Cassie said. "I'll get you some paper towels in the lav."

She glanced at Jenn again after she thought she'd heard her snort, then ran out of the room, debating whether to return to class.

❖

By lunchtime, Cassie's appetite had only partially returned.

Ever since she and Dominic celebrated their anniversary a few weeks earlier, she'd been experiencing a strange, anxious feeling in her stomach. And sometimes she had to rush out of class to use the private bathroom in the nurse's office when her stomach really started acting up.

As she and her friend, Lisa, stood in the cafeteria line, Cassie craned her neck to scan Monday's menu options for the one least likely to cause another eruption like she'd had in Greek Myth. She chose a ham-and-cheese sub, Doritos, and Jell-O, knowing that what she didn't eat, Dominic would finish.

As they made their way to their jock/cheerleader lunch table,

Cassie noticed the notorious school bully, a boxy, hard-faced girl, Sherry Malone, nicknamed "Monster Malone," hovering over the table where a few of the theater geeks sat. Cassie veered toward the table out of curiosity and discovered that Sherry was taunting that quiet girl, Maggie, who, in the span of one full school day, had since been christened Marty McFart.

"What the hell is she doing to them?" Cassie asked Lisa.

"Who cares? Let's go," Lisa replied.

She stopped. "No. Wait a second."

"What are you doing?"

"I'm so sick of that douche bag always picking on the defenseless."

Lisa regarded her with disbelief. "You want her to pick on you instead? Forget about it."

Cassie stood, tray in hand, watching poor Maggie shrink further into herself as Sherry encroached on her personal space. Inspired by that big-boobed demon slayer Jenn was sketching that morning, Cassie squared her shoulders. "That Atilla the Hun needs to be stopped once and for all. Are you with me?"

Lisa scoffed. "Cass, I'm sitting down. My meatball sub is getting cold."

After Lisa breezed past her and headed to their table, Cassie remained, mesmerized as she stood on the precipice of heroism. This wasn't the first time she had borne witness to Sherry's reign of terror against the downtrodden and defenseless in their class. But this time, something wouldn't allow her to just keep walking.

She crept closer to the table. Holding her lunch tray in front of her like it was her last line of defense, she muttered, "Hey, leave them alone."

Sherry whipped her head toward her, disdain in her eyes. "Excuse me?"

"I said leave them alone." Although quivering like the Jell-O on her tray, Cassie's voice grew louder and more assertive. "You're always bothering them. Cut it out."

Sherry's eye twitched as she seemed to process the audacity someone had to call her out. Her voice coming out strained, she replied, "I'm not bothering anyone. Just having a chat with my friend, Marty McFart here, so take a hike, pom-pom girl."

Cassie stood her ground and kept glaring at Sherry, who was now baring her teeth like an animal.

"Are you deaf? I said get out of my face before I rearrange yours."

Maggie managed to make eye contact with Cassie. "Don't," she said softly. "You'll get in trouble."

"Nobody's talking to you," Sherry said and flipped Maggie's lunch tray, sending a thermos of what looked like tomato and rice soup into her lap. Maggie leapt up, and the surrounding students roared with laughter and jeers.

"You asshole," Cassie shouted.

Sherry then whacked Cassie's tray of food to the floor and shoved her in the chest, causing her to stumble backward. At that point, the burnout, Jenn, appeared seemingly out of nowhere and body-checked Sherry from the side, knocking her into the theater geeks' lunch table. Sherry slipped on Cassie's spilt Jell-O and fell on the floor. She flopped around like a fish as she struggled to her feet.

The crowd of onlookers grew larger and louder as they heckled and cheered. Cassie and Jenn looked at each other grinning until they got pelted with a spray of cold green beans.

Suddenly, food was flying everywhere. Macaroni and cheese spattered the walls, shredded lettuce rained down on everyone, and an aerial assault of milk cartons exploded like grenades. Dominic pulled Cassie away from the fray and over to their table in the front of the cafeteria before the administrators arrived to shut it down.

"Everybody just sit here and be cool," Dominic said.

"Everyone saw me yelling at Sherry," Cassie said.

Lisa glared at her. "Why did you get involved? You could get kicked off the squad for this."

"She's not gonna go down for that skank, Sherry," Dominic said. "We'll all say she was sitting with us the whole time."

"Oh yeah, so we all get caught lying and thrown off the team," Bruce, the quarterback, said. "No way. I didn't see anything anyway."

"Yeah, because you were stuffing your fat face with everyone's food," Dominic said.

"All because Cassie wanted to play hero of the dweebs," Lisa added.

As her friends argued among themselves, Cassie watched Jenn get escorted from the cafeteria by one administrator while Sherry was led out by another. "Oh, no. They nabbed Jenn."

"Good," Lisa said. "It's not like she has anything to lose."

Cassie's stomach sank. How could she just sit there playing innocent while Jenn got dragged down to the office? That wasn't fair.

"Cass, where are you going?" Dominic called out behind her.

She followed the suspects in custody to the principal's office, determined to advocate for Jenn, who clearly shouldn't have been penalized for coming to her and Maggie's defense.

"Mr. Mezzanotti," Cassie said as she followed the group into his office. "There's been a big mistake here. That girl shouldn't be in trouble." She pointed at Jenn.

"Cassie, nobody appointed you Miss Ferrano's lawyer. Now go to your fifth-period class before you get detention for being tardy."

"You don't understand. Jenn didn't start anything. Sherry did. Jenn was just coming to my defense."

His fat forehead wrinkled with surprise. "Your defense? You were involved in this?"

"She started it," Sherry said, leaping up from her chair. "She called me an asshole."

"Sherry started it," Cassie said. "I was trying to stop her from picking on the theater geeks—I mean theater kids. She spilled Maggie Lavery's soup all over her."

"You fucking narc," Sherry said.

The principal glared at her. "I have no doubt of your involvement in this, Sherry. You're out for the rest of the week. Now go wait in the main office until your mother comes for you."

The assistant principal tugged at her arm and led her out of the principal's office.

"Okay, Ferrano," he said. "You got yourself two days in ISS."

Jenn huffed and leaned her head against the wall.

"No, Mr. M. You can't do that to her," Cassie said. "It's not fair. She was defending us."

He removed the pen he'd just started to chew. "She shoved another student and instigated a food riot in the cafeteria. I'm most certain I can do that."

"But—"

"She's getting off easy, thanks to the additional information you've provided. Now I suggest you simmer down and get back to class, or you'll be joining her in in-school suspension."

"Fine. I will."

He looked up, seeming confused. "You'll what?"

"If you're punishing her for standing up to a bully, then I deserve to be punished, too, because that's exactly what I did."

"Ms. Burke, please…"

Cassie folded her arms and glared at him defiantly. "What kind of message are you sending to the student body if two students commit the same infraction and only one gets punished?"

He studied her for a moment. "Are you planning a career in politics or something?"

She continued to stare at him as her heart pounded with the thrill of standing her ground.

He sighed and began filling out the suspension slips. "All right then. Consider yourself suspended as well. I'll see you both bright and early tomorrow in suspension hall. Now go to class, both of you."

Once out in the hall, Cassie and Jenn began walking in the same direction silently.

"I know we've barely spoken in more than three years of high school," Jenn finally said. "But I have to ask…are you out of your fucking mind?"

"It's only fair," Cassie said. "We barely know each other, and you still stepped in and saved my life. I'm sure I'd be missing a few front teeth right now if you hadn't."

Jenn shrugged. "I've always wanted a reason to body slam that twat, Sherry. Thanks for giving it to me."

Cassie chuckled at her response. "I just felt bad for that girl, Maggie. She's always getting shit from people. I mean, what kind of person picks on such a sad waif?"

"Yeah. Bullies suck."

Cassie stopped at the corner. "Well, I'm headed to trig. Thanks for your help."

Jenn nodded with an unexpectedly shy smile. "See ya tomorrow."

❖

Early the next morning Cassie reported to the in-school suspension classroom in the bowels of the building across from auto shop. The drab subterranean halls reminded her of what the corridors in maximum-security prisons must look like. She'd heard stories but had never been down here before, never having broken the rules or taken shop. The first one to arrive, she chose a desk directly in front of the teacher's desk in the likely event the room filled up with dope heads, violent offenders, and your average, run-of-the-mill menaces.

As Cassie arranged her Trapper Keeper notebook and decorative pens on the sticky, graffiti-marred desk, the bell rang, startling her already frayed nerves. A group of rowdy boys rolled in with a harried gym teacher following them.

"All right. Sit down, and shut up," gym teacher said, clutching the whistle dangling from his neck. "I don't want to hear a word out of any of you delinquents until the first-wave lunch bell. Got it?" He sat down in the squeaky chair, pulled a newspaper from under his arm, and spread it across the desk.

Cassie listened as the whispering and bustling settled down behind her. Was she the only girl in here? Where the heck was Jenn? She gingerly opened her granola bar, fearing the noise from the wrapper would spark a riot among the boys behind her. After chewing a few bites, she settled into copying her vocabulary words onto index cards to study with Dominic later that day.

As her pen moved across a card, the gym teacher's booming voice shouting, "You're late, Ferrano," jolted her and sent her pen careening off onto the desk.

"Thanks, Big Ben," Jenn said on her way to the empty seat next to Cassie.

"You're a funny girl, Ferrano," gym teacher said. "Now you can entertain the detention-hall teacher as well tomorrow after school."

"Fuuuuck," Jenn hissed as she plunked herself down.

"Good morning," Cassie whispered.

"Is it?" Jenn replied.

"Not really."

Gym teacher lowered his newspaper and glared. Jenn opened a ratty-looking spiral notebook and continued working on a sketch of a beautiful girl with long, flowing hair. Cassie kicked herself for selecting the seat right up front, then decided to switch modes of communication. She pulled out a sheet of paper, wrote *I'm glad you're here* with a smiley face, and in a calculated move handed Jenn the paper.

Jenn replied, *Detention aside, it's actually not that bad. I get to do what I truly want to do. Draw.*

You're so talented. I watch you draw in Greek Myth. I can barely manage stick people. Cassie was suddenly conscious of her excess use of smiley faces. Was Jenn going to think she was a dweeb, too, like Maggie? She'd better cool it with them.

Thanks. You're pretty good at making towers of people at football games. That's a talent, too, Jenn replied.

Cassie caught herself mid-chuckle, but gym teacher had already dozed off. *That's cool that you come to football games. I didn't think you were the school-spirit type.*

I'm not. We go there to make fun of everyone....Just kidding.

Cassie smiled at the comment. She was finding a lot to smile about with Jenn. While she came off as scary and unapproachable, she was just the opposite. And the way she'd swooped in yesterday when Sherry was about to whale on her? That was still making Cassie smile on the inside.

Surprisingly, the day went by much faster than Cassie had anticipated. By the time the dismissal bell rang at 1:50, she felt like she knew everything there was to know about Jenn. And she'd certainly told her everything about herself. The twelve sheets of lined paper containing their day-long stream of silent communication was proof.

They'd hung back and let the stampede of boys leave first. Out in the hall, before they went their separate ways, Jenn gently grabbed Cassie's arm. "Listen. Tomorrow, get us seats all the way in the back, okay?"

As Cassie watched Jenn trot off ahead of her, the thought that they would be able to do this all over again tomorrow filled her with delight.

❖

The next morning when Cassie's mom woke her up for school, she sprang right up, eager to go. That alone was surprising, the springing-right-up part, but stranger still was that she was excited to go to suspension hall.

Then at school, as Dominic escorted her to the room, the flutter inside her grew harder to ignore.

"Hang in there," he said. "Only one more day of misery. Then you're a free woman." He backed up to the lockers and pulled her against him.

It was part of their usual morning make-out ritual before first period, but that morning it didn't feel the same. She felt anxious, and all she was concerned with was peeking into the room to see if Jenn was already there.

"What's wrong?" Dominic asked. "Did anyone bother you in there yesterday?"

"No, no. Everything's fine." She put on a confident face. "I just can't wait to get it over with." This time her cavalier attitude felt forced as she realized she'd just lied to him. She didn't want to get it over with. She couldn't wait to pass notes with Jenn and try not to crack up when she read Jenn's funny comments.

"Okay. But don't be afraid to tell me if anyone screws with you. I don't mind kicking some ass if I have to."

"I know you don't," she replied. "But remember, kicking ass is what got me two days in ISS in the first place...as half-assed as the ass-kicking was." She smirked as she tried to think of a time Dominic had ever kicked anyone's ass aside from tackling opponents on the field.

He kissed her again with tongue. She shrank from his morning breath and received the warning bell as a gift from the gods.

"See you at lunch," she said and backed into class before he could kiss her again.

She turned to where she and Jenn had sat yesterday, and both seats were empty. Ugh. If Jenn was absent, this day was going to be endless. She remembered Jenn's request that she get seats in back and meandered toward the back row to claim two in the corner.

The second bell rang, and after a few seconds, Jenn came tearing around the corner, her black Converse high-tops squeaking on the linoleum. Cassie's autonomic sigh of relief came out audibly. If any of the kids in class had been awake or not listening to a Walkman, she would've had some explaining to do.

"You gave me a heart attack," she whispered as Jenn sat down.

"No way I was gonna stay home and have to do this tomorrow without you."

It was a small sentiment, but it made Cassie smile inside. "Me either," she said as she took out loose-leaf notebook paper. "What do you think Sherry will do when she sees us on Monday?"

"Are you scared of her?"

"No," Cassie lied. "I just want all this crap to be over. If I get in trouble again, I'm off the squad."

"Then don't try to be a cafeteria superhero anymore." Jenn playfully elbowed her.

"I didn't try to. I don't know what came over me. I saw Maggie getting hassled yet again, and I just lost it."

"Well, I think what you did was totally awesome, sticking up for her."

"Yeah?" Cassie doodled spirals on her paper as her face flamed from the compliment. "Speaking of superheroes, you acted like one, too, coming to my rescue. No telling what that brute Sherry would've done if you hadn't stepped in." That was weird. Why did that come out sounding like flirtation?

Jenn blushed. "I didn't save you," she said with a cute, scrunched face. "I just couldn't pass up a chance to give Sherry a good shove. She's been needing one forever."

Cassie giggled. "Aww. I thought I was special or something."

"Uh…" Jenn seemed speechless.

"But yeah, Sherry totally earned that shove." Cassie began rustling with her trig textbook to deflect the awkwardness building between them.

After she'd completed her math classwork and finished reading the assigned section of the *Odyssey*, she glanced over at Jenn's notebook.

"Did you finish the reading for Greek Myth?"

Jenn shook her head as she sketched in her notebook. "It was putting me to sleep," she whispered back.

"How are you going to answer the questions?"

"I'm probably not, but I made this killer sketch of Odysseus and his ship." She held it up.

"Ay, Ferrano," gym teacher said. "This is ISS, not Show and Tell. Now both of you better get back to work, or I'll separate ya's."

Guess it's time we switch over to note passing, Cassie wrote and drew a screwy face after it.

❖

The day after Cassie and Jenn were freed from incarceration in ISS, Cassie was delighted to be back in class listening to one of Mr. Pike's lethal lectures. Giving her hand a break from note taking, she let her pen glide in the margin, lightly doodling "Dominic" with hearts over the I's. Her pen might have been on autopilot, but her mind kept drifting back to Jenn and the fun they'd had the past two days when they were supposed to be serving out their punishment.

It was crazy how instantly they'd seemed to connect. Cassie felt that Jenn, a different kind of social outcast from Maggie, was more like a friend she'd known her whole life. How had they gone through almost four years of high school together and only now got to know each other?

Cliques, that was how.

When she glanced at the side of Jenn's face, as if instinctually,

Jenn looked up and smirked. She must've been reliving their awesome time, too. She turned her eyes back to her open textbook when she heard the tap of a piece of paper folded up so small it could've been mistaken for a Scrabble tile land on her desk. She scanned the sides and front of the room to see if anyone was making eye contact, to no avail.

Upon prying apart the many folds, she observed ornate bubble lettering that read, *Thank you. I don't know why you did it, but thanks.*

She turned almost completely around and saw Maggie sitting directly behind her. She offered the slightest twitch of a smile and dropped her eyes back to her notebook.

"You're welcome," Cassie whispered. She was suddenly attacked by a deep pang of empathy for the awkward geek, uh, girl. "I hope you didn't—"

"Miss Burke," Mr. Pike said. "Is something more interesting happening on Miss Lavery's desk?"

Cassie whirled around and stared straight ahead. In her periphery, she thought she'd caught Lisa and another cheerleader, Debbie, scowling in her direction. They'd already gotten in her face about nearly getting herself kicked off the squad for brawling in the cafeteria over that, to use their word, dork, Maggie. But now they had a problem with Cassie simply talking to her?

The bell rang, and the entire class spilled out into the hall while Mr. Pike was still mid-sentence.

As Cassie, Lisa, and Debbie walked down the hall, Jenn raised her head from the water fountain and joined their stride.

"Hey, did you just get a note from Maggie?"

Cassie nodded.

"She left me one inside my locker," Jenn said. "Does she even know how to speak?"

"Don't be dense," Cassie said through laughter. "She's just wicked shy."

Lisa wasn't at all subtle about clearing her throat.

"Oh, Jenn, you know Lisa, don't you?"

Jenn glared. "No."

Obliviously, Cassie continued. "And Lisa, you know Jenn, from Greek Myth."

"The class we just left forty seconds ago? Uh, yeah." Lisa's contempt wasn't even slightly veiled.

Cassie felt the tension fall onto her from both sides. "Well, yeah, she…"

"Listen, I gotta run," Jenn said, walking backward facing them. "Catch ya later, Cass." She glared at Lisa and Debbie before trotting past them, making it clear the feeling was entirely mutual.

"Catch ya later?" Lisa repeated. "You spend two days in the slammer with that felon, and now you're hanging out?"

Cassie tried to downplay it. "We're not hanging out. Besides, she's cool. Don't have a cow over it." She scoffed to try to make Lisa's suggestion sound ridiculous, but after the last two days, hanging out with Jenn again wouldn't be the worst thing in the world.

That was if somebody as rad as Jenn wanted to hang with a cheerleader.

CHAPTER THREE

Turned out Jenn had wanted to hang out with a cheerleader outside the walls of a high school reformatory. When she'd asked Cassie a couple of weeks later, Cassie didn't hesitate to say yes. But after the plans were made, Cassie panicked at the thought of telling Lisa and the others what she'd planned to do that Thursday night—and with whom.

Her solution was swift and simple: Don't tell them.

Cassie grinned as Jenn stood on the hood of her friend Ronnie's jacked-up, yellow Plymouth Duster, screaming along to Joan Jett's "I Hate Myself for Loving You" as it blared from his boom box. A month ago, this was the last place she could've imagined herself—a mountain overlook where all the burnouts hung out drinking and smoking pot.

Ronnie was facing Jenn, rocking his head back and forth, poking the air to the beat, stopping only to take a drag from the joint they were sharing.

"Goddamn, I love that song," Jenn said when it was over. She lowered herself onto the hood and reclined against the windshield. "C'mon up," she said to Cassie, tapping the space next to her.

Cassie swallowed a lump of nerves gathered in her throat. Jenn was so cool in her worn leather jacket and hair dyed Joan Jett black. When Jenn looked her in the eyes she just couldn't turn away. "I'm okay standing," she replied. She leaned into Jenn's space, resting her elbows on the front quarter panel.

"How about I pick the next song since it's my radio," Ronnie said. He took a hit from the joint and passed it to Cassie.

"Oh, no thanks."

"Ronnie, man, she said no already," Jenn said. "Don't be peer-pressuring her. She's got a rep to protect." She nodded at Cassie, making her feel even more like a nun.

She studied them both as they giggled. They seemed to enjoy how the pot made them feel. "You know what? What the hell. Maybe I will give it a try."

"Yeah?" Jenn looked impressed as she handed the joint to Cassie.

Cassie swallowed again. Why had she just agreed to try drugs? Did she want to impress Jenn? Or maybe it was the end of her senior year, and she was still a virgin, had never finished a whole cigarette, and had never tried a single drug in her life outside of baby aspirin.

Ronnie raised an eyebrow. "You're not gonna get high just sniffing the smoke. You gotta take a hit."

"Oh, right," Cassie said, and they all cracked up. "Here goes nothing." She sucked hard on the moist end, inhaled, and promptly coughed the smoke out into the night air, squinting against the burning in her eyes.

"The first time is never pretty," Jenn said as Cassie continued to hack. "You all right there?" She slid off the hood and started patting Cassie's back.

Burning throat and watering eyes aside, Jenn's hand on her back patting, then rubbing suddenly made everything feel better.

"You gotta try it again," Ronnie said, passing it to Jenn. "Don't suck on it so hard this time."

Jenn snorted at his wording.

"Really?" Cassie had hoped that one time would've been enough to impress them.

Ronnie propped a hand on his hip. "How're you supposed to get high if you don't hold the smoke in?"

Jenn slid her hand from Cassie's back over to her upper arm and held it gently. "Look, you don't have to. This isn't for everybody."

Cassie stared into Jenn's eyes that by now were slits. "I'll take another whack at it."

Jenn bit her lip as her mouth slid into a smile. "Go for it."

A little while later, Cassie understood why the burnouts hung out there all the time. She and Jenn were leaning shoulder-to-shoulder against the car as Ronnie undulated to a George Michael song, kicking up a cloud of dust from the dry dirt clearing as he moved.

"Ronnie's the only seventeen-year-old guy I know who's into George Michael," Jenn said discreetly to her. "I wonder if he's trying to tell me something." She chuckled at her own joke.

"What do you mean? Like he's gay?" Cassie widened her heavy eyelids at the scandalous suggestion.

Jenn nodded. "I asked him once, and he got so defensive about it."

"Maybe he's not. That's why he's defensive."

"My gut says he is, but he's just afraid to admit it to anyone."

Cassie tried to process the idea. "I've never known a gay person before."

"I have an uncle I swear is, but he lives in New York and hardly ever comes to family stuff."

"You think Sherry Malone is a lez?"

Jenn laughed. "Wouldn't doubt it. She acts like a guy. That's probably why she's always starting shit with girls. She's probably in love with poor Maggie Lavery."

For some reason, Cassie found that hysterical and began cackling uncontrollably.

"Yo, Ronnie, you gonna bogart that last Budweiser while you're dancing to your boyfriend's tunes?"

He tilted his head all the way back for the last sip and whipped the empty can at her.

"Oh, dude! You almost clocked Cassie in the head."

"Well, shut up with that boyfriend shit."

"Kid, it was a joke," Jenn said. "Lighten up."

"You've made that joke before," he said. "I'm not a fag."

Cassie crossed her arms, cringing at being caught between them.

"Okay, buzzkill," Jenn said. "You don't have to get so defensive."

"I'm not," Ronnie said, keeping his distance from the car. "How would you like it if I kept asking why you're so into Joan Jett? I don't know any other girl as obsessed with her as you are. Are you hot for her or something?"

The zeal with which Ronnie bombarded her left Cassie as stunned into silence as Jenn. *Obsessed* made it sound weird. As awkward as this was getting, Cassie was intrigued.

Jenn touched her spiky hair, apparently styled as an homage to Joan. Okay, so maybe Jenn was a little excessive in her devotion, but come on. The woman was a rock goddess.

After a long silence, Jenn seemed to have regained her cool. "Just because I think she's pretty and totally rad doesn't mean I'm obsessed with her."

Ronnie's glare was a full-on accusation. "Your bedroom walls are covered with her pictures, and you play her cassettes until the tapes snap. Not to mention your hair…"

Jenn was silent and seemed to be stewing over the incessant

barrage of accusations. Was it possible they were both gay? They were rumored to be dating in school, but while neither one ever denied it, they didn't act like a couple at all. Maybe that was why.

"So what if I idolize her?" she finally replied. "I don't have to answer to you. It's my business."

"Touchy," Ronnie said, then displayed a satisfied grin. "That's enough of this stupid conversation." He approached the car and checked the rumpled paper bag. "Fuck."

"That was the last one, wasn't it?"

"Good guess, Detective," he said.

"We should probably bolt outta here," Jenn said.

Cassie's head was spinning from the beer and the weed, but she was having too much fun to leave them. And she would certainly have a lot of explaining to do if she went home now and her parents were up. "Where to next?"

"Diner?" Jenn said.

"I'm broke," Ronnie said.

"I think I have seventeen dollars on me," Cassie said. "I'll treat."

"Cool. I'll pay you back," Ronnie said.

"No, he won't." Jenn grinned and gave him a nudge.

"Fuck off. Yes, I will," he said as they all climbed into his car.

"Yeah. No, he won't."

"Well, we'll just have to do this again soon and find out," Cassie said. The cloud of sadness that had come over her when she thought the night was over suddenly lifted at the idea of hanging out with Jenn again sometime. And Ronnie. Jenn and Ronnie.

"I hope your cheerleader friends don't get jealous," Jenn said. "You know how petty girls can be sometimes."

Cassie leaned forward and poked her head between them. "They don't have to know all my business. I didn't tell them we were hanging out tonight."

"Oh, so we're a deep, dark secret?"

"No. That's crazy. I can be friends with anyone I want." Cassie wanted to sound unfazed, but Jenn wasn't far off. Lisa and the others had had a few choice words about her new friendship with Jenn, and she didn't want to have to deal with any more unpleasant repercussions. "Hey, we should have Maggie join us next time."

"Fuck, yeah," Jenn said. "Imagine how she'd be high."

They all laughed.

"I wonder if it would make her more weird or less weird," Cassie said.

"I can't wait to find out," Jenn said.

Cassie's cackle added to the hilarity, but inside, all she could think about was another night hanging out with Jenn.

For the past couple of weeks, Cassie had been thinking about the fun she'd had with Jenn and her friend Ronnie that night up on Totoket Hill. She was dying to be with her again, but with her cross-country practice and meets, spending time with Dominic and her own friends, it hadn't happened. Now with a month left of school, she worried that it would never happen before school was out, and then with summer, who knew if Jenn would even be interested in doing stuff with her.

Before the bell rang in Greek Myth, as usual, Jenn was sketching in her notebook. Cassie surreptitiously glanced at the page, but instead of some half-naked female war lord or succubus creature, she saw a blond girl in a sweater and jeans rolled at the ankles. She had a movie-star smile and held a Trapper Keeper notebook to her chest. What the...

Cassie leaned closer to get a better look, but Jenn flipped her notebook shut.

"Excuse you," Jenn said. "Private property."

"Since when? You always show me your sketches."

"You can see my work when it's done."

Just as the bell rang, Mr. Pike scurried in with his tatty, overstuffed briefcase and Styrofoam cup of coffee decorated with brown spill droplets. "Good morning, good morning, students," he said as he plopped his briefcase on the desk. He sipped his coffee and then hiked up his wrinkled trousers. "Today's the day we're assembling teams and topics for the final unit project on the gods and goddesses of Mount Olympus."

Cassie raised her hand. "Do we get to pick our teams?"

"I knew you'd ask that, Ms. Burke. But no, this time I've assigned the teams I think will work best together. You are free, however, to choose your topics as a group."

Cassie led the chorus of groans at his response. Unmoved by their protests, Mr. Pike read off the roster of teams. "And last but certainly not least, we have Cassie, Jenn F., and Maggie."

From the other side, Lisa gave Cassie a vehement look, as though cajoling her into saying something. Cassie feigned a helpless look, but in reality, she wasn't unhappy about her team.

Lisa raised her hand and didn't wait to be called on. "Mr. Pike, can't we have four people? We need Cassie."

"I'm sorry, Lisa. Only three per team. I spent the weekend meticulously arranging them, so I have no doubt that you're all in good hands."

"But Cassie and I always work together," Lisa said.

"I'm aware," he said. "You all choose your friends as your partners, and I think it's time you diversify. It's important that you all experience different personality dynamics and points of view, especially those of you heading off to college in the fall. Now come on, everyone. Get together with your teammates and brainstorm your topics."

Cassie nodded to Jenn, and they both moved into seats near Maggie. While she was initially excited about being partnered with Jenn, the idea of "working" seemed to have eluded her this marking period. And her other partner, Maggie? The girl didn't even speak.

"So, Maggie…We meet again," Jenn said as she plopped into the desk to Maggie's left.

"But under much better circumstances," Cassie added with a smile as she sat to Maggie's right.

"You can ask Mr. Pike to switch me out with your other friend over there." Maggie indicated Lisa, who was still scowling in their direction. "I won't mind."

Cassie puckered her lip with sadness. "Oh, no. I'm fine with this group."

"I'd mind," Jenn said. "Being stuck with one cheerleader is bad enough."

"Ha. Ha. Very funny," Cassie said. "Cheer season is over. I'm an athlete now."

"Ooh, my mistake. You're a jock now." Jenn nudged her with a cheeky grin.

Cassie couldn't help but smile as their eye contact lingered until Maggie's awkward throat clearing broke it.

"So, what should we do the project on?"

Jenn shrugged.

"How about the goddesses of the Pantheon?" Cassie asked.

"Won't that be a lot of research?" Jenn asked.

"Yeah, if only one person had to do it. We're working as a group. We can research together in the library after school. Or on Saturday mornings."

"Whoa. I don't do school on Saturdays," Jenn said. "This isn't *The Breakfast Club*."

"Fine. Let's meet in the library today right after seventh period. Okay?"

By the end of class, Cassie felt good about her group. She and the girls already had the outline completed for the project. She and Maggie would handle the heavy lifting on the research end, and Jenn, naturally, would take the lead on creating the collage for the presentation.

When the bell rang, they went their separate ways. But Cassie wouldn't be alone for long. Lisa sidled up to her.

"Why didn't you speak up to Pike when he announced these stupid teams?"

"Because you already did, and he said he wasn't changing anything."

"Way to go, butthead." Lisa picked up her pace and moved ahead of her.

"Lisa," Cassie called out as she caught up. "It's just a dumb project. What's the big deal? You're with Wayne. He'll probably do the whole thing for you, and you'll get an A on it."

"Whatever," she said, still snotty. "Come to the lav with me. I need a cig."

Cassie complied, as always, but these days, it was more out of habit than allegiance.

That afternoon, promptly after seventh period, Cassie met Jenn and Maggie in the library to begin their project research. Behind their mountain of encyclopedias, Cassie and Jenn found interviewing Maggie more fascinating than facts and myths about the goddesses.

"So, when you're not building sets for the theater club, what you do for fun?" Cassie asked.

"Nothing," Maggie said as she scanned a paragraph with her index finger.

Cassie and Jenn exchanged looks.

"Well, none of us really do anything, but you must do something on the weekends."

Maggie regarded her with a blank expression.

"What did you do last Saturday night, for example?"

"Watched *The Golden Girls* with my Mema."

Jenn appeared horrified. "You spent a Saturday night with your Mema?"

Cassie kicked her under the table. "That's nice that you got to spend a night with your grandmother. Mine lives two hours away."

"I live with mine," Maggie said. "I always spend time with her."

Cassie's eyes almost watered at the thought of this girl doing nothing but hanging out with her grandmother. She was in high school. These were supposed to be the best years of their lives, and Maggie Lavery was spending them getting bullied at school and on weekends watching old-lady TV shows with an old lady.

Jenn's suggestion of taking Maggie out and getting her high suddenly came into focus for Cassie. "What are you guys doing Friday night?"

Jenn's head jerked toward her. "Not going to any stupid pep rally, that's for damn sure."

Cassie's mind was already off and running with the idea. "No, no. I'm not either. Why don't the three of us get together and go up to Totoket Hill for some tunes and some...you know." She nodded knowingly at Jenn. "Ask Ronnie if he wants to come."

Maggie looked worried as she stopped copying things from the encyclopedia into her notebook.

Jenn seemed to pick right up on the plan. "What do you say about giving Granny a rain check and come out with us?"

"She's Mema, not—"

"We won't take no for answer, Maggie," Cassie said. "Come on. It'll be a fun night."

Jenn grinned at Cassie as she addressed Maggie. "Trust me. Watching *The Golden Girls* with Nana will be a whole different experience after you hang with me and Ronnie for a night."

❖

Cassie paced the floor in her bedroom between applications of eye makeup, rouge, and lip gloss. Why was she feeling so...nervous? Or was it excitement about being with this new group of kids? Whatever it was, Ronnie and Jenn were coming by any minute, and she wanted everything just right. Remembering how windy it was up on the hill, she sprayed her teased and feathered hair with one last layer of Aqua Net like a coating of shellac.

She and the girls had just finished their Pantheon project for Mr. Pike's class, and as a sort of pre-presentation celebration, she and Jenn had convinced Maggie to join them and Ronnie for a little party on the hill. Their previous attempts to convince her to go out with them had been unsuccessful when they'd tried to pry her from her standing Saturday night date with her grandmother. To their surprise, Friday night took relatively little coercing.

Not surprising, though, was Dominic's reaction when Cassie told him she'd have to miss another Friday night with him. After she'd bewildered him with a rather dense explanation that it was important for couples in a healthy relationship to spend time apart, he'd finally dropped the argument.

By eight thirty, they'd gathered around a small, makeshift fire pit with a cooler filled with sodas, beers pilfered from various refrigerators, and bags containing Doritos, Fritos, and Funyuns. Cassie made sure to secure her spot next to Jenn, a habit that had become a ritual since they started working on their project and hanging out regularly.

As soon as she was comfortably seated around the small pit surrounded by stones, Jenn lit one of the two joints that were her contribution to the evening's festivities. "How did you escape another Friday night with your boyfriend and the jock squad? I know you didn't tell them you're hanging out with us again. That'd be social suicide."

"I'm not afraid or ashamed of our friendship." Cassie winced at her lie. She was very afraid of the wrath she'd been experiencing from her friends. And with senior prom and graduation around the corner, it wouldn't do to become the black sheep of the group.

"Then what did you tell them?" Jenn asked.

Cassie shrugged. "That I'm sleeping over at my cousin Stacey's house in Ellington."

Ronnie: "Ellington?"

Maggie: "Connecticut?"

Jenn: "Do you even have a cousin Stacey?"

"Okay, guys," Cassie said. "Can we just get to the reason we're here? Ronnie, where's the tunes? Jenn, pass the...you know..."

"The pot?" Jenn asked aloud. "You can say the word, Cass. Nobody else is here tonight."

"Except maybe a psychotic murderer," Maggie said softly as her big eyes searched the surrounding darkness.

Jenn looked at her. "You mean out there or in our group?"

Cassie laughed and fanned the small campfire to keep it going.

As they smoked, they listened to Van Halen, a compromise to curb the abuse of Joan Jett and George Michael songs. At long last, she was finally starting to experience the relaxational properties of the doob.

And so was Maggie, who was on her maiden marijuana voyage. She'd gotten up and was doing some sort of slow, interpretive dance to "Dance the Night Away" as the others watched in jubilant fascination.

"I can't believe this side of her," Cassie said.

"I know, man," Jenn said as she inhaled her hit. "Where's that painfully awkward chick from class?"

"Is marijuana some type of magic potion that brings out the real you or something?"

Jenn cracked up and nudged herself into Cassie's shoulder.

"Wanna know what I used to do with my cousin, Chrissie?" Ronnie said after his hit. His glance was darting between them.

"What?" Jenn said.

"Have fancy-dress-up parties. My aunt Harriet had bins full of wigs and dresses in the basement from her theater days, and we'd pretend we were Daisy and Jordan from *The Great Gatsby*."

Cassie looked at Jenn, who was still staring at Ronnie.

"What?" Ronnie asked innocently. "It was my aunt's favorite movie."

"Those were the girl parts," Jenn said. "Why weren't you Gatsby?"

"Duh," he replied impatiently. "Because she only had dresses and wigs in the bin."

"Dude!" Jenn cracked up and crashed into Cassie's shoulder, then practically into her lap.

Cassie laughed and pushed Jenn upright again as she watched Ronnie's movements to the music grow more effeminate. He sucked at the joint again and passed it around with delicately poised fingers. Through her mental haze she was beginning to experience a moment of intense clarity.

"Ronnie," she blurted. "Are you gay?"

Jenn coughed out a cloud of smoke that alerted Maggie to rejoin the circle.

"What? Why are you asking me that? So you can tell all the jocks, and they can kick my ass in gym class?"

"No." Cassie was hurt that he would think that of her. "I'd never do anything like that."

"She wouldn't," Maggie said. "Cassie's not like that."

"Thank you, Mags."

"That's right," Jenn said. "She's a champion of justice for all us outcasts."

Cassie glared at her. If that was a compliment, it sure didn't sound like one. Or feel like one. "I just think that nobody should ever be bullied for being who they are, whether they're a burnout," she looked at Jenn, "a theater geek," she glanced at Maggie, "or a cheerleader." She pointed a thumb at herself.

"Or a fag?" Ronnie said softly, and he suddenly looked very sad.

"Or a gay person," Cassie said. "If that's what you are." Ronnie didn't say anything more, so she didn't either.

"Look. Why don't we make a pact," Jenn said. "Whatever we want to tell each other up here stays in the circle. This right here is the zone of sacred secrets."

"That's right," Cassie said. "No matter what goes on off this hill or at school or anywhere else, whatever we say here is said in strict confidence."

Ronnie finally smiled, and Cassie felt infinitely better. At that point, they all began tearing into the bags of chips.

On the way home, Cassie and Jenn sat in the back seat as Ronnie drove and Maggie rode shotgun. They were leaning against each other, their heads supporting one another, Cassie trying to stay awake. She'd wondered what other secrets lurked in their group. Surely, Ronnie wasn't the only one who'd been hiding part of himself.

Their moment of candor up on the hill had her trying to recall if being with Dominic had ever felt the way it did being with Jenn.

CHAPTER FOUR

With just a few days left until graduation, the girls clamored into Mr. Pike's class to give the final school presentation of their high school career on the goddesses of the Greek Pantheon. They'd spent a lot of time together working on the project, more than Cassie ever had with her cheer friends, and she was incredibly proud of the result.

Mr. Pike stood before the class like he was emceeing the Grammy Awards in his short-sleeve dress shirt and tie, his hairy hands clasped together. "And now I'd like to call my Pantheon Girls up to present. Cassie, Jenn, and Maggie, would you please come up?"

They dragged the enormous, detailed collage board up the aisle to the front of the class. When they turned it around, a rumble emanated from their audience of peers. Loaded with flow charts and neatly written facts, clearly it was Jenn's killer illustrations of the goddesses in action that wowed them.

Cassie's attention gravitated toward Lisa, Debbie, and a couple of defensive-end goons, whose desks were pulled closer together than usual. The perpetual sneer on Lisa's face was unmistakable, but this time it was obviously directed toward Cassie. Why was she still being so bitchy toward her? It wasn't her fault she was in a group with Jenn and Maggie. Mr. Pike chose the groups.

But that meant little to Lisa, who'd pointed out more than once Cassie's failure to protest the injustice when it occurred.

Whatever. Cassie refused to let Lisa or anyone else psych her out. While they all had a hand in the research and collection of information, each of them excelled in a specific area that made their group dynamic so effective, Cassie's being the speaking part of the presentation.

With Maggie and Jenn flanking each side of the collage board,

Cassie swung into action, narrating a brief introduction before explaining each level. She held flashcard notes but rarely needed to consult them.

Each time Mr. Pike interrupted with a question meant to test the depth of their knowledge, Cassie or her team members replied with an accurate, confident answer.

When it was Maggie's turn to explain a section, one of the jocks coughed out "McFart," a reference to the now-historic time she'd slipped that fart out in class.

Mr. Pike quickly quelled the uproar but without admonishing the jock's interruption.

As Cassie brought the presentation to a close, savoring the rush of victory adrenaline, Lisa coughed out "nerds," after which followed more laughter from the class. Cassie stumbled on her words, thrown off by Lisa's public betrayal. She flipped through her flashcards in a panic, trying to find where she left off.

Finally, Maggie leaned into her and whispered the phrase she needed, so she could recover her train of thought. But it was too late. Her cheeks burned with humiliation, her otherwise flawless oration of their project desecrated.

When they were done, Mr. Pike led the applause, but Cassie didn't hear any of it. Seething, she walked past Lisa, Debbie, and the jocks and checked her hip into the side of Lisa's chair.

"Oh. Watch it," Lisa said and continued giggling with her group.

As Jenn and Maggie reveled in their team's success, Cassie stewed. She and Lisa had been friends since the fifth grade. How could she turn on her like this? Was she so petty that Cassie's finding interests outside their group could compromise an eight-year friendship?

"Cass, what's the matter?" Jenn asked. "We aced this."

"You and Maggie aced it. I screwed up my part at the end."

"No, you didn't," Jenn said. "Your part was the hardest, especially with those Neanderthals in the audience. You were great."

"She's right," Maggie said. "You were great."

"Yeah, fuck them, man," Jenn added. "Their project sucked."

Maggie nodded. "That's because the three of them had to share one brain."

That brought a smile to Cassie's face and some needed perspective about perceptions. She'd enjoyed nearly all her high school years in a popular clique, taking the benefits of it for granted: admiration from other students, favor from the teachers, and a rich social life. But the first time her friendships within that clique were tested, the people she'd cared most about let her down.

"Thanks, guys," she said. "You're the best."

As the dismissal bell prompted the Pavlovian students to get up and file out, Cassie stood proud, reaching her full height as they left. As she passed Lisa, she said to Jenn, loudly, "And you're right. Our project kicked ass."

The party Cassie had been hoping to avoid was Saturday night. Since presentation day, things had been more strained than ever between her and Lisa and Debbie. Out of necessity, she'd made excuses about studying for finals to avoid them. Dominic and the guys, of course, hadn't noticed anything, so he was talking to Cassie about the party as though she were just as jazzed about going as he was.

"What do you mean, go to the movies instead?" He stared at her like she'd just said that Lawrence Taylor was just an okay linebacker. It was a hail Mary play for her to suggest the movies, and clearly, it hadn't worked. "Not only is this the last team kegger of the school year, but it's the last one of high school. Ever."

"All the more reason for you guys to just hang out together," she replied. "Dudes drinking and bonding together as a team for one last time."

"Are you trying to bail on going?"

The sadness in his query over what she thought was obvious tugged at her heartstrings. "Noooo. Of course not. I wouldn't dream of it."

But she had dreamed of it. Sadly, with a week left until graduation, she didn't want to spend the last Saturday night of senior year with the friends she'd gone through all four years of high school with. Tradition or not, she didn't even want to spend it with her boyfriend of over a year.

But with less than an hour until the party started and with Dominic standing in the foyer of her living room, she didn't have the courage to voice her desire to spend it with Jenn and Maggie. So they said good-bye to her parents, sneaked into the garage to fetch a couple of wine-cooler six-packs her older brother had procured for her, and headed to Nicky's house.

Soon after they arrived at the party, she'd readily accepted a shot of peppermint schnapps from Lisa, Debbie, and the other girls, but not because she'd liked it. She didn't. She just disliked tension even more. Although they'd all been civil to each other since the infamous presentation scandal, the vibe hadn't returned to their original sisterhood.

When Cassie came out of the house and approached the girls gathered on lounge chairs on the patio, they'd abruptly stopped talking. The smiles on their faces seemed forced and didn't hide their guilty expressions—the ones on all their faces except Lisa's and Debbie's, the ringleaders.

Clearly, they were talking about her when she was inside changing into her bathing suit. She said nothing, but her heart was wounded. Feeling like a fool, she grabbed a wine cooler out of the foam container and chugged it.

"What are we sitting around for," Lisa said. "Let's go in the pool." She indicated the guys splashing around, jumping on top of each other as they passed a football.

"I just opened this," Cassie said. "I'll be there in a minute." A little chilly in the night air, she wrapped her towel around her shoulders and sat at the shallow edge, away from the splashing guys, so she could dangle her feet in the water.

"Cass, come in so we can have chicken fights," Debbie said.

"Yeah, don't be a chicken," Lisa added as she waved her hands through the water.

"I told you I wanted to finish this." She held up her wine cooler. "Besides, the water's cold. Aren't you guys freezing?"

"It's nice once you're in," Debbie said.

"You just need to get wet." Lisa splashed a little water at her.

"Stop." Cassie recoiled.

"Come on," Lisa said, splashing harder. "It's not cold. See?"

"Cut the shit," Cassie shouted as she scrambled to her feet.

Lisa then shoved armfuls of water at her, soaking her towel. She shuffled across the wet patio to the guys' side, but Dominic was clearly engrossed in the game.

"Dom," she called out, but he didn't answer. "Dominic," she shouted, finally winning his attention. "The girls want to play chicken."

His eyes lit up. "Then come on in."

She placed her wine cooler on a table and inched down the ladder into the chilly water away from the boys, so she wouldn't get splashed.

Lisa and Debbie, with beer cans in hand, jumped in on either side of her, creating walls of water that soaked her to the bone.

She shrieked at the jolt of cold.

"What's the matter?" Dominic called out.

"It's freezing," she shouted back while glowering at them.

"Don't be such a baby," Lisa said. She dove under and kicked up more water at Cassie.

She swam toward Dominic. He kissed her hard, then dove down between her legs and lifted her out of the water.

The night air filled with rowdy hoots and shouts as the rest of the girls got onto boys' shoulders.

Someone shouted a gruff, "Yeah! Let's go!"

"What are the teams?" Dominic said as he rubbed Cassie's shins.

"Let's do the teams we had in Mr. Pike's class," Lisa said.

"That's not fair," Cassie said. "My teammates aren't here."

"Not our fault you partnered up with the social outcasts," Debbie said.

"Don't be a jerk, Deb. You know I didn't have any say in who I was put with for the project. You guys really need to get over that shit."

"Ooh" resounded in deep, post-pubescent male voices.

"Why don't you get over your obsession to have everyone in school love you," Lisa said.

"What are you even talking about? Just because I'm not a bitch to the less-popular kids doesn't mean I need their approval."

"Did you just call me a bitch?"

A stern, defiant tone pushed out Cassie's reply. "I was looking right at you when I said it, wasn't I?"

Dominic and Nicky were snickering beneath them at the brewing tension.

"I dare you to come closer and say it again," Lisa said.

The boys finally backed away from each other to prevent the real brawl that was about to replace a chicken fight.

As Dominic and Cassie were backing away, someone came from behind and shoved Cassie so hard in the back, she slid forward into the water.

Furious, she swam toward the ladder and climbed onto the deck. She grabbed her towel and dried her face.

"Cass, come on," Dominic said. "Come back. Let's get even with them."

"Where are you going?" Debbie asked. "Sorry. I thought the game had started already." She began laughing before she'd finished the sentence.

When all the others joined in, Cassie ran into the house and into the bathroom. She cried into the towel so nobody would hear her. She had to pull herself together before they all came in to apologize and beg her to come back into the pool.

But no one approached her.

❖

Monday after school, Cassie and Jenn had gone home with Maggie to further discuss Cassie's indignation at the way she was treated at the pool party. As usual, Jenn brought along their fourth guest, a doobie brother, and they made it a bitch session in Maggie's musty basement.

"Man, that's so fucked up," Jenn said. "And they never apologized?"

"Not until yesterday when I told Dominic if they didn't, I'd never speak to either one of them again."

"Dominic never came to check on you either?" Maggie asked.

"He did, eventually, but by that time, I was already gone. Luckily, my brother had just walked in from work and answered the phone when I called. He came and got me."

"I would've come if you needed a ride," Jenn said.

"You don't have a license," Cassie replied.

"A mere trifle," Jenn said as she sucked on the joint like a high-society woman. "It wouldn't be the first time I borrowed my mom's car while she was in a chardonnay coma."

Cassie admired her rebelliousness. "Well, it all worked out, so you didn't have to commit grand theft auto."

"Worked out? You mean you've forgiven those asswipes?"

"Yeah." Jenn's question surprised her. "Dominic bought me roses and a pair of jeans I've been wanting. He was really sorry. He just had too much to drink that night."

Maggie and Jenn stared at her. While they hadn't offered any more critiques, Cassie felt the disappointment they were telepathically bombarding her with. Should she have been disappointed in herself? Was she the type that forgave too easily?

"Anyway, we're graduating next week. After that, I never have to see them again if don't want to."

"You don't have to see them now," Jenn said, one eye closed

against a rope of smoke coiling up to her eye. "What does graduation have to do with anything?"

Jenn didn't get it. She hadn't understood what graduation had meant to Cassie's whole group of friends. Cassie had gone through just about everything with them throughout high school. Of course she intended to spend the biggest night of all with her boyfriend and their friends.

"It's just an important night for all of us," Cassie said softly.

Jenn shrugged. "Yeah, well, hopefully, they won't drive off on you when you're in the bathroom."

Cassie sighed. Jenn and Maggie both looked so sad. Had they assumed that just because they'd started hanging out together occasionally that Cassie would blow off her main crew on the last night of high school ever?

❖

With New Kids on the Block blaring from Debbie's car stereo, they pulled into the school parking lot near the football field. It was a balmy June night, and the girls piled out of the car, adjusted their caps and gowns, and gabbed away as Lisa finished her cigarette. Cassie tugged at her bra as she sweated and handed a passer-by her Kodak camera to take their picture together.

"I cannot believe that an hour from now we'll officially be graduates," Debbie said.

Lisa crushed out her cigarette under her white pump. "How psyched are we?"

"So psyched," Cassie replied, but her attention was elsewhere as she glanced around the massive crowd. Where were Maggie and Jenn, and what would she do if she found them? Invite them to join this group? Not likely.

For more than a week she'd agonized about the terrible choice she'd been forced to make. Graduation night. The most meaningful in their entire high school career. But should she have chosen to go with the group she'd been friends with throughout the last four years yet felt disconnected with lately? Or should she go with Jenn, Maggie, and Ronnie, the "misfits," the group she'd only recently fallen in with but the one she truly wanted to be with?

In the end, sticking with tradition had won out over rugged individualism, and there she stood, at the entrance to the football field with Lisa, Debbie, and the rest of the squad, smiling but wracked with guilt.

"There's the guys," Lisa said. "Let's go."

The girls migrated toward Dominic, Nicky, and the rest of the team before heading to the rows of chairs set up in front of the risers where the administration and distinguished guests were assembling.

Dominic tugged at Cassie's waist. "Hey, baby." As he kissed her, the sweat from his thin, soft mustache hair dampened her top lip. "You're riding with me after the ceremony, right?"

She froze with indecision but was saved when their class advisor hurried them into their alphabetically arranged seats. He'd meant riding with him to the after-party at Nicky's house.

The sand in the hourglass of her virginity was about to run out. Ugh. The senior prom had been so much easier to navigate. With neither Jenn nor Maggie going, she didn't have the stress of trying to please everyone. The after-prom party at Nicky's house had been easy, too. She'd faked her period that night and managed to escape the traditionally inescapable rite of passage for high school couples, the losing of the virginity.

As the principal rambled, Cassie glanced behind her to try to make eye contact with Jenn or Maggie, both seated several rows behind her. She regretted not joining the guys in the shot of Jäger they'd done under the bleachers. Her nerves were frayed, and she was tired of thinking. After a glance up in the bleachers to get a visual on her parents, she closed her eyes and listened to the droning voices and whines and whistles of the PA system.

After the ceremony and the photo ops with friends and family, the crowd began to dissipate. Dominic took hold of her hand and led her into the parking lot.

"Wait till you see Nicky's graduation present," he said.

Cassie did a double take when she saw Nicky leaning against his "present" with arms folded across his chest. A brand-new, shiny white IROC Z-28 Camaro.

"Holy crap, Nick," she said. "We're riding in style tonight."

He grinned. "You better hang tight when we blow it outta here."

"This is gonna be sweet," Dominic said as he climbed into the back.

Lisa ran around to the passenger side, opened the door, and lifted the seat forward for Cassie to get in behind her.

"Yo, Cass," someone shouted out over a loud rumbling muffler.

With one leg in Nicky's car, Cassie twisted at the waist.

Jenn was hanging out the back window of Ronnie's Duster. "You're getting in the wrong car."

"What the hell?" Lisa sneered in Jenn's direction. "Just get in, Cass."

But Cassie didn't move. She continued staring at Ronnie's banana-yellow car, then finally let her leg fall from the car to the ground.

Maggie suddenly appeared across Ronnie's lap out the driver's side window, more animated than Cassie had ever seen her. "Come on, Cassie. Let's go." She waved frantically at her.

"Cass, there's nothing to think about here." Lisa's tone was ominous. "Ignore them and get in."

Dominic called out from the back seat. "What's the holdup? Let's go."

The indecision must've been plain on her face. Lisa grabbed her upper arm as if she was about to jerk her into the car.

"But I…" Cassie pulled back.

"You what? You wanna get in that loser-mobile?" Lisa said.

Cassie froze. She looked at Dominic, then at Ronnie's car, then back at Lisa, a caged animal with the door open a crack.

Lisa challenged her with a look of disgust. "Go ahead then." She let go of her arm with a little shove.

As Cassie started a slow, deliberate walk to Ronnie's car, cheers emanated from his open windows.

"Cassie, what the fuck are you doing?" Dominic shouted.

She kept walking.

"Let her go," Lisa shouted. "She belongs with those dweebs."

"Cassie, if you get in that car with them, we're through," Dominic shouted.

Jenn flung open the back driver's side door, and Cassie climbed in. When Dominic started for them, Ronnie peeled out of the parking lot before the door was closed and ran over the curb. Cassie and the girls screamed with exhilaration as she looked out the back window, fearful Nicky might chase them.

"Oh, man, I can't believe you blew them off," Jenn said.

"Who's a loser now, Lisa Sankowicz?" Ronnie shouted into the rearview mirror.

Maggie leaned over from the front seat. "I can't believe you chose to be with us on this most hallowed of adolescent milestones." Her innocent, jubilant smile melted Cassie's angst. And her heart.

"I'm tired of people telling me what to do," she said. "This time I just followed my gut."

Jenn responded to Cassie with her usual show of affection, a punch in the arm.

"Where are we off to?" Cassie said.

"My place," Jenn said. "My mom is away with her boyfriend for the weekend, and she filled the fridge with food before she left."

"Aces." Cassie sat back and reveled in her crazy, impetuous decision. She was proud of herself for finding her voice. She wasn't sure how she would explain this decision to Dominic and her friends after the dust settled, but if their threats were sincere, she wouldn't have to.

When they arrived at Jenn's modest house, they all stripped off their graduation gowns and left them in a heap on Jenn's back patio. With a few bowls of various chips and a box of Entenmann's chocolate-chip cookies on the table, they opened the first of several bottles of cheap wine and sparked their first joint.

By around one a.m., they'd moved the party inside so Jenn's neighbors wouldn't call the cops after their initial warning. Cassie felt herself losing steam. Maggie and Ronnie were passed out on the living-room sofa while she and Jenn, on the love seat, continued talking about life after graduation, drinking wine from plastic cups, feeling like grown-ups.

"I'm just happy to have the summer to chill out before starting college," Cassie said. "My brain needs a break from thinking."

"Mine doesn't," Jenn said. "My hand needs a break from sketching."

"It's gonna be so strange being in a different state surrounded by people I don't know."

"You're lucky to be going out of state. My mom said art school tuition alone was going to make her broke, so forget about paying to live on campus somewhere."

"If you really want to go away somewhere, you could get a student loan and work on campus."

Jenn wrinkled her nose. "I really don't. I wanna draw and sketch and paint. I don't care where I do it. Except maybe Paris."

"I know. Right?" Cassie repositioned herself on the love seat. "That's always been my dream, to go to France. The shopping, the food, the romance…Did you ever see the movie *An American in Paris?*"

"No. I'm just a fan of Toulouse-Lautrec. Ever see his paintings?"

Cassie shook her head.

"Wanna look at my scrapbook of some of his stuff? I can't stand listening to Ronnie snore anymore anyway."

Cassie nodded and followed her down the hall. "Are you sure you don't mind me sleeping over? I've already told my parents we were all staying at Nicky's tonight."

"Yeah. No problem. My mom won't be home till Sunday. Late Sunday."

"You'll be alone here all weekend?"

Jenn nodded as she pulled out a photo album. As cool as the idea sounded, Cassie felt bad for her in a way. She couldn't imagine what it would be like to be alone all the time. If she wasn't home with her parents or bickering with her brothers, she was out with Dominic or her friends.

"I just realized that I left my overnight bag in Debbie's car," Cassie said.

"No biggie. I can spot you a shirt and shorts to sleep in. And a toothbrush."

They plopped on Jenn's bed, resting on their elbows as they flipped through the photo album of small reprints of Toulouse-Lautrec's paintings. When they were done, Jenn whipped out a roach from earlier in the evening. "Let's finish this," she whispered.

"Ronnie's gonna be mad," Cassie replied, but she loved the added element of risk.

"I'll tell him we all finished it. He won't know the difference." They giggled as Jenn lit the roach, then took a hit. "You ever shotgunned it before?"

Cassie shrugged. "I don't know. I've only ever smoked with you. Have I?"

Jenn shook her head as she laughed out smoke. "Here. Let me show you." She took another hit, pulled Cassie's head close to hers, and blew the smoke into her face.

Cassie coughed and giggled. "What the hell was that?"

"You're supposed to open your mouth," Jenn said, almost doubling over in amusement.

"You didn't tell me that."

"I forgot what an amateur you are. Okay. When I get close to you, you have to open your mouth." She took a big hit and leaned toward her.

Cassie closed her eyes and opened her mouth slightly. Jenn's warm lips pressed against hers, followed by a puff of smoke. She inhaled it and opened her eyes, but instead of the blast sending a mellow wave into her, she didn't feel anything but the residual effects of Jenn's lips.

They were amazing, a feeling like nothing she'd ever experienced with anyone else.

"Let's do it again," she whispered, and Jenn complied.

This time hardly any smoke came out, but Jenn's lips lingered on hers. They weren't shotgunning anymore. They were kissing. Was the pot making them act weird? Cassie was experiencing a cascade of all sorts of things she'd never felt before, not with Dominic or any other boy she'd kissed. She wanted Jenn to put her arms around her, to push her down on the bed. She desperately hoped Jenn wouldn't pull away.

And she wasn't. In fact, she was moving closer, almost climbing into her lap.

"Jenn." Ronnie knocked and opened the door at virtually the same time.

She and Jenn sprang back from each other on the bed as though a bomb had exploded between them.

"Are you two doing what I think you're doing in here?"

"We're not doing anything," Cassie said.

"Bullshit." He sniffed the air. "You smoked my roach."

Cassie released her breath, but her heart was still thrumming against her chest.

"Big deal," Jenn said. "You were passed out only five minutes ago."

"Well, I'm awake now."

"Have some wine." She handed him a nearly empty bottle of Cold Duck.

"Eww," he replied. "I'm going to microwave some pizza rolls."

After he stormed off down the hall, Cassie stared back at Jenn, and they both smiled awkwardly. Cassie was about to say something about the kiss, but Jenn spoke first.

"Want a French-bread pizza?" She stood abruptly and went to the door.

"Uh, yeah, sure." Cassie followed her out of the room, trying to make sense of what had happened over the last several minutes, until the smell of pizza rolls coming from the kitchen overtook all rational thinking.

❖

The next morning after they left Jenn's, Cassie had Ronnie drop her off home. She looked out the window at a blue jay splashing in her mother's bird feeder as she ate a peanut-butter-and-jelly sandwich. What a strange sensation she'd had since waking up next to Jenn. While part of her had wanted Jenn to kiss her again, the rest of her had slept on the edge of the bed to prevent Jenn from thinking she was trying to make a pass at her.

Maybe it wasn't a kiss at all. Maybe Jenn really was "shotgunning" her, and she was the one making it be all weird.

"Oh, you're home?" Cassie's mom came into the kitchen carrying a couple of grocery bags. "Dominic called this morning asking where you were and what time to pick you up for Lake Compounce."

Shit. That's where they all were today—riding roller coasters, eating fried dough, and having a blast.

"We had a fight last night," she said as she helped put away the groceries. "That's why I slept over at my friend Jenn's house."

"What a shame you picked graduation weekend to fight."

"I didn't pick the time. It just happened. I don't care anyway. I've outgrown Dominic and my snotty girlfriends."

"Who's this Jenn you're always with now?"

Cassie didn't like the implication. "I'm not with her all the time. It's actually Jenn, Maggie, and Ronnie. We met on our class project in Greek Myth."

"That's right. You told me about them during your suspension. Well, you'll be meeting even more new friends when you go off to college."

Cassie nodded.

"If I were you, I'd just enjoy the rest of the summer doing what you want with whomever you want and not let anyone pressure you into anything. This is the last time in your life you'll ever truly be free."

Cassie nodded again. She wasn't always keen on her mother's advice, but this time, she'd nailed it.

CHAPTER FIVE

Cassie's breakup with Dominic helped facilitate her parting ways with Lisa and Debbie as well. They couldn't fathom how she could decimate Dominic's heart like that when this was supposed to be their last summer as a group before they all went off to college. And her former "friends" had little trouble deciding who out of the pair deserved their loyalty after that "stunt" Cassie had pulled at graduation.

After driving around all night, blasting songs, then getting shakes and fries at Burger King, Cassie and Jenn ended up at the town beach. They'd picked their way across the cold sand and perched on an outcropping of rocks, a forbidden act during daylight hours.

The new moon kept its light hidden, so only a few streetlights and porch lights of nearby beach houses illuminated the area around them.

"Do you miss Dominic and the rest of your clique?" Jenn was staring out into the dark water when she asked.

"A little bit. But I don't regret breaking up with him. I refused to stay with a boy just so my friends would approve of me."

"Why did you break up with him?"

"I wasn't in love with him anymore. The pressure was getting too much."

"Pressure for what?"

"To do it. I'm not ready yet, but that's all he talks about lately."

"Eww. I'm still a virgin, too. But I don't want a guy."

"Well, yeah, you have to have the right guy to pop your cherry. It can't be just anyone."

"I don't want any guy. I'm not interested in them."

Jenn was still facing the water as she spoke, and now Cassie knew why. She was making a confession, the kind Cassie had no clue how to respond to.

"Aren't you going to say something," Jenn said. "Or are you going to stop being friends with me, too?"

"I wouldn't stop being friends with you over something like that."

Jenn finally turned her head toward her. "But it's the same thing we whisper about Ronnie behind his back."

"We have to whisper it behind his back because he won't admit it. He's as gay as an Easter bonnet, and he thinks we don't have any idea."

"I'm sure he knows we do. He's probably afraid of the same thing I was."

"Did you tell him about you?"

Jenn shook her head. "You're the first person I've felt comfortable enough with to tell."

"Really? That's cool."

"Cool? You're not grossed out?"

Cassie shook her head and gushed a little at Jenn's vulnerability, a side she'd never revealed to her before. She always came across so tough, as though nothing could intimidate her. Nothing except a deep, dark secret about herself. She was flattered that Jenn placed so much trust in her. It made her feel safe, like she was that friend she could bare her soul to in confidence.

"You wanna know a secret about me?"

"I didn't think goody-two-shoes cheerleaders had any secrets." Jenn chuckled and nudged her in the shoulder.

Cassie wanted to laugh, too, but was getting anxious. "Do you want to hear it or not?"

"Yeah, yeah. Go ahead."

"You promise not to say anything? Even to Ronnie?"

"I won't tell anyone. I swear."

Cassie's hands suddenly felt as damp as the rock beneath them. They'd had dozens of conversations before, yet a sudden fear gripped her before she could utter the words. "Okay, well. Remember last week...when you shotgunned me?"

"Yeah..."

She hesitated before finishing her thought. "Well, it made me feel a certain way..."

"High?" Jenn laughed, clearly missing the tacit confession in Cassie's sincere tone.

"No. It was something else." Again she struggled to articulate her feelings. "It's like what I would've felt if we shotgunned…without the pot smoke."

"Well, if we weren't smoking, that would just be like we were kissing."

Cassie looked at her, afraid to say another word. Since it had happened, she'd been dreaming about kissing Jenn again. Without the smoke.

"Is that what you meant?" Jenn asked gently.

Cassie shrugged.

"What did you mean that it made you feel a certain way? Like a bad way?"

Cassie shook her head.

"Like in a good way?"

A shy smile broke through as she nodded.

"I felt it, too," Jenn said. "Is that weird? It's weird, isn't it?"

"I don't think so. I mean I don't know."

They both stared out at the undulating water, a heavy silence growing around them like moss. Cassie wanted to touch Jenn's hand but didn't dare.

"Should we try it without the weed?" Jenn finally said. "You know, to see if it feels the same?"

"Okay," Cassie said. She turned toward Jenn, her heart beating harder than the tide against the rocks. "Are you ready?"

"I've been ready," Jenn whispered and leaned near to kiss her.

As they kissed, a breeze blew off the water, adding to the chills Jenn was already giving her. Cassie was swept away in the softness of her lips and the excitement of her touch. Butterflies flitted through her insides as if she were experiencing her first kiss for the first time.

"Let's go down there where nobody will see us." Jenn indicated the sand below them.

After glancing around, Cassie knelt with Jenn in the cold sand, and they resumed kissing with fervor. Jenn laid her back onto the sand and got on top of her. The deep kissing with tongue stirred her like never before. She wanted to lie on that beach and kiss Jenn all night long, even when the chilly night tide started rolling up around their feet.

They laughed as they kicked their feet in the water, splashing it on themselves before resuming their passionate make-out session. As Jenn squeezed her breasts, Cassie imagined her fingers roaming down to relieve the ache concealed inside her cut-off jeans.

But would Jenn want to go that far? Kissing was one thing, but if they actually fooled around like that, would they still be friends in the morning?

The sound of a group of teenagers approaching the beach scared them both back to their feet. As Cassie wiped the sand off the back of her legs, she sensed the same awkwardness between them she'd felt that night when Ronnie almost caught them.

"We better go," she said. "It must be getting late."

"Yeah, totally," Jenn said as she brushed sand off her butt. "We're not gonna say anything about tonight, right?"

"To who?" Cassie was horror-stricken. "No. We said nobody, and that includes Ronnie."

"You don't think Maggie will be mad we didn't tell her? What if she finds out?"

"She better not. And what do you think she'd expect, a threesome?"

"Eww. No," Jenn said. "But she may feel like we don't think she's a good enough friend to tell her. It might hurt her feelings."

"Look," Cassie said as they walked toward the parking lot. "She won't be hurt about anything if she doesn't find out about anything. Nobody can know about this, Jenn. My parents will forbid me from hanging out with you if they do."

She hadn't known for sure if they would, but it seemed like a plausible threat to prevent Jenn from getting ideas about blabbing.

Whatever was happening between them, it was definitely supposed to stay between them.

❖

Weeks after blowing them off at graduation to hop in the car with the "nerd brigade," Cassie remained out of favor with Lisa and Debbie. They hadn't called her to gab or invited her to any of the elite post-graduation parties. Experts at freezing out those who displeased them, they likely were having a good and satisfying laugh over the punishment they believed they were meting out to her. Cassie grinned to herself. If they only knew she couldn't care less. All she cared about was hanging out with Jenn.

Dominic, on the other hand, was slightly more forgiving. When he showed up unannounced looking like Eeyore, she sat with him on her front steps.

"I don't know why you're being like this," he said. "This is our last summer before we go away to college, and you're acting like you don't care if you ever see me again."

Cassie shrugged. "Well, you did say that if I left with Jenn and Maggie we were through."

"I only said it because I was mad. And kinda shocked. I didn't think you'd actually do it."

"I didn't mean to hurt you. I was just so fed up with Lisa and Debbie. They'd been ragging on me for so long because I became friends with Jenn and Maggie. I just didn't want to spend the night partying with them."

"So you ran out on your own boyfriend." He sat up and flicked out the back of his mullet. "Not that I cared that much. I had a bitchin' time anyway."

Cassie indulged his bravado. "I'm glad you did. We all deserved to have the best night."

"Didn't you miss me? Do you miss me now?"

"Yeah." Her enthusiasm level sounded lower than she'd intended. She grabbed his hand. "I think it's good that we stopped spending all our time together. It'll be easier for us when we go off to school in the fall."

"I don't think it's good," he said. "I'm miserable without you. I don't wanna break up."

"Don't think of it as breaking up. Think of it as we're both eighteen, and we're going to have a whole new world to explore."

"We can still explore the world while dating."

"We'll be meeting so many new people and doing new things, Dom. We'll enjoy it much more if we don't have the pressure of trying to keep a relationship together."

"I guess you've already made up your mind," he said softly.

She immediately thought of Jenn and how excited she was about seeing her later. Maybe at one time she'd felt that way with Dominic, but not anymore. "I think we should just take a break, at least through the first semester, and see where we are in January."

"January?" He retracted his hand. "That's six months from now. Are you going to lose your virginity to someone else?"

"Eww. Oh my God. That's the first thing you think of?"

"I've been a good boyfriend, Cass. I've been waiting patiently for over a year. Don't you think I've earned it?"

He was making her job a lot easier. "Whatever, Dominic." She stood up and dusted off the back of her shorts. "I have to go now."

"Can we go get something to eat this week? Maybe a movie? *Batman* and the new *Star Trek* both look good."

"I'll let you know," she said, distracted by Jenn whizzing around the corner on her ten-speed bike.

"Hey," Jenn said as she hopped off and let it drop on the lawn. "'Sup, Dom."

"'Sup," he replied and returned his gaze to Cassie. "How about Saturday?"

"I said I'd let you know," Cassie said.

"Okay, but don't wait till the last minute. I might not be available if you do." He jogged to his car and peeled off down the street.

"What about Saturday?" Jenn asked.

"Oh, he just wants to go to a movie or something."

"Like a date?"

"I don't know. I guess."

"I thought we were all going to the carnival Saturday. Are you blowing us off again?" Jenn's usually stoic face turned into a pout that was unfamiliar to Cassie.

"I'm not blowing you off. I just forgot for a second. He put me on the spot."

"If you'd rather go out with your boyfriend, go ahead. Who's stopping you?" Jenn turned and picked up her bike from the lawn.

"What are you doing?" Cassie lurched from the steps and grabbed the handlebars.

"I'm getting out of here. I'm nobody's second choice." She tried to move the bike, but Cassie held on.

"Jenn, don't be dumb. You're not my second choice at all." She studied the hurt in Jenn's eyes. Or was it fear? It had to be both because Cassie was feeling it, too. "Please don't leave. Just come in for a minute. Nobody's home."

Once she released her grip on the handlebars, Jenn leaned the bike against the porch and followed her inside.

They grabbed a few cold cans of soda and a bag of mini doughnuts from the cabinet and went into Cassie's room.

"Didn't you say you broke up with Dominic?"

Cassie nodded as she chewed. "I did, but I guess it didn't take."

"Why didn't you tell him again when he was here?"

"I got nervous. I've never dumped anyone before. I didn't know you had to do it more than once. It's so awkward, especially when they're standing right in front of you."

"I never dumped anyone either. Never had to. I'm not the relationship type."

"I liked being in a relationship. It's fun to have someone to do things with and buy presents for and make out with."

"Are you sure you never had sex with him and aren't telling me?"

"Jenn!" Cassie laughed in embarrassment. "No. I mean we fooled around and stuff but never went all the way."

"How come?"

"Eww. I don't want that thing inside me."

Jenn almost spewed out her soda. "That's where it's supposed to go."

"No, thank you. Who needs to worry about getting knocked up? I'm leaving for college at the end of next month."

Jenn turned to face Cassie. "That's gonna suck...for me anyway."

"For me, too." Cassie's heart began to pound as she studied Jenn's face. She was so tough but so cute. If she were a boy, Cassie would be totally head over heels in love with her. "But we have like six weeks of summer left, so let's be positive."

Jenn smiled and took a small bite of a powdered doughnut. Cassie reached up and gently wiped some powder residue from the side of her mouth.

"We didn't take any napkins," she said.

Jenn kissed her, her lips sweet from powdered sugar. Cassie had been dreaming of making out with her again since their romantic kiss on the beach. Something about her softness, her gentle nature, and her pretty scent made it so different from being with a boy.

Without a word, they climbed onto Cassie's bed, Jenn getting on top and Cassie falling open to every part of her. She wanted Jenn to touch her in places she'd kept hidden away from Dominic.

And that afternoon she did.

With her parents at work, her brother off somewhere for the day, and her bedroom door locked, she and Jenn explored each other from head to toe. Wrapped together with her in cool bedsheets in her air-conditioned bedroom, Cassie experienced the thrill of sexual pleasure for the first time in a way she'd never imagined it could be.

They stared into each other's eyes as they kissed and touched and whispered beautiful words. So unsure of herself, Cassie followed Jenn's lead with each stroke and caress. When Jenn's fingers trailed down, it wasn't long before Cassie closed her eyes and dug her head back into the pillow, writhing in a pleasure she'd never experienced.

After she'd done the same to Jenn, they lay face-to-face on her pillow, smiling as they caught their breath.

"It all makes so much sense now," Cassie whispered.

"What does?" Jenn asked as she caressed Cassie's lips.

"What I've been saving myself for."

Jenn smiled. "I think I'm in love with you, Cass."

Excitement rippled through Cassie. She'd heard "I love you" before from Dominic, many times, but the words had never pierced her heart like they did now. "I think I'm in love with you, too."

"Are you still going to the movies with Dominic Saturday night?"

"Not a chance."

Cassie rolled on top of her, and they picked up exactly where they'd left off.

❖

For the rest of her secret summer with Jenn, they'd hung out alone or with Maggie and Ronnie. But no matter what they did—mini golf, the beach, clothes shopping, nights on Totoket Hill, sleepovers—they'd done it together. Ronnie and Maggie had both made casual inquiries regarding the nature of their relationship, and soon she and Jenn had both stopped making outright denials. How could they when they were constantly orbiting each other? Even their mothers had questioned them at several points throughout the summer. Cassie's mom had gone so far as to ask if Jenn was why she'd broken up with Dominic. The air of suspicion that had surrounded them, coupled with Jenn's growing possessiveness, had begun to suffocate Cassie.

By the end of August, she was dreading what she had most looked forward to for the last few years. She hadn't been able to wait for the independence of moving away to college, living on her own, and meeting new people. She'd planned to try out for the university's cross-country team, maybe join a sorority, make new, lifelong friends—all the experiences she'd heard college offered beyond the rigors of academic life.

But it was going to come at a cost well above tuition.

"I can't believe you're really leaving." Jenn sat on Cassie's bed and watched her fold sweaters and place them in a box.

The forlorn look on her face crushed Cassie and added to her own angst about leaving. "I'll be home for Thanksgiving," she said with a bright smile. "And before you know it, it'll be winter break."

"Thanksgiving is three months away." She rolled onto her stomach and shoved Cassie's pillow under her chin. "You really couldn't transfer to Southern?"

Cassie shook her head. Her parents would flip if she even suggested rearranging her plans and opting for a state university instead of Georgetown. How would she possibly explain chucking her dreams of a communications/political science double major after all her hard work to get accepted? She couldn't, so she didn't, despite telling Jenn she would in previous conversations to keep the peace. Truthfully, despite knowing how much she'd miss Jenn, she wanted the experience of going away and seeing what life could be like beyond New Haven County.

"Maybe after the fall semester, you can say you hated being away so much that you couldn't focus on your studies. Then they'd have to listen to you."

"That's an idea, but I doubt it would fly if I got good grades." Cassie taped the box of sweaters closed and moved on to the personal trinkets she was taking to ward off homesickness.

"I don't know how I'll get through these next three months without you."

"You're gonna work and take your art classes. Pretty soon you'll be so busy, you won't even know I'm gone."

Jenn sat up on the bed. "Why are you blowing off everything I'm saying, Cass? I'm gonna miss you so bad. Aren't you gonna miss me?"

"Yes. Of course I am." She sat down next to her and held her hand. "I'm just trying to look on the bright side. This is hard for me, too."

Jenn pulled her hand away and flopped back down onto the bed. "You're probably gonna meet a guy as soon as you get there anyway."

"I highly doubt that. I'll be so preoccupied getting used to everything, I won't have time to date. Besides, I'll be too busy missing you."

That response brought a smile to Jenn's perpetually dismal face. It was true. She had no interest in meeting guys at school, and she would miss Jenn. A lot. Just not enough to derail her exciting future.

Jenn leapt off the bed and draped her arms around Cassie's neck. "Promise me you won't forget about me."

Cassie looked into her glassy eyes and felt terrible. Her stomach had been in knots in the days leading up to this. While she was thrilled about leaving, she was anxious herself, wondering if, despite all her claims of devotion, Jenn would wait the entire four years it would take for her to earn her BA.

She kissed her to reassure Jenn and herself. "I could never forget you. We're gonna talk on the phone every weekend. Maybe you and Ronnie could take a road trip down sometime in the fall."

"Who knows where he'll be in the fall? Besides, I'm getting my own car soon. I won't have to wait for him to drive me down."

Cassie smiled. It would be nice to see Jenn before Thanksgiving. But Jenn was more of a dreamer than a go-getter. Soon after Cassie was gone, she'd likely be losing herself sketching and painting and procrastinating getting a job so she could afford to buy her own car.

The knock on her bedroom door launched them apart. "Cass, let's start taking your stuff down to the car," her mom said. "Your dad's getting antsy to hit the road."

"Okay," she replied as she wiped away a tear.

Her mother took that as an invitation to enter. "Aww, you two. I remember what it felt like when my best friend left for college, too." She inserted herself between them and threw an arm around them, pulling them in for a group hug.

Cassie looked at Jenn and tilted her head toward the boxes stacked near the door. They each grabbed one and marched down the stairs and out to the car.

And that was the end of their Shakespearian-style farewell.

In the spring semester of her sophomore year, Cassie and one of her roommates, Shavone, were studying for midterms in their dorm. They were sitting comfortably in sweats in the common living area of their dorm suite surrounded by a couple of bottles of red wine and an empty pizza box. When someone knocked on their door, Shavone jumped up to get it.

Cassie stopped reading when she heard a familiar voice ask if she was here.

"Sure. Come on in."

Shavone stepped aside, and Jenn walked in with a duffel bag slung over the shoulder of her beat-up bomber jacket.

Unnerved by the surprise, Cassie jumped up, made a quick introduction, and pulled Jenn into her bedroom.

"Hey," Jenn said and threw her arms around her.

"Hi," Cassie said while being smothered with kisses. She kept her eye on the door that wasn't closed tightly. "What are you doing here?"

"I couldn't wait till spring break to see you."

"You should've called first."

Jenn finally released her grip. "Why? Am I interrupting a romantic evening or something?"

"Oh, yeah. A romantic evening studying for midterms that are starting Monday. If you'd called first, I would've told you that."

"I'm sorry. Jeez." Jenn plopped down on her twin bed. "I thought I was doing something nice, surprising you."

"I love that you thought of me. Don't get me wrong. But it would've been nicer if your timing wasn't the absolute worst. I really do have to study this weekend, Jenn."

"Fine." She jumped up and grabbed her backpack off the chair. "I'll just take the next fucking train home."

Cassie grabbed her arm. "No. That's ridiculous. Stay tonight, and you can leave in the morning."

Jenn jerked her arm free and reached for the doorknob. "Please don't let me be a burden to you while you study with your very pretty roommate. How rude of me to miss my girlfriend and want to be with her."

Cassie tried to subdue her flailing arms. "Jenn, please calm down," she said softly. "I'm sorry I overreacted. I want you to stay."

"No, you don't. You just don't want me to cause a scene in front of your roommate."

That, too, Cassie thought. She wasn't out to any of her three suitemates and wanted to leave well enough alone. Plus, she was happy to see Jenn, even though it would mean she'd have to stay up cramming till all hours Sunday for her Monday exams.

"Please stay," she said sweetly. "Let me finish what I'm doing in there, and then we can go to dinner."

A smile was making its way back to Jenn's face. "It's okay if I crash on the couch out there tonight?"

Cassie laced her fingers through Jenn's. "You can crash in here with me. Shavone sleeps in the other bedroom, and my roommate is away for this weekend."

"Still think I have the worst timing in the world?"

Jenn kissed her, and suddenly Cassie decided she'd earned a break from studying.

CHAPTER SIX

After Jenn's ill-timed surprise visit that semester, she'd never attempted another, much to Cassie's relief. Jenn had seemed to become more respectful of Cassie's schedule as her classes and internships took up more of her time.

During winter break of her senior year, Cassie had decided to return to DC right after Christmas instead of staying through till the start of the spring semester. She'd gotten a job as an assistant copy editor for a local political magazine and had been advised by one of her poli-sci professors that if one aspired to some sort of career on the political scene, one would want to establish a foothold in that city.

The decision had been the final nail in the coffin of her romantic relationship with Jenn, even though they didn't have much left of it by that point. Luckily, this time they were on the same page.

"I was going to tell you while you were home for the holidays," Jenn said. They were having one of their heart-to-heart phone conversations that had grown sparse over the last year. "But since you took off so soon…"

Cassie sighed, bored with the melodrama. "You could've just told me when you started seeing her."

"How? In a letter? Over the phone? I thought you deserved better than that."

"It doesn't matter." Cassie twirled the phone cord around her finger. "All I care about is if you're happy. Are you?"

"Yeah. For the first time since you left."

"Good. 'Cuz I don't wanna have to come up there and flip any-one's food tray on them for being mean to my friend."

Cassie moved the phone away from her ear as Jenn roared on the other end of the line. "You must've forgotten who you're talking to," she said when she'd finally calmed down.

"All kidding aside, you sound happy, and I'm glad for you," Cassie said softly. And she'd meant it. She was in a different place in her life now, no longer caught up in the throes of their all-consuming first love. Although they'd slowly, steadily drifted apart over the three years she'd been away, still, it stung a little to know the thing she'd been bracing for the whole time had finally happened.

"Are you?" Jenn asked. "Happy?"

"I am. I love my job at the magazine, and I'm so excited about graduating."

She hadn't mentioned the hot bartender at Hoya Saxa, the off-campus watering hole in Georgetown that a classmate had introduced her to once she'd turned twenty-one. She'd been going every Saturday night for weeks, and their flirting game was intense.

"Are you coming home in May after you graduate?" Jenn asked with what Cassie felt was a tinge of wistfulness.

"Yeah. Of course. What else am I gonna do?"

"It'll be nice to have my best friend back in my life."

"Ditto," Cassie said. "We have so much to catch up on. And I can't wait to see Mags."

"We'll have to have ourselves a wild summer before she goes off to grad school."

"For sure."

A thick silence hung on the line for a moment.

"I still miss you, you know," Jenn said. "As a friend."

Cassie got a little choked up. "Miss you, too, ya jerk. Now behave yourself till I get back there."

"Behave myself? What's that?"

They shared a laugh before hanging up. Cassie exhaled, satisfied that she and Jenn had been able to straighten things out between them while keeping their friendship intact.

That Saturday night, as if the universe had cleared Cassie a path, Lorna, the hot bartender, upped the flirtation ante. After bestowing on Cassie her usual unfair share of attention, she'd sauntered over to her and thrust a tray of colorful test-tube shots under her nose. "From that dude at the end of the bar." She followed up with a vague nod to a cluster of college guys to Cassie's left.

Cassie groaned after assuming it was from the clearly drunk guy who was squinting and straining to focus as he tried to return her gaze. By that point, she knew she preferred women. After Jenn, there was no going back. But that was no reason not to accept the gracious gift. She plucked a melon-flavored shot, raised it to the drunk guy, and downed it. "Yummy." She looked at him again, but he was no longer focused on her. That's odd, she thought. He must've been drunker than he appeared. "Can you thank him for me. He hasn't looked this way once."

Lorna smirked.

"What's so funny?"

"The shot's from me," she replied.

"From you?"

She nodded as she popped open a few bottles of beer and placed them on a serving tray.

"Why?" Cassie cringed as soon as she'd realized what a stupid question that was.

Lorna seemed to find it endearing. "Isn't that what you do before you ask someone to dinner? Buy them a drink first to see if they're interested?"

Cassie was floored. Even after all their flirting, it had never occurred to her that Lorna would want to date her. For starters, she had to be a dozen or more years older. And rumor had it that she wasn't just the Saturday-night bartender; she was actually the bar owner, a filthy rich one, who got a kick out of flirting with college girls on Saturday nights.

"Are you, uh…" Cassie was trying to keep it together, but Lorna's smoldering stare was no match for her. "Are you asking me out?"

"I don't buy shots for just anyone."

Cassie guffawed. "Yeah, right. You buy shots for everyone. All the time."

"Well, that's true, but you're the only one I want to take to dinner." She winked. "Think you can fit a couple of hours with me into your busy co-ed schedule some time?"

"Sure." Cassie was trying so hard not to beam. "I think I can make it happen. When did you have in mind?"

"How about tomorrow?"

"Tomorrow?" Her response sounded like a parrot squawk. She

thought she'd have at least a week to mentally prepare for a date with that much woman.

"I figured it was a good day since you didn't have work or class." Her triceps flexed as she shook a cocktail shaker.

"Yeah, okay. I can do that."

Lorna pretended to wipe sweat off her forehead. "Phew. That's a relief. Now I don't have to buy you any more drinks tonight."

Cassie giggled, and she gazed at Lorna's ass in tight Guess jeans as she turned to serve a couple of butch lesbians who were clearly eager for her attention. What a way she had with women. They were practically fawning over her. They must've been melting under the heat of her stare the same way she was.

Hopefully, Lorna didn't line up dates weeks in advance. She wanted to believe that she was the only one Lorna had set her sights on that night. Something about Lorna's devil-may-give-a-shit attitude lured her in, sort of the way Jenn's rebel appeal had done back in high school, and she wasn't about to say no, despite the risk.

When Lorna made her way back to the bank of beer taps, she gave Cassie another wink. "See those girls I was just talking to?"

"Yeah…" Cassie dragged out the word.

"They said your tab is covered for the night." There was that goddamn irresistible smirk again.

"Did they really say that?"

"Dyke's honor." Lorna held up her right hand and slipped her tongue between her index and middle fingers.

Cassie knew she was lying and giggled at the joke. From that night on, she never paid for another drink at Hoya Saxa again.

❖

The night before Cassie's graduation, Lorna had ordered sushi from Cassie's favorite Georgetown Asian-fusion restaurant and opened an expensive bottle of white Bordeaux. Sitting at the small table in the dining area of her townhouse, she'd explained that she wanted to give Cassie her graduation gifts before Jenn and Maggie arrived from Connecticut the next morning to stay with them.

The first gift was lavish beyond Cassie's wildest imagination. Ten days in Greece to visit, among other things, the Greek ruins, a gift inspired by Cassie's stories of meeting her best friends in high school.

After Cassie had finished jumping up and down and all over Lorna, she tore into a small box, the size and ornate design of which indicated it was some type of jewelry. She lifted the lid, and a gold rope necklace bedazzled her…until she saw the key nestled underneath it.

"What is this key to?"

Lorna spread her arms apart to show off her luxurious townhouse.

"Really?" Cassie was flabbergasted, and Lorna clearly read her reaction on her face.

"It's not a proposal or anything," she replied. "I just don't want the pressure of financial security to factor into your decision to stay here. Use it, don't use it. It's totally up to you."

"Oh my God. That's so thoughtful." Cassie laid a wet kiss on her. Secretly, she was ecstatic. She'd fallen madly in love with Lorna during the five months they'd been dating and was afraid Lorna's feelings weren't as intense as hers. "And I don't even know what to say about the trip to Greece."

"You don't have to say anything, baby. Your smile says it all." She caressed Cassie's cheek while gazing intently into her eyes. "I know it's been only five months, but I see in you, in us, everything I've ever wanted. I want to take care of you, Cass, so you can pursue all your dreams."

Cassie's nose tickled as emotion welled up inside. "I'm so over-whelmed."

"I'm hoping those are happy tears," Lorna said.

"They are," Cassie said as she swiped her fingers under her eyes like mini windshield wipers. "I'm madly in love with you, Lorna, and I was scared I was moving too fast or, worse, it was totally one-sided."

"Oh, my sweet thing." Lorna pulled her from her chair into her lap. "It isn't just you. I'm crazy about you. And when I hold you close like this, I know I've finally met the love of my life."

❖

The day after graduation Cassie took Maggie and Jenn to lunch in Dupont Circle alone, while Lorna took Cassie's parents and younger brother on a museum tour. The girls couldn't stay more than a couple of days, and she wanted to hear their honest opinions about Lorna before they left, especially since they were about to make it official by moving in together.

Cassie picked at her Cobb salad as she tried to think of clever ways to casually broach the subject. That was going to be the tricky part since Jenn and Maggie had both mentioned in separate phone conversations that they couldn't wait for her to come home after graduation. Hopefully, the subject would just organically come up during their chat, and it wouldn't be the big deal she was making it out to be in her head.

"Are you sure you guys don't want to do or see anything specific today?" Cassie said. "I wish I'd thought about arranging a White House or congressional tour."

Maggie grimaced.

"We've been here before," Jenn said. "This time we're here to celebrate you."

Cassie smiled. "We did that last night."

Maggie glanced around from their outdoor table. "The weather's gorgeous. Let's just walk the Mall, then stop for a drink somewhere later."

"And take advantage of this time alone." Jenn leaned in as if she were about to hear something salacious.

"What?" Cassie thought they planned to spring something on her.

"She just wants the scoop on you and Lorna," Maggie said.

"Isn't she amazing? She's a woman with her shit totally together."

"She's goddamn hot, too," Jenn said.

"And rich, if that townhouse of hers is any indication," Maggie said.

Cassie sighed. "And she's the sexiest, most romantic, sophisticated woman I've ever met. One night we went to a French restaurant, and I almost passed out when she ordered for both of us in fluent French. It was so hot. She studied abroad in Paris for two years in college."

Jenn and Maggie exchanged puzzled looks.

"Oh, don't let all the tattoos and the bartender gig fool you. She's a brilliant, well-educated businesswoman."

"You seem very in love," Maggie said.

"I am. I am." Cassie leaned back and took a breath. Lately, she'd been in a whirlwind with graduation, her job, and then Lorna offering her a commitment...key. She'd only now started to feel like her feet were returning to the ground.

Jenn wrinkled her brow. "What are you guys going to do when you come home? Try the long-distance thing?"

"I'm not coming home." Cassie blurted it out and braced for the fallout.

"What do you mean?" Jenn said.

Maggie elbowed her. "She's staying here with Lorna."

"Oh." Jenn's smile seemed forced. "Oh, yeah. Duh."

"And the magazine. They offered me a full-time assistant editor position. It's a huge opportunity. It could open all kinds of doors for me."

Maggie glanced at Jenn, who'd suddenly gone silent. "Yeah. You're in the perfect place at the perfect time."

Jenn's new sullenness blanketed their conversation with an awkward air.

"And it's not even that long a drive from here to Connecticut," Cassie said. She'd felt that old need to walk on eggshells around Jenn arise again.

"Uh-huh." Jenn stared out on the circle. "I'm sure we'll see each other all the time."

"It'll definitely be easier now that I don't have school to contend with."

Cassie's suggestions clearly weren't helping defuse the tension. When Jenn returned her attention to the table, her attitude showed all over her face. "At least when you become a famous political correspondent, we can see you on TV."

"That's not gonna happen," Cassie said. "It's an incredibly competitive market down here. I just want to work in some capacity in the political environment."

"Then you can do that in any state, even Connecticut."

Cassie was starting to feel cornered. "I know, but Lorna is here," she said timidly.

"I have to hit the ladies' room," Jenn said as she jumped up from the table.

As soon as she disappeared, Cassie turned to Maggie. "What is her problem?"

"She wants you to come home."

"Everyone wants that, but why does she have to be the only one making me feel like shit about it?"

"Maybe she thinks you two will rekindle your old flame."

Cassie knew that Maggie was being ironic, but still, the thought had also briefly occurred to her. "That's not gonna happen even if I come home. We've both grown up and moved on to other people."

"You certainly have."

Cassie's heart nearly melted at the thought. "I can't believe how crazy I am about Lorna."

"She seems crazy about you, too," Maggie said. "While the other one"—she jutted her chin toward the restrooms—"just seems crazy."

"Let me go talk to her." Cassie got up and went into the ladies' room. Jenn was rubbing her hands under the dryer. "What's up with you?" she asked. "Are we gonna have another one of our stupid fights over this?"

"No." Jenn slumped against the sink. "I'm just fucking bummed you're never coming back. I've missed my best friend."

"I miss you, too."

"No, you don't. You have a whole new life."

"That doesn't mean I've forgotten the people I care about."

Jenn folded her arms and stared at the tile floor.

"Look. I've given this so much thought in the weeks leading up to graduation," Cassie said. "I've been so looking forward to going home, but everything is just falling into place for me here."

"I know, goddammit. I only want the best for you. It's just so hard to be happy for you and sad for myself at the same time." She stood up straight and scratched the back of her head. "I'll get over it, though." She flashed her signature crooked grin. "I got over you dumping me, didn't I?"

Cassie laughed, relieved to hear the playfulness in her voice again. "You sure did. And got right under someone else."

"Several someones."

"Come here, you jerk." Cassie pulled her in for a hug, and they both held on as if making a silent vow to each other. When Jenn released first, they both were trying to conceal the tears that spilled from their eyes. "Now if we could only figure out a way to get Maggie under someone."

"That's gonna be a tall order," Jenn said as they left the ladies' room. "If it didn't happen while she was away at college, I'm pretty sure she's gonna be a virgin for life."

"Impossible. She just hasn't met the right person yet."

"Unlike you," Jenn said. "I really am happy for you despite my mini tantrum about you not coming home."

Cassie stopped her in the foyer before they headed outside. "Thank you. I needed to hear that from you. And I promise. We're going to make our friendship stronger than it's ever been, separate geographical locations be damned."

"As long as Lorna keeps a guest bedroom in her townhouse, you'll be seeing my face."

"I better. Maggie's, too."

They shared a quick embrace and headed back to their table.

CHAPTER SEVEN

January 1999

Over the last six years, Cassie had molded her life to fit snugly into Lorna's dichotomous world of high culture and saloon-style bars down in DC. Although part of her never got used to being so far away from her family, friends, and roots in Connecticut, she was in love with Lorna and couldn't imagine life without her.

Lorna had made it easy for her. Financially stable thanks to an inheritance from her father and her highly profitable college bar, Hoya Saxa, Lorna let Cassie want for nothing. She seemed to assess her own value according to how much she could give her partner, whether it was material luxuries or an overabundance of love and flattery. Anything to make her woman feel like she was her queen. After four years, she'd even agreed to move up to Connecticut with Cassie when the magazine she was working at folded. Indeed, life with her first real love had been everything Cassie dreamed it would be.

Until it wasn't.

She woke up again one morning with the same awful feeling that had greeted her each day for several months—like some level of intuition was eating at her gut and no amount of antacid could bring relief. After six years together, she and Lorna were drifting apart despite Cassie's efforts to get them to reconnect and recover the magic that had drawn them together back in Cassie's senior year.

When Lorna and she had moved to Connecticut, Cassie thought that meant they were working toward a new start in their relationship as well. She'd developed quite a talent for living in denial, convincing herself that they'd power through whatever "rough patch" they were experiencing. But as Lorna's distance increased, Cassie realized their promises to make more time for each other and try harder to meet each other's needs were as sturdy and impenetrable as a ship made of cardboard.

Never one to give up easily, Cassie had become an expert at going through the motions rather than confronting the inevitable. With Lorna's fortieth birthday less than a month away, she chose to focus on the finishing touches for a surprise party at Pantheon the next weekend. Cassie had been planning it for weeks, and it was no small task to keep it from Lorna since she was now the owner of Pantheon—well, they both were, but Lorna had had the money to back the place initially when she decided to take over a once-popular lesbian club. And it worked. Lorna let Cassie rename it, and together, they created Pantheon, taking it to new heights over the last year and a half.

"Lorna?" Cassie padded out of the bedroom and into the bathroom. She turned on the shower and waited for a response. Before stepping under the warm water, she called out again. "Babe?" Nothing. She'd probably run out to do some errands.

Still tired from a late night at the club, Cassie stood at the kitchen window and scratched at her half-dried, wavy hair as she poured a huge cup of coffee. Lorna must've been up early because the coffee was only lukewarm.

She sat at the desk in the sunny alcove off the kitchen, intending to pay some bills after checking her email. When she brought up the browser, she saw that Lorna hadn't logged out of her private email…an address unfamiliar to Cassie.

Downing a large sip of black coffee, she entertained possible reasons why Lorna might have an email account Cassie hadn't known about. One click and she'd be in it. Would she find anything that might shed light on how or why things had changed between them? Maybe she was just overthinking the situation. Maybe Lorna was just freaking out at turning forty. At twenty-eight, Cassie had heard of people having midlife crises, but she'd thought it only happened to balding men who'd dealt with it by buying a Corvette. Surely, an attractive lesbian nightclub owner didn't have such lame insecurities.

Her index finger rested on the mouse as she contemplated the weight of this decision. *Come on, Cass. Is this what you've become? The suspicious, snooping girlfriend?*

She stared at the computer screen over the edge of her mug as she sipped and contemplated…sipped and contemplated. It wasn't really snooping if Lorna hadn't signed out of her account and Cassie accidentally opened it thinking she was signing into her own email.

As if without permission, her index finger clicked and brought up Lorna's mystery account. There were only a couple of messages, all from Jane203@hotmail.com.

Who the fuck was Jane203?

She clicked on the email, and by the end of the first line, the persistent knot that had been resting in her stomach turned into a full-on punch, blocking any air from entering her lungs. The virtual love letter was signed "love, me."

Suddenly, it came together like the plot of a bad film noir. Jane was that grungy biker chick who'd been hanging around Pantheon with her buddies the last few months. She was well aware that Lorna and Cassie were a couple. In fact, she'd acted like she wanted to be friends with both of them, make her way into their group. Cassie had caught a bad vibe from her from the start, but being the girlfriend of the club owner, you had to deal with women like that—social climbers who didn't let a little thing like morals get in the way of chasing what they wanted.

After reading the entire email exchange again, Cassie realized that Lorna wasn't going to let anything get in her way either.

She slunk back in the chair and continued to stare silently at the words on the screen. They flashed in and out of focus as tears began pooling in her eyes. She labored to take in enough oxygen, couldn't move as her brain struggled to process what she'd read. So much flirting, Jane lathering Lorna up with compliments, and Lorna playing the misunderstood martyr wanting to be faithful to her wholesome, loveable girlfriend but fearing she was losing the fight to Jane's bold energy.

Cassie swallowed against the coffee threatening to gush from her stomach like a geyser. How was this happening? They were supposed to be solid, lovers forever. Lorna was her first real girlfriend, the college crush she'd wanted to build a life with. She'd thought their awesome romantic and professional partnerships proved they were. How could Lorna do this?

She couldn't stop reading their exchange, getting sicker each time. It seemed like they hadn't slept together yet, but they talked like it was imminent. Maybe fate had caused Cassie to find this when she had. Maybe she could stop it from happening and help Lorna see what a mistake she was making.

She brushed the tears off her cheeks, closed the browser, and leapt up, her legs weak and unsteady. She held the wall as she walked back into the kitchen, trying to reorient her thinking for what was next. She should get dressed and go out and get Lorna some fresh flowers. This had probably happened because Cassie was taking things with her for granted. She could've been a better, more attentive girlfriend.

Yes, she'd start with a beautiful bouquet. And tonight, a dinner reservation at their favorite Italian restaurant. She loved Lorna and felt bad that she hadn't done enough to make her realize that fact, not just on special occasions but every single day.

And then the car door slammed in the driveway. Cassie leaned against the kitchen counter and broke down. Streaming tears turned into sobs, and when Lorna walked in with a grocery bag and gas-station coffee cup, Cassie slid down the front of the cabinet to the floor and covered her face to try to muffle her wailing.

"Babe, what's the matter?" Lorna said. She laid her stuff on the table and rushed to help Cassie. "What happened, Cass? Are you okay?"

A soft "no" escaped Cassie's lips as she continued to cry.

"Talk to me, babe." Lorna rubbed Cassie's forearm. "Tell me what's wrong."

"You forgot to sign out of your email."

"What?" Lorna sounded sincerely confused.

"When are you going riding with Jane? Or steal a kiss in the bathroom of Pantheon?"

"Oh, God," Lorna whispered. "Cass, I'm sorry."

"I bet you are." Cassie climbed to her feet and flung off Lorna's supporting hands. "How long have you two had this thing?"

"Not long." Lorna's head was down.

"Did you fuck her?"

"No. I swear. It never got that far." Lorna finally looked at her, her eyes brimming with contrition.

Finally, Cassie could breathe again, but just barely. "I'm assuming you'll end it now. I mean I guess I can understand why it happened." She heard herself babbling, and she sounded desperate. "I know I could've given you more attention, especially since—"

"No," Lorna said softly.

Cassie's eyes met hers. "What do you mean 'no'? No, I gave you enough attention?"

Lorna shook her head, her eyes wild like a cornered animal's.

"No, what, Lorna?"

"No. I'm not going to end it with Jane." She folded her arms and looked away, as though Cassie no longer had any influence on her life whatsoever.

"What do you mean?" Cassie stared hard at her, willing Lorna to switch back to the woman she was before she left for errands that morning. But she just gazed out the window. "Lorna?" She hadn't meant to yell it. "Why are you doing this to me?"

"I'm sorry, Cass. But you know we haven't been happy for a while."

"You mean you haven't been happy."

"No. I think if you're honest with—"

"Don't put this on me. Your shit's obviously spilling over onto me, and you don't want to take the blame for it." Cassie took a moment to breathe as her heart caved in on itself. "I love you, Lorna. I've wanted to work on fixing what's wrong. I've been trying, but it's like I've been the only one. Don't you want this anymore?"

Lorna chewed the inside of her cheek as she stared at the floor.

Her silence was like a backhand to the face. "Do you still love me?"

"Yes, I love you." She extended her hand but retracted it soon after Cassie refused to accept it. "I'm just not *in love* with you."

Cassie had no more words. With a guttural grunt, she shoved Lorna hard into the kitchen island and ran upstairs to their bedroom, slamming the door behind her. She dropped onto the bed and wept quietly into her pillow, waiting for Lorna to come upstairs and knock, a pattern they'd established long ago when Lorna got in the mood to push buttons.

But no knock followed. No sound at all except the front door closing.

Cassie ran to the window and watched Lorna get into her car and back out of the driveway. She closed her eyes and then crumpled down to the carpet.

❖

After spending most of the winter sealed away in the home she'd shared with Lorna, Cassie was climbing the walls. Lorna had become a ghost, contacting Cassie only through email when it related to Pantheon business. The cruel but necessary freeze-out helped her come to terms with the reality that Lorna wasn't coming back.

One Saturday in March when she trudged out to the mailbox in her sweats, she noticed her favorite first sign of spring: crocus buds pushing their way up from the cold, softening soil. She reveled in the sight for a moment as it reminded her of one late summer weekend after graduation with Jenn and Maggie. The three of them were crammed in the front seat of Jenn's mother's old Pontiac screaming the lyrics to "Ballroom Blitz" by Krokus as they drove around downtown New Haven yelling and waving at the returning Yale students swarming the intersection of York Street and Broadway.

Nature's message had awakened something in her as well. It was time for a fresh start. Her winter hibernation of self-pity had lasted long enough. She'd come to terms with the fact that her six-plus years with Lorna and all her promises of "happily ever after" had been just a fairy tale. It was beautiful and magical while it had lasted, but like with all good stories, when it was over, one had to lay the book down and reconcile with life in the real world.

As she thought about moving forward, Cassie wanted to attempt to get the Pantheon Girls back together as the first item on her list.

Ten years after they graduated high school and exchanged only phone calls and a few visits in between, she sat in a big, round booth at a pub with Jenn and Maggie and couldn't believe how no time or distance seemed to have passed.

"Cass, are you all right?" Maggie asked.

"Yeah, why?"

"*Why?*" Jenn said. "You've just gone through a major breakup, and the way you're smiling? The term 'powerful sedatives' comes to mind."

"Look at us," she replied. "Lorna dumping me has put us back in contact. This is better than any kind of pharmaceutical remedy."

After a double high-five, Jenn said, "Well, I don't know about *any* pharmaceutical, but I have missed you guys. We need to hang out more. No excuses."

"I miss you both, too," Maggie said. "Now that my Mema's gone, I don't do anything but work."

Cassie patted Maggie's hand. "I'm sorry about your Mema. And sorry I couldn't make it to her funeral."

"At least Lorna was good for lavish vacations to faraway lands," Jenn said. "My girlfriends are barely employed."

"You should probably date women who are done with college," Cassie said with a straight face. "That might help."

Jenn raised an eyebrow at her. "Maybe we should both date women our own ages. Wanna date me again?"

Cassie chuckled in the spirit in which Jenn obviously meant it. "We can't ruin our pact. We've already said if we're still single at fifty, we'll date again."

"Fifty. Phew. Can you imagine?" Jenn swiped at her forehead dramatically.

"I hope you'll let me in on it this time," Maggie said.

"We didn't let anyone in on it, Mags," Cassie said. "That was taboo stuff back then. Speaking of letting people in on your romantic antics, are you dating anyone?"

Maggie shook her head. "I'm asexual."

"What's that?" Jenn looked between them.

"I don't have sex with anyone."

"That's called being single," Cassie said. "We're all in the same boat now."

"Uh, being single doesn't mean you don't have sex with anyone," Jenn said. "You two are in the same boat. I'm out there on a yacht of sex."

"Yes, Jenn. We all admire your ability to be totally indiscriminate in your sex partners. But I prefer an emotional connection first." Cassie turned to Maggie. "Okay, so then what is asexual?"

"I don't want to have sex with anyone," Maggie said. "I don't have a desire to."

Cassie and Jenn exchanged not-so-subtle looks of disbelief.

"You just haven't met anyone who's floated your boat," Jenn said.

Maggie sucked the onion out of an onion ring. "You guys are really stuck on that boat metaphor."

"Look, whatever Maggie wants or doesn't want is fine," Cassie said. "We support you fully in any and all of your endeavors."

"Speaking of, let me know when you're ready to start dating again," Jenn said. "I'll put out the feelers."

Cassie vehemently rejected the suggestion. "It's only been a few months. I need some time to regroup."

Jenn stared at her. "Don't tell me you're waiting for Lorna to come back. It really seems like that ship has sailed." She turned to Maggie. "Sorry."

"Um, no," Cassie said. "Despite the inevitability of those two narcissists eventually imploding, I'm definitely not waiting for anything from Lorna. My therapist says that I'm still too raw and need time to reflect on who I am and what I want."

"What *do* you want?" Maggie asked.

Cassie sipped her beer, then exhaled. "I have no idea. But I need to get out of Lorna's house and find a job outside of her bar."

"I'm surprised she hasn't thrown you out of both yet," Jenn said.

"Why would she? She's renting a fancy apartment in downtown New Haven with Jane. And since I handle most of the day-to-day business at Pantheon, she's not looking to kick me out of that."

"Plus, this way she still gets to keep tabs on you," Jenn said.

"All the more reason to cut the cord," Maggie said.

"Is that your professional advice?"

Maggie shrugged. "Yes. It's the advice I'd give anyone I care about. It's the only way you'll truly be able to move on."

"I know, but it's like…" The gravity of her situation pulled her under. "How did I allow my life to become so intertwined with Lorna's?"

"It happens, especially in your first serious adult relationship."

"We were supposed to be together forever." A wave of emotion surprised her. "She just kind of took charge of things over the years, like I hadn't a single thing to worry about, and I let her do it. Then one day she just decides she wants to move on with someone else, and I'm left trying to piece myself back together." She looked away so they wouldn't see the tears pooling in her eyes.

"I'm sorry, Cass," Jenn said.

"It wasn't supposed to end this way," she replied.

Maggie placed a hand on top of Cassie's as she stuffed another onion ring into her mouth.

Cassie sucked in a deep breath and flicked an escaped tear off her cheek. "What do you say? Should we drive around Yale later and scream out the windows?"

"Thought you'd never ask," Jenn said, and they all laughed.

CHAPTER EIGHT

Deana Godwin, wife of US Senate hopeful Jeffrey Godwin, walked into the new Fairfield County children's center a week before its official opening. She'd volunteered to meet the artist who was painting the mural on the wall, a "sacrifice" she was willing to make since she'd gotten to know her well over the last several weeks. In that time, she'd developed what she'd considered an "innocent" crush on the sexy, beguiling butch with a slender, sinewy frame and half-shaved jet hair hidden under a backward baseball cap.

The artist, Jenn Ferrano, was freakishly intuitive and always seemed to know when Deana could use a friendly conversation, which was often, since her marriage of political convenience had left her restless and searching.

"Good morning," Jenn said as she entered with a tray of coffees for them. She lugged her painting supplies in her other hand as she breezed past Deana with a wink.

"Morning," Deana said over the usual butterflies Jenn caused. "Can I help you carry anything?"

"Nope." She dropped her stuff and handed Deana a coffee. "Skim, two Equals."

"You remembered." Deana railed against the urge to look away from Jenn's warm, dark eyes. They always made her self-conscious, as if Jenn were reading something about her that she wasn't ready or willing to reveal.

"I remember every word of our chats over the last few weeks, Mrs. Godwin."

Jenn's arched eyebrow sent a current of sensation throughout Deana. In spite of herself, she remained cool as she sat on top of a children's picnic-style table. "I'm going to miss those chats. I feel a little guilty, like I've gotten free therapy sessions for the price the benefactors paid for your services as an artist."

Jenn shot her a seductive glance. "No problem at all. Mural gigs are usually a solitary experience. I've enjoyed your company."

"I've loved watching you," Deana said. "You're very talented."

After sipping her coffee, Jenn licked her lips, her gaze lingering on Deana in what seemed a suggestive way. "Thank you."

A rush of heat spread over her. She walked away for a second and tugged at her blouse to let some air in. This young woman was incredibly sexy and had reignited physical desire in her that had burned out long ago with Jeffrey.

"Listen. I hope things work out for you…"

Deana turned back to Jenn standing there with a strap from her overalls hanging down, her tight tank top revealing thin, muscular arms and shoulders.

"You know," Jenn said, "with your marriage."

"Thanks, but there's nothing left to work out. I wasn't entirely honest when I said we're having trouble." She started to walk toward her coffee cup on the table. "Our marriage is over. It has been for a while."

Jenn's expression grew somber as she moved toward her. "I'm sorry, Deana."

"After the election, I'm going to file for divorce. But until then, I promised him I'd play the dutiful politician's wife."

"It must be so hard living like that, keeping your desires restrained." With brush in hand, Jenn continued to move closer.

Deana picked up her coffee cup but didn't sip from it, fixated on Jenn's full, glistening lips. "You know what the hardest part is?"

Jenn shook her head, never breaking her intense gaze traversing Deana's face.

"Not being touched. I mean, you know…" Deana tapped her hand innocently on her own forearm to lessen the charge of sexual inuendo. She then crossed her arms over her chest, creating an invisible barrier against the woman she'd been fantasizing about.

"He must be a real fool." As Jenn slowly dragged her gaze up and down her body, Deana could almost feel it.

"It's not *his* touch I've been craving." Deana looked away in embarrassment. She hadn't meant to be so brazen, but now that the confession was out, she realized she no longer wanted to restrain her desires.

"You don't mean…" Jenn pointed at herself with her paintbrush.

Deana smiled awkwardly as she dropped her gaze to the floor. She thought about shutting this interaction down before it went too far, but Jenn was moving closer.

"Do you know how incredibly sexy you are?" Jenn whispered in her ear.

Deana tingled with arousal at Jenn's warm breath against her ear. She hadn't been with a woman since a drunken night at her liberal arts college in the early eighties, and that was just a little clumsy kissing and touching.

"I take it from your silence, it's been a while since someone's reminded you," Jenn said.

"Wives aren't usually a politician's first priority," Deana said. "Something this wife has grown increasingly grateful for."

Jenn's eyes seemed heavy as her hand crawled up through the back of Deana's hair and gently pushed their heads closer. Her lips parted and slowly slid against Deana's. At first Jenn's kisses were soft and sensuous, but when Deana could no longer contain her moans of pleasure, they grew hungry and aggressive.

"Do you know what you're doing to me?" Deana whispered.

As Jenn's tongue swirled around in her mouth, she slid her fingers into Deana's pants and explored her wetness. "If this is what I've caused, then I should do something about it."

"Yes," Deana said in a whisper as she leaned into her.

Jenn grabbed her hand and hurried them into the back room. As soon as she locked the door, Deana breathed heavily as she anticipated Jenn's next move. And she did not disappoint. She moved closer and cradled the back of Deana's head, running her lips up her neck and grabbing hold of her earlobe with her teeth. Her body was screaming to feel Jenn's fingers rubbing her again as she throbbed.

Backed against the counter, she nibbled at Jenn's lips, trying not to bite them too hard. She was losing herself in desire as she grabbed Jenn's hips and began grinding into her. Jenn hoisted her onto the counter, rolled her knit pants down to her ankles, and attended to her ache with a sensual expertise Deana had never experienced. The force and skill of Jenn's tongue left her spent after a round of orgasms.

Afterward, they fumbled through a little awkward conversation as though it were just another business exchange. Jenn went back to her mural, but Deana needed a moment to pull herself together—physically and mentally. Her mind blown, she tried to remember if she'd ever experienced sex like that with Jeffrey or the other men she'd dated before they'd married.

❖

At the request of Jenn, Cassie stayed at Pantheon after she'd finished working in the office that evening. Still secretly mourning the loss of Lorna, all she'd had the energy for lately was to work and go home. Or go for dinner or drinks when Jenn and Maggie had insisted. And if she planned to have drinks with them, Pantheon was the last place she wanted to hang out. Although the club was half in her name, thanks to Lorna's magnanimous love-bombing early on in their relationship, she'd never considered the club hers. She'd always felt like Lorna's employee because the money had all come from Lorna—via her rich daddy.

But now that Lorna was hot and heavy with Jane, she was only too happy to leave the responsibility of running the bar to Cassie. Same for the house they'd shared. Cassie needed a new job and a new house but hadn't gained the emotional strength to pursue any of it yet.

Seated at her usual spot at the corner of the main bar, Cassie sipped a Jack and Ginger while Jenn danced around anxiously awaiting the arrival of her new "friend."

"What time is your girlfriend arriving?" Cassie asked.

Maggie added a yawn to the conversation.

"She's not my girlfriend," Jenn said. "We had a little thing, but we decided it would be best to be just friends."

Cassie sucked her lip. "You both decided or just you?"

"Is that a dig at my 'love 'em and leave 'em' reputation?"

"If the rep fits…"

"No, no. She's still married. It would be really complicated, you know, so I suggested we stay friends. She's cool with that. Besides, she's from Fairfield County. Imagine all the referrals I'm gonna get."

"There it is," Cassie said.

"No. Listen. She's a really cool woman. You'll see. She's just in a tight spot right now in her personal life and wants to make some new acquaintances."

"Sounds like a lot of work," Maggie said. "I don't have to do anything, do I?"

"You just be your usual warm, captivating self," Jenn said and rolled her eyes at Cassie.

"She must really want new friends if she's willing to traipse to New Haven for them," Cassie said.

"When I told her my good friend, Cassie, owns the hottest lesbian bar in CT, she said she just had to check it out."

"This is the one married to the guy, right?"

"How many married ones do you have in your stable?" Maggie asked.

"One," Jenn said, annoyed. "Only one ever…that I knew about anyway."

Something drew Cassie's attention toward the entrance. Walking in was the most beautiful woman she'd ever seen come through those doors. Fortyish, brunette, curvaceous, it could've easily been her mom's favorite actress, Ava Gardner, later in her career. The sight rendered Cassie mute as she absorbed every inch and aura of the woman carefully exploring her surroundings as she sauntered in.

In the midst of her trance, she heard Jenn say, "Okay, shut up, everybody. That's her."

The woman lit up at Jenn's frantic waving and headed toward them.

"That's her? That's the married mess?" Cassie mumbled it to herself in awe and disbelief.

Jenn embraced her, then introduced her to them.

"It's so nice to meet you both," Deana said, shaking their hands. "Jenn told me so much about you while she was designing her amazing mural for the center. I'm assuming you've seen it."

"Yes. She's shown us pictures," Cassie said.

"Lots of pictures," Maggie mumbled.

"Oh, pictures simply can't do it justice. You should all come to the grand opening next weekend—I mean if you're available, of course."

"They're available," Jenn said. "I guarantee it."

Cassie reminded herself to stop staring at this woman, although, with a smile like hers, she must've been used to people getting all googly-eyed around her. Was she crazy, or did Deana even have a little scar on her cheek like Ava did after the horse kicked her in the face?

"This is a beautiful club you have," Deana said. "Impressive for someone your age."

"Thanks. Technically, it's my ex's, but she's too busy with her new girlfriend to care about the place."

"Oh." Deana gave an awkward smile.

Cassie's head felt like it might explode in embarrassment. "Would you excuse me for a second?" She fled the scene and headed to her office, closing the door behind her.

Nearing the verge of tears, she took a few deep breaths. What had possessed her to say something so stupid and pathetic in front of a perfect stranger? A perfect gorgeous, personable stranger. Over the last couple of months, she'd welcomed plenty of moments where she'd felt like she was finally moving on. Then like a crackle of thunder out of nowhere, something triggered her, and she felt consumed with indignation over Lorna doing her dirty that way. And that calculating creep Jane, who'd pretended she wanted to be friends with both of them.

The gentle knock on the door stirred her back to reality. Maggie or Jenn was coming to check on her. They'd both been so caring and concerned for her during and after her breakup. "Sorry for being so dramatic…" she said as she opened the door.

"There's a bit of drama in all of us," Deana said with a sweet smile. "I was going to the ladies' room, so your friends asked me to check on you."

Disarmed by Deana's warmth, Cassie grinned. "That's really nice of you…considering you met me and witnessed me having a meltdown all in the span of three minutes."

Deana chuckled. "Jenn said you had a dark sense of humor. I like that in a person."

"Then you definitely picked the right group to drink with tonight."

"When you're ready to rejoin the party, I'd like to buy a bottle of the finest champagne you have."

They started walking back into the bar. "What are we celebrating?"

"New beginnings," Deana said.

"I'll drink to that," Cassie replied.

"I hope you don't mind, but Jenn shared that you're dealing with a painful breakup."

Cassie shrugged. "At this point, everyone knows."

"I'm stuck in a rather unpleasant holding pattern myself now. But hopefully, that'll be changing soon."

"Oh, are you filing for divorce?"

"After the 2000 election. Sooner, if I can manage it."

Cassie hoped Deana wasn't pinning her hopes on a relationship with Jenn after the divorce. Since they'd broken up while Cassie was away at college, Jenn had become a serial dater, easy to catch but hard to contain. Despite them closing in on the big three-O, Jenn hadn't seemed motivated to change her MO.

After the bartender poured four flute glasses full of champagne, Cassie handed them out. "Thank you, Deana," she said, and they clinked glasses.

"Thank you all for this lovely companionship tonight," Deana said.

Cassie thought Deana's gaze lingered a little extra longer on her, but in her state, it was probably wishful thinking.

"Here's to more nights and days of lovely companionship to come," Jenn said.

What wasn't wishful thinking was the way Jenn's gaze lingered on Deana.

The night of the opening of the children's center in Fairfield, Cassie was way more jazzed about the event than she'd had reason to be. Obviously, Jenn was psyched that her mural was being unveiled in front of a large, affluent crowd of people eager to spend ridiculous amounts of money. That kind of exposure could elevate her from house and business painter to a full-time artist painting on commission.

But Cassie was still working her way back to life among the living. She could handle socializing in small doses, but a charity event of this caliber would require her to be on her best game. Maggie had canceled at the last minute in a fit of panic at the opportunity for a new social experience. What kind of a friend would she have been if she'd bailed on Jenn, too?

Adding to her apprehension was that she'd thought about Deana and her Ava Gardner smile and sweet disposition all week long. Seriously. Every single day since she'd met her the previous weekend. Then again, Cassie was sure anyone who met Deana would inevitably be chased in their dreams by her screen-goddess face.

"I'm so pissed at Maggie for bagging on us," Jenn said. "This night really means a lot to me."

"I know, but her anxiety's been bad lately."

"Yeah. What else is new with her?" Jenn sighed as she backed up her pickup truck into a spot on the street.

"Come on. Show some compassion. Imagine going through life so awkward you can't make a relationship work with anyone?"

"I'm sure it's horrible," Jenn replied as they walked toward the center. "Hey, I heard Martha Stewart sometimes shows up at things like this."

"I know how you feel about blondes, so I'll make myself scarce if she graces us with an appearance."

Jenn giggled. "I wish. Although she does like art. Maybe I can woo her with my brushstrokes."

Cassie wanted to ask the question that had been burning in her since last weekend, but how would one ask that kind of thing without revealing some sort of motive? Now, with Jenn's mind focused squarely on herself, seemed like a good time. "So, are you and Deana really just gonna keep it friends?"

"Yeah. I told her that her life is too messy for me. She's got a kid, too, you know."

"No. I didn't."

"Besides, not only is she married to a guy, but she's like forty."

"So? What's a dozen years? And I mean she's gorgeous in like this ridiculous old-Hollywood, glamorous way."

"You like the older ones. You should go for her." Jenn seemed unmoved, but Cassie had sensed a territorial vibe coming from her since that night at Pantheon when she and Deana flowed off on their own in a stream of easy conversation.

When they walked in, Cassie zeroed in on Deana immediately and almost let out an audible gasp at the vision. Her hair and cream-colored pantsuit looked fresh off Fifth Avenue, and she beamed with the pride of ownership over such a classy affair. She gave Jenn a quick hug, then moved over to her, holding on for a second longer, long enough for Cassie to inhale her exotic scent.

Cassie glanced down at her own outfit. While her beige dress pants and black blazer fell short by comparison, standing next to Jenn in her grunge artist outfit of black leather pants, tank top, and plaid flannel wrapped around her waist, it all seemed to fit.

"I'm so happy to see you both," Deana said. "Just to give you a quick rundown of the evening. We're having cocktails and hors d'oeuvres till eight. Then the unveiling of Jenn's mural and the silent auction for the specially commissioned piece of yours." She patted Jenn's shoulder in a collegial way.

"I still can't believe people are going to bid on one of my paintings."

Cassie tried to be attentive with Jenn during her shining moment, but Deana's glance kept tugging at her.

"Typically, the highest bid comes in at around fifty. That would give you about twelve thousand. I can't thank you enough for taking such a cut on one of your originals."

"It's for the children," Jenn said.

Someone pulled Deana away, and Cassie snorted. "You're taking a cut? When have you ever sold an original for more than a hundred bucks?"

"Wild, isn't it? Deana is just the coolest woman ever."

Cassie released the breath she'd been holding as she watched Deana work the room, especially the way she moved—so sensual and fluid, like a Nereid accompanying sailors to safety. This woman was the closest thing to a goddess anyone would find here on the Earth.

Near the bar, a well-dressed, polished guy drew his arm around her waist and whispered something in her ear. She gave what seemed like a forced smile and slipped away from him. Clearly the husband.

Cassie grabbed a glass of champagne off a passing tray to wash down the distasteful feeling the sight evoked in her. Was he aware his wife had banged the artist he'd probably be bidding on later in the evening? Or that she was fraternizing with a group of lesbians one county over?

Draining the last of the champagne, she imagined him a smug politician who was having affairs of his own. Deana should dump him sooner rather than later. She was too good to play trophy wife for the rest of her life.

"Can I get you something to eat?"

Cassie jumped as Deana's voice crept over her shoulder.

"I'm sorry," she said in a giggle. "I didn't mean to startle you."

"I was just meandering over to the hors d'oeuvre table." Cassie couldn't take her eyes off Deana's magnetic smile. "What a great gathering you've put together."

"Thanks. I'm so happy with the turnout, especially since it includes my new friends." She gave Cassie a little wink that set her stomach tumbling.

"It's a great cause, and of course, Jenn's mural is just to die for."

"It is. I can't wait for the unveiling," Deana said enthusiastically. "She's so talented. I've passed her name to a few friends in the city. I'm sure some work will be coming her way."

"I hope so," Cassie said. "She's the most expressive, creative person I've ever met. You should've seen her notebook sketches in high school. They were the first thing I noticed about her."

Deana giggled. "She told me the story about how you became friends. It's just adorable—the two of you playing superhero to your bullied friend and then causing a food fight."

"In a weird way I'm grateful to that bully. If she hadn't been such a shitty kid, I never would've become friends with Jenn and Maggie. We were all so opposite."

"It's wonderful that when things are meant to be, they'll happen no matter how unlikely the circumstances." She lowered her eyes in a way that seemed almost...flirtatious? "Kind of like you and I meeting through Jenn."

Cassie nodded. "I could definitely use some serendipity these days. Or at least a new friend or two."

"Well, if it's new friends you're looking for, I'd like to volunteer." Deana raised her hand and smiled so sweetly, she totally disarmed Cassie. Was this woman just the most innocently charming human on earth or a master of flirtation?

She absolutely meant to find out.

After Deana returned to making her party rounds, Cassie walked off in search of Jenn or a quiet corner to contemplate what was going on with her hormones. She was obviously having some kind of rebound reaction to Deana. No surprise. The woman was amazing. Her only flaw was the dude leaning against the bar looking like a life-size Ken doll in an Armani suit.

Why did forbidden fruit always taste so much sweeter?

❖

As the night's festivities were winding down, Cassie suggested they find Deana and say their good nights before a mass exodus of muckety-mucks descended and swallowed her up.

"You want to go already?" Jenn said. "It's not even ten yet."

"It's almost over, and I really don't want to be the last ones here with Deana and her husband."

Jenn sneered. "The illustrious state rep, Jeffrey Godwin. What a dick."

"Do you know him?"

"Just what Deana's told me about him." She leaned closer to the side of Cassie's face. "He's having an affair."

"Well…" Cassie indicted her with a raised eyebrow.

"We're not having an affair. We had one smoldering encounter in the back room over there. That's it. We're just friends."

"You fucked her in the children's center? That's so depraved." Cassie tried to maintain her grave expression but broke into a grin.

"It's not like we planned it."

"I'm sure next time you guys'll do it in a more dignified locale… like a cheap motel."

"There won't be a next time. I don't want to ruin our friendship— and potential business relationship."

Deana turned as they approached her. "Oh. You're heading out?"

Cassie nodded. "We had a great time."

"I'm so glad. I wish I'd been able to chat more with you gals."

"Hey, we get it," Jenn said. "How about a happy hour next Friday? Come to Pantheon."

Deana had to peel her glance away from Cassie before replying to Jenn. "I would love to make that happen. Let me see how the week goes."

Cassie looked away to deflect the heat from Deana's gaze.

"Or we can meet closer to you if that works," Jenn said.

"That sounds like fun." Deana suddenly seemed distracted. "Jenn, I'll call you and let you know about Friday."

Representative Godwin sauntered over and looped his hand under her arm as though claiming his property. "Are we all set to go, hon?"

"Yes. Just saying good-bye to my friends."

He offered them a prepackaged smile. "I'll bring the car around. 'Night, ladies."

Cassie watched him walk away. She couldn't picture Deana with a guy like him. Sure, he was polished and rich but oh, so arrogant. Deana, on the other hand, was so authentic, down-to-earth, and warm. She seemed that way anyway.

She was looking forward to possibly hanging out with Deana on Friday, getting to know her better without the shadow of him looming over her.

CHAPTER NINE

While Deana and Jeffrey drove back to Greenwich, the silence rankled her. She had nothing meaningful to say to him, but tension filled the air. She should be glad they weren't sniping at each other. That's all they'd been doing lately. More than lately in fact. After fourteen years of marriage, their relationship had run its course. Yet there they were, playing the happy Fairfield County power couple—a political star in state politics and his dutiful, selfless wife.

Deana stared out the window at the passing manicured lawns and stone fences of their upscale neighborhood and imagined the world she'd be entering next Friday when she met Jenn and Cassie at Pantheon. She could easily arrange a sleepover for Sean, but how would she explain that she was going out again on a Friday night without him?

"Eclectic group you assembled tonight," he said.

"Yes. I was happy so many diverse people showed up. I'm certain the night's receipts will be impressive."

"Mmm-hmm." He sounded distracted...as usual. "You were certainly drawn to that artist and her friend."

"*That artist*, Jenn, was a huge part of the event. It's her mural." She reeled back her attitude. "It just happened that she and her friend, Cassie, were very nice and very not pretentious."

"Suddenly our circle is pretentious?"

"You know what I meant, Jeff. Sometimes it's just pleasant to be with people you don't have to always be 'on' with."

"It must've been. You spent most of the night talking with them despite the steady stream of generous donors who deserved your attention."

"Most of the night?" Deana felt the venom seeping into her blood. "I hardly spent most of the night with them. I'm well-versed in how to work a room full of donors. I know whose egos need stroking."

"I'm just saying it seemed like every time I turned around to look for you, you were with one or both of them."

"Jenn created the mural for the center. I had to engage with her."

"And what about the tall blonde? Is that her girlfriend?"

"No. I don't know." She was getting flustered. "I think they're just friends."

Jeffrey's grunt of a reply annoyed her. He'd always had a way of questioning her that made her feel like she was doing something wrong. Of course, in this case she had been. Having sex with Jenn was wrong, but she'd craved it. With the intimacy gone in her marriage and Jeffrey having his own affairs over the last few years, she allowed herself that indulgence and wasn't about to look back on the incident with regret. It had revitalized her, opened her world up to a brand-new pleasure that she deserved to experience.

"I'm going out for happy hour with them both next Friday," she said and waited for the fallout.

"The hell you are."

"I'll check the calendar, but I'm sure nothing's on it."

"That's not what I'm talking about. What do you think it'll look like if my wife is seen hanging out with lesbians?"

"That your wife isn't a bigot?"

"Enough of this nonsense, Deana. You have plenty of girlfriends in our circle to have happy hour with."

"And I've met two more. Now if you don't mind, you can spare me the lecture."

His hands tightened their grip on the steering wheel. "I don't understand your attitude. You agreed to support me for my senate run, and the first time I'm asking for a favor, you put yourself first."

"That's not fair, Jeffrey. The first favor you asked was that I not file for divorce. I complied and have tried to make things work again with us, but what have you done? Do you really think I don't know what goes on when you're suddenly called away on business?"

He was quiet for a moment. "That was the past," he said softly. "I've changed and am focusing now on my political career and keeping my family together."

"Is trying to control me part of that effort?"

He exhaled slowly. "I'm not trying to control you. Do whatever you want. Just don't embarrass me."

She returned her gaze to the passing night. *After the election. Just make it till the election.*

❖

Friday night had come along, and the anticipation that had been roiling Cassie's insides all week was about to boil over. She took a shot of bourbon, and after it warmed her throat and stomach, she took one more. She was way more excited to see Deana than she should be, but when she finally saw her walk into Pantheon in black jeans, white V-neck tee, and a denim jacket rolled at the sleeves, the jumpiness melted into raw desire.

As Deana approached them, Cassie hoped her excitement wasn't as glaringly obvious as it felt.

"Damn," Jenn muttered.

Maggie gawked. "She looks like a goddamn supermodel."

"She was a model in her early twenties," Jenn said.

"And you're not involved with her?" Maggie asked.

Jenn shrugged. "No. She's married."

Maggie eyed her. "As if that would matter."

Cassie leaned in for Jenn's response.

Jenn arched an eyebrow. "I detect an insult in there somewhere. Anyway, yeah, we had sex once, but we're just friends. It's cool."

"Hey, Deana." Cassie nudged Jenn to turn around.

"Hey, guys." Deana offered each of them a hug.

"You remember our other best friend, Maggie," Cassie said.

"So nice to see you again." Deana extended a hand that Maggie shook with only a couple of fingers and a shy smile. "You really have a great place here, Cass."

"Thanks. You should've seen it a couple of years ago in its heyday. We were shoulder to shoulder in here practically every weekend."

"How fun," she gushed. "I was probably taking my son to Boy Scouts on any one of those weekends."

"Life was definitely a party back then," Jenn said.

Cassie gave her the eye to go easy on that party talk.

"Oh?" Deana was clearly intrigued. "What brought the party to an end?"

"A DUI," Maggie said. She sipped her drink and glanced away as though someone else had spoken.

"Jenn's DUI, not mine," Cassie said.

Jenn glared at her. "Oh, like you weren't right here with me wiping your nose as we walked out of the ladies' room. You just had Lorna to drive you home."

Cassie stuck her nose in her drink for a long sip, but her mortification didn't go unnoticed.

"Is that a Jenn Ferrano original I see there on the wall?" Deana asked.

Wow. What a save.

Jenn's gaga-eyed reaction to Deana's compliment gave Cassie a twinge of jealousy. Jenn repeatedly said she wasn't into her, that all they'd had was a hot one-nighter, but that look in her eyes indicated a clear spark of interest.

They all glanced up at the painting of a sexy demon woman tempting a 1950s housewife with an apple. "Yes, it is. I'm the proud owner of the first Ferrano ever commissioned for a business."

"She got it for a steal," Jenn said.

"The number of free drinks you've received over the years has more than compensated you for the low-end price you charged when you were an unknown."

Resting her elbow on the bar, Deana seemed to be getting a kick out of their banter. "You two sound like an old married couple."

"They could be today if Cassie hadn't gone off to college and broken Jenn's heart," Maggie said.

Jenn looked as horrified as Cassie felt. "Oh, yeah, right. She wishes."

Cassie shook her head. "Why is everyone putting me on blast in front of our new friend?" She turned to Deana. "I really am a respectable woman."

Deana giggled. "I have no doubt. I didn't get to see much of your respectable establishment the first time I was here. Care to show me around?"

Cassie glared at her friends as she replied. "I'd love to. Follow me."

She led Deana into the video room, where the walls were lined with televisions that played music videos that customers selected from a jukebox.

"This place is amazing," Deana said. "I've never seen a nightclub like this outside of New York City."

"Thanks." Cassie looked around at the decor she'd selected when designing this room years earlier. "Makes me kinda sad to think I'll be selling it by the end of the year."

"Really? Why?"

"It doesn't do the business it did in the mid-nineties. I'm ready, especially since I own the place with my ex. I can finally cut the cord."

Deana seemed to look deeply into her eyes. "Is that what you truly want? To cut the cord?"

Cassie nodded. "I'm finally there. Took me long enough."

They sat at a high-top table for two, and Cassie signaled the bartender to pour them another round.

"I'm finally there, too," Deana said. "My life's just a bit more complicated these days."

"I'll say…a mom and the wife of a notable politician. That's as complicated as it gets, especially if you're leaving to pursue an alternative lifestyle."

"That's not why I want a divorce. Jeffrey and I aren't in love anymore. We haven't been in many years."

"Oh" Cassie hesitated. "I didn't mean to presume…So, are you straight or not sure or…?"

"After the time I recently spent with Jenn, it's safe to say I'm bisexual. I'd had a brief involvement with a girl back in college, but then I met Jeffrey at the end of my senior year. We clicked, and two years later we were married. After that I didn't have a need or desire to question my sexuality. I was in love with him."

"That's funny. I met Lorna my senior year at Georgetown. She owned and tended bar at the local off-campus watering hole. She was older, a biker, and totally wrong for me, so of course, I fell madly in love."

She watched Deana laugh and felt slightly self-conscious about how childish her relationship with Lorna sounded. Sitting and sharing war stories with Deana, she felt something let go inside of her, like a fist holding her heart had finally released its grip. What had she been holding on so tightly for? In her late twenties now, she wasn't the same person who'd fallen for Lorna. She'd grown up during their six years together. But Lorna had remained the same. She would always be that person hiding her narcissism in flirtation, forever seeking validation in the high from new-relationship oxytocin.

"How did things with Lorna end?"

"In the typically anticlimactic fashion they usually end—she met someone else."

"She just came home one day and told you?"

Cassie scoffed. "No. That would've required a level of integrity and courage she didn't have. I found out about the affair while we were still together. I think she was trying to make sure she had things buttoned up with someone else before leaving me."

Deana grimaced. "That's awful. So cowardly."

"And selfish."

"Exactly." Deana grew pensive. "But I suppose it's easier to judge when you're on the outside looking in. I know Jeffrey's having an affair."

Cassie's heart sank for her.

"He doesn't go to great lengths to hide it from me, but he also won't own up to it. In his weird way, I'm sure he's trying to spare me the humiliation he knows it would cause while I stay with him until after the election."

"I know we've just met, but I can't begin to imagine how your husband could think he can find better than you. You seem to be the whole package."

"Thank you. That's sweet of you to say." She sipped her drink, then took out the stirrer to play with. "Our troubles began when I couldn't get pregnant. Infertility can sometimes be the kiss of death in a young marriage. It was so stressful—the hormone injections, the expense of it, the complete lack of spontaneity with sex. We finally went the IVF route and had Sean. We were a happy family for a while after. Until he wanted another child, and I said I didn't want to go through all that again."

"He got mad at you for that?"

"More like resentful. We've never been able to pull it together since. That was about seven years ago."

Cassie cringed, imagining herself stuck in that awful holding pattern with Lorna for five more years. Living those last two in her unhappy relationship, Cassie had felt trapped, like she was slowly, almost imperceptibly dying from suffocation. She recalled the day Lorna moved the last of her things out of the house. Cassie had felt like her lungs could finally breathe in crisp, clean air.

Poor Deana. No wonder she went for that wild time with Jenn at the Center.

"I'm sorry you're going through all this. God. It sucks all around."

Deana smiled. "Thanks. I simply stay focused on Sean. He just turned eleven and is the absolute light of my life. Would you like to see a picture?"

"I'd love to." It was obvious that Deana felt motherhood was her greatest achievement, and her enthusiasm for it was almost infectious.

She handed Cassie a photo from her wallet.

"Wow. This kid looks exactly like you."

Deana grinned. "I think that was another thing that pissed Jeffrey off. After all the effort he put in to accommodating my infertility issues, his own son doesn't look a thing like him."

"That's some delicious karma there."

They laughed out loud with the same cadence. Cassie couldn't remember the last time something had made her feel so light and easy. As much as she adored her time with Jenn and Maggie and as priceless as their friendship had become when Lorna left, something about Deana's energy made her want to be in her presence.

Jenn and Maggie finally made their way into the video room. "I thought you were giving her the tour. Didn't you ever make it out of this room?" Jenn asked.

"You don't leave a room when the music is good." Deana winked at Cassie and indicated the Eurythmics video playing.

"Let's go to the patio," Cassie said. "It's a gorgeous night."

"I'm going to pop into the ladies' room first," Deana said as the group headed out of the room and into the main bar area.

Jenn waited until the door closed behind Deana. "And what were you two talking about all this time?"

"Mostly relationships and stuff. I felt so bad when she talked about her fertility struggles."

Jenn looked confused. "We didn't talk about anything like that while I was doing the mural."

"How about her son? Did she show you his pictures?"

"If we were discussing any of those topics, do you really think we would've ended up doing it against the counter?"

"I suppose not, but didn't you want to get to know her at all as a person?"

Jenn's eyebrows scrunched. "Not really. It was just a job opportunity that turned into a sex opportunity. I mean, look at her."

Cassie felt better about her investment in Deana after hearing that. It had been tough to gauge Jenn's level of interest without giving away her own. "So you probably wouldn't want to be with her even if she was single."

"I didn't say that. As Maggie suggested, I guess I'm a serial dater, so yeah, I'd definitely ask her out, but I don't think we're a good match in the long run. She's way too straitlaced for me."

Maggie snorted. "You certainly have an interesting interpretation of 'straitlaced'—a woman married to a man who had sex with you in a storage room."

"Yeah, and it was incredible. I love getting my hands on women starving for the touch of another woman." Jenn licked her lips. "They're so...grateful."

"Eww, you're gross," Cassie said.

Deana returned to the group. "This round is on me. Do we all want the same?"

"I'll help you carry them," Cassie said.

Jenn nudged her way between them. "I'll do it, Cass. You and Maggie relax."

As Deana and Jenn headed to the bar, Cassie turned to Maggie, who had a knowing gleam in her eyes. "What?"

"You know what," Maggie replied. "I know what, too."

Cassie huffed. "Okay, Mags. What's your point?"

"I have no point other than if I can tell you're into Deana, so can Jenn."

"And?" Cassie's palms started to sweat. "What does it matter who's into her? She's married."

"That doesn't seem to be stopping her from pursuing her interests."

"What's Jenn's deal with her anyway? One minute she's saying she's not her type, and the next she's herding her like a sheepdog. Has she suddenly become interested in her because she senses I am?"

Maggie shrugged and began gnawing on her cuticles.

"I don't want to say anything to Jenn and create a problem where there isn't one. On the other hand, I don't want Deana to become this pink elephant we have to avoid tripping over."

Still gnawing, Maggie listened.

"I'm not saying anything about this to Jenn. If Deana was available, that would be a different story. Why stir the pot?"

"Stirring the pot never results in anything positive."

"Exactly." Cassie took a breath, satisfied with her quick resolution. "Are you spitting your fingernails on my floor?"

"I forgot my nail clipper at home."

"Here they come. Just play it cool."

"I don't know how to do that," Maggie said.

"I wasn't talking to you."

"Okay, Cassie, here's your Manhattan," Deana said. "Are we going to dance? I have a little time before I have to go."

"We're not so much the dancing crew," Cassie said.

"And Maggie's already used up a month's worth of social energy hanging out with us past nine." Jenn chuckled as she elbowed Maggie.

"This is fun. Thanks so much for inviting me." As Deana sipped her white wine, her gaze lingered on Cassie.

"We enjoyed having you." Cassie caught it as soon as she said it while Jenn snorted, Deana smirked, and Maggie pursed her lips awkwardly. "You guys are fucking jerks."

Deana brushed Cassie's arm. "So this is what it's like to be a Pantheon Girl?"

"Usually," Jenn said. "You think you're up for joining?"

"Well, I don't know. Is there room for another?"

Cassie sensed this move could be trouble, but the chance to welcome Deana into her friend fold and perhaps see her more often was too enticing to pass up. She raised her drink glass. "And then there were four."

They all clinked glasses to solidify the deal.

"I hope we can do this again soon," Deana said. "There's a café in Fairfield that makes a mean espresso martini. If you don't mind taking the ride."

"I wouldn't mind," Cassie said. "I'll be glad to drive if the girls are up for it sometime."

"Sounds good to me," Jenn said.

"Fabulous," Deana said. "Cass and Maggie, I'll give you my cell phone number so we can all stay in touch when we make a plan."

Cassie watched her walk over to the bar, captivated by her smooth, confident stride that must've been a holdover from her modeling days.

She returned with a pen and a napkin. As Jenn observed them exchanging numbers, Cassie couldn't help feeling she felt something more than a casual interest. If Jenn genuinely had her sights on Deana, why wouldn't she just admit it? And if she didn't, why was she still giving off that vibe?

Maybe she was just conflating the rush of her own attraction to Deana with whatever Jenn might have had left over from their hookup. Whatever the case, she had to stop overthinking it.

After announcing several times that she had to leave, Deana finally put down her empty glass and asked Cassie if she would mind walking her to her car. As they stood on the sidewalk under a streetlight smiling nervously, Cassie would've given anything for a glimpse into Deana's thoughts.

"Thank you for inviting me to your club and giving me the VIP tour. It was such a fun night."

"I'm glad you enjoyed yourself." Cassie threw her arms open like she was starring in a commercial. "That's always been the goal here at Pantheon, showing the ladies a good time."

Deana chuckled. "Mission accomplished." Her expression lost its mirth. "I needed this night, to get out of my sometimes-stifling world and my own head for a while. I'm sure I'll pay for it tomorrow."

That last part unnerved her. What was Deana implying? Whatever it was, Cassie wasn't about to let it slide. "I hope not too severely." She seasoned the inquiry with a casual grin. "It's not like you ran off to Mexico and got a quickie divorce."

"Now that sounds like my idea of a good time."

"I always wanted to go on a Mexican vacation. I'll call my travel agent."

Deana nodded as though she were ready to go. "I meant what I said earlier. I'd love to get together again with you gals."

"We have each other's numbers now. All we need is a time and a place."

"Okay." She looked down and stuffed her hands into her denim-jacket pockets.

This sudden shyness was a stark contrast from the Deana she'd encountered at her charity event last weekend. And even earlier that evening inside the club when her sparkling personality was attracting everyone she came across into her radiant sphere. Now she had that look that Cassie recognized as the one a woman gets at the end of a first date when she anticipates the good-night kiss.

Cassie leaned against the passenger side of Deana's car and licked her lips. Deana seemed to be edging closer to her, her eyes fixed on her mouth. Was this going to happen? God, Cassie hoped...

"There you are," Jenn called out. They immediately widened the space between them as she approached. "Jeez, Cass. We thought you got abducted or something."

"Or something," Cassie muttered.

The original Deana came back in full force, accentuated with a brilliant smile. "We were just discussing when and where we could all get together again."

"Cool," Jenn said. "We'll talk."

After Deana's car pulled away, she and Jenn walked back to the club. "You left Maggie alone in there? You realize you set her up in the perfect Irish good-bye scenario."

Jenn didn't reply in the jovial spirit Cassie had expected. "We were worried. I mean, how long does it take to make sure someone makes it to their car safely?"

"Okay. Looks like someone needs a shot of Fireball."

Cassie tried hard to ease the strained vibe with a pat on her shoulder as she led Jenn to the bar. Luckily, Maggie hadn't bolted when she'd had the chance. Seated at the bar, she was playing tic-tac-toe on a napkin with a trans woman.

"Are we doing a shot or calling it a night?"

Maggie shook her head. "I'm ready to go."

"I have a job tomorrow. I can't be hungover." Jenn took out some cash for a tip and laid it on the bar.

After the high she'd felt in Deana's presence, Cassie was frustrated with the downward turn the night had taken. It wasn't so much Maggie's desire to go home at ten o'clock but Jenn's uncharacteristically dour mood. And Cassie knew precisely why it was dour.

They said their good-byes to Maggie, and Cassie signaled Brittany, her bartender, to bring over shots for her and Jenn. Jenn frowned as Cassie lifted the glass to her lips.

"I told you I don't want a hangover."

"Then don't drink it. God." Cassie did her shot and gave Jenn's to Brittany. The friction between her and her best friend was getting too awkward to keep dismissing. "Is something else bothering you tonight?"

"No. I'm just tired."

Cassie knew by her glare that she was lying, but she wasn't about to press her. She was still so excited from her near-kiss with Deana. The mere implication that it could've happened had her all atwitter.

She just wanted to savor the thought of Deana's lips touching hers a little longer before Jenn admitted she was in love with her, and Cassie had to stand down.

❖

In the grocery store, Cassie walked beside Maggie as she shopped and had occasionally dropped in an item she hadn't known she needed.

Although she hated grocery shopping, as her empty fridge would attest to, she wanted to talk to Maggie alone, but getting her out of her hovel during the week for a social call was generally a non-starter.

"Have you noticed anything strange about Jenn lately?"

"No." Maggie scribbled off an item on her list with a pencil and pushed on.

"I mean like her mood. She seems so crabby."

"I hadn't noticed."

That response could've been taken two ways: that Maggie hadn't noticed because she didn't usually concern herself with the moods of others or that Jenn had been crabby only around Cassie. She chewed her lip, dreading it was the latter.

"Has she said anything to you about Deana recently?"

"No. Why? Did they sleep together again?"

"I don't think so. I'm sure she would've announced it to both of us if she had."

"For sure. Why do you think she's crabby?"

Maggie was pulling out her school-psychologist script, something she did frequently when she didn't want to have a certain conversation but still wanted to be a supportive friend.

"Will you promise that this conversation stays between the two of us?"

Maggie opened a box of Devil Dogs and tore into one as she continued pushing her cart. "I'll consider it therapist-patient privilege."

"Okay. Good." Cassie waved away the Devil Dog Maggie offered her. "I think Jenn's attitude is coming from Deana. More specifically, Deana's attention toward me."

"Is Deana into you?"

"Well, I can't say for sure, but I kinda get the feeling."

"Hmm, if that's true, and I trust your judgment, then it can become an issue."

Cassie hadn't decided what kind of answer she'd wanted from Maggie, but that certainly wasn't it. "It can? Why? Jenn's said repeatedly that she doesn't want to pursue anything with her."

"Of course she's saying that. Deana's not available. But that's not to say she wouldn't want Deana to pursue something with her. It's almost like Deana got what she wanted with Jenn and dropped her for you."

Cassie groaned and grabbed a Devil Dog out of the box. "That's not true. She didn't drop her. We're all friends."

"Yes, but there's a nuance here that you're missing."

"You mean that Jenn keeps protesting against Deana to save face because she's unavailable, but deep down, she really does want something with her?"

"I have no idea if that's the case, but if she's getting an attitude only with you when Deana's around, that would be my guess."

Cassie bit halfway into the Devil Dog and let the processed sugar and lard soothe her soul. This was exactly what she was afraid of. After devouring it in her second bite, she took a deep breath. "Should I talk to her about it?"

"Why? Do you want to pursue Deana?"

"No, but she's sort of pursing me…for friendship. You know the weird situation she's in with her husband. She asked me to meet her for breakfast this Friday."

"How convenient." Maggie's tone clearly suggested an ulterior motive.

"Why's that convenient? She's a stay-at-home mom. She's probably bored to tears when the kid goes to school."

"And she knows you work nights while Jenn and I work weekdays."

"Jenn works all the time, whenever she gets a painting job."

Maggie crinkled her eyebrows at her, then headed toward the registers. "Do you need anything else?"

"No. I just needed some yogurts and Coffee Mate."

"I meant do you need any more advice about the situation that you'll completely ignore?"

Cassie glared at her. "No. I'm all set. Thanks."

"Fine. I'll just leave you with this tidbit. If you only intend to be friends with Deana, you have nothing to concern yourself with or feel guilty about."

"Not even about seeing Deana without Jenn?"

"No. We're all adults. You can certainly go out with her if Jenn can't make it. But I'd be careful about squeezing her out of the equation. It's just not good form."

"Well, yeah. I'd never disrespect either of you like that. I'm not a douche."

"It only takes one douche to cause a problem."

"Roger that," Cassie said, happy to end the conversation there.

CHAPTER TEN

As much as she loved the idea, Cassie wasn't big on believing in the magic of fate. She thought that if you wanted something to happen, you made it happen. But exactly one week after she and Deana talked for hours, then had that awkward moment at her car, she was sitting across from her at a cute country luncheonette in Westport.

Now that she was here studying the nuances of Deana's wholesome beauty in the light of day, Maggie's words replayed in her head. Had Deana really suggested Friday for breakfast knowing Cassie would be the only one able to make it?

It was a rather cynical assumption. Staying home to raise one kid who was in school all day had to be an awful bore. Why was it so hard to believe that she'd want to make new friends who'd be available to meet during the day? Even her important charity work wouldn't take up all her time.

Despite Maggie's sinister insinuation, Cassie intended to view Deana as being as sincere as she was altruistic.

"Thank you for suggesting this place." She took in the country-farmhouse decor. "I absolutely love it."

"I'm so glad you were free to join me." Deana sliced into her veggie omelet.

"The best thing about working nights is when someone says let's go to breakfast." She watched Deana sip her Bellini and wondered if that sweet, clean aroma was coming from her or the two gardenias stuffed into a tiny vase on their table.

Every time Cassie was around her, the allure of Deana's scent led her to distraction.

"I'm sorry the girls couldn't join us."

"Yeah. Those poor dayworkers."

Deana put her fork down, leaned back in her chair, and gave her an intense stare. "I really like Jenn and Maggie, but if I'm totally honest, I don't mind that it's just the two of us. You and I seem to connect on our own level."

Cassie needed a sip of her black coffee and a moment to convince herself that Deana just meant as friends. "I think so, too. As much as I love them, they can't truly understand what I went through—am going through—with Lorna. I'm the only one who's had a long-term relationship. And the only one who's had to endure it turning to shit."

"I can definitely feel your pain there."

After their server refilled Cassie's cup, she leaned forward. "If I'm honest, it's nice to be able to talk with you without worrying if I'm ruffling any feathers. Don't get me wrong. Jenn is my best friend, and I love her dearly, but…"

"I understand." Deana smoothed out her napkin and reorganized her flatware. "I sort of regret having that encounter with Jenn. If I had known she had a friend like you…"

Okay, clearly this was going there. She blotted her lips with her napkin after taking a sip of her refill. "Are we like flirting with each other?"

Deana chuckled. "I think so."

"I thought so, too, but I had to ask because it's been so long for me."

"Even longer for me. Plus, I had to figure out if flirting with women was the same as with men. That's where Jenn was really handy."

"You couldn't have found a better tutor if you searched the Yellow Pages."

The laugh they shared helped dissipate some of the building sexual tension. While Cassie loved the repartee, she wasn't sure if she liked the way Deana was occupying so much of her mind when they weren't together. She was appealing for so many reasons, not the least of which was her "damsel in distress" aura. Cassie found comfort in meeting someone who seemed to be as adrift in her personal life as she was. She loved the idea that she could help distract Deana with flirty playfulness.

As long as it remained only playfulness.

"You don't have any feelings for Jenn?"

Deana shook her head emphatically. "I admit I was very attracted to her aloof Bohemian-artist vibe, and she seemed to dig my lonely Fairfield County housewife, but our one encounter satisfied that itch."

A weight tumbled off Cassie's shoulders. With both her and Jenn insisting there was nothing between them, she could relax into her new friendship with Deana and not feel guilty over a little harmless flirting.

"I'm sure Jenn will join us next time. Maggie? I'm not so sure."

"Either way, I look forward to a next time. By the way, I have a pedicure appointment around noon. Would you care to join me?"

Of course she wanted to join her, but she automatically paused to think of her other responsibilities. *Wait. What responsibilities?* She had no partner to consult anymore, and with Lorna all but abandoning Pantheon to her, she didn't have to do anything except open the bar for Thursday happy hour at four o'clock.

Two hours later they were side by side at a posh salon having their feet massaged as they drank herbal teas. Deana had just breezed in and politely assumed they'd accommodate the wayward friend she had in tow. The elegance she effused eliminated any sense of obnoxious entitlement the rich are often accused of tossing about. Had the salon not been able to accommodate, Cassie was certain Deana would have gracefully accepted defeat.

For a moment they lay back in their massaging chairs and absorbed the classical music while they were pampered. But Cassie kept cracking open her left eye to catch glimpses of Deana's long legs and her exposed shins and calves. Exquisite. She retreated into darkness behind her eyelids again and wondered how it was possible that Jenn hadn't fallen madly in love with Deana. They'd been together a lot at the Center while she was creating the mural. And then to have passionate sex with her?

She cringed. The thought of Jenn having sex with Deana chafed her. It must've been as hot as Jenn had claimed it was. But she'd never know. She wouldn't dare jump from the frying pan of grief over Lorna's betrayal into the fire of a married woman.

As the aestheticians began to massage their calves, a murmur of pleasure escaped from Deana. Cassie felt a slight tingle, and it wasn't from the chair massage. Was that what Deana sounded like when she was having sex? When she began that slow, luxurious ascent to orgasm? Cassie's entire endocrine system surged into overdrive.

Maybe accompanying her to the salon after breakfast was a bad idea. Too much too soon. Deana was the type of woman one had to exercise caution with. She was a bad habit waiting to happen, and Cassie was in no way ready to get swept away in the savage current of another woman who would leave her smashed against the rocks. She had to be careful no matter how irresistible Deana was.

In the car on the way back to the luncheonette where Cassie had left hers, Deana had interrogated her about Lorna, specifically if she still had feelings for her or hope that they would eventually find their way back together.

"That timer's definitely run out," Cassie replied. "Not that she would ever come back begging, but I'd absolutely not take her back."

"Really? For some reason I assumed you were still in love with her. You don't seem like you're over her."

Cassie sighed as she contemplated exactly what she was still mourning. "It isn't really Lorna I'm not over. It's more what she represented. She was supposed to be my life partner. And she betrayed me. She pulled the rug out from under me. And for what? Some new conquest?"

Deana rolled her eyes. "Are you sure she's not a politician? I swear, with some of those men, it's like women are leases, meant to be turned in for a new one every two years."

Cassie laughed. "Although she hated to admit it, Lorna's a trust-fund baby. When you have all that money can buy, apparently you start wanting to acquire things money can't buy."

"If you're talking about people, I have a state-rep husband who will eagerly disagree with you."

"Fair enough." It was so refreshing to talk with someone who had a sense of what it felt like to be fooled by someone you loved and trusted. And had a sense of humor about it.

"Well, even though I'm a bit older than you, I believe the best is still yet to come, for both of us. Obviously, we're going through some heavy stuff that will only make us stronger coming out the other side."

"I hope your optimism is contagious," Cassie said. "I can use a new perspective."

"Me, too." Deana lifted her head and opened her eyes. "It's a very good thing we've become friends. I'll make it a point to thank Jenn for welcoming me in."

"You're part of us now," Cassie said. "Pantheon Girls stick together."

❖

As Deana drove to her son's school, she kept thinking how badly she didn't want to go home. She just wanted to pick Sean up and take him to meet Cassie. Anywhere. Even if it was to sit in another restaurant ordering food she wouldn't eat. She wanted to talk more with her, find out more about her. It had been years since she'd had a female friend she could truly confide in, one who wasn't simply playing the part of confidant because their husbands ran in the same power circles. Jeffrey's career aspirations had taken her miles away from her hometown and the friends she'd grown up with and deposited her in a world of social climbers, label queens, and all manner of insincerity associated with the wives of wealthy, powerful men.

Jenn and Cassie were so different. But Cassie was the one she couldn't stop thinking about.

As she waited in the pickup line for the dismissal bell, her car phone rang.

"Deana Godwin," her friend, Johanna, sang out in an accusatory tone. "Where have you been? We've missed you at garden club and last week's brunch."

She flung her head back in defeat. "Hi, Jo. I miss you gals, too. I've just been running around like crazy getting Sean ready for summer camp and such. We'll lunch soon."

"We better, missy."

"A promise is a promise." The whimsy in her own voice was making her sick. She hung up the phone as Sean came trotting toward the car.

"Hey, Mom." He dumped his book bag on the floor by his feet and waved to his friends as they drove off.

"Hey, honey. Did you have a good day?"

He nodded as he played with the radio buttons.

"What was the best part?"

He went into extensive detail about what he did in each of his classes and ended the discussion with a request to stay at his grandmother's beach cottage in Westbrook next week after school was over for the summer.

In the past she'd cringe at the idea of letting him spend a week without her at her in-laws', but he was eleven now and soon would be an official sixth grader.

And with her son occupied, she would have free time to occupy herself with something that had caught her fancy. Or someone.

❖

Cassie had had the best time ever with Deana at breakfast. Any time she thought about it, she smiled. And she was doing that a lot during the last couple of days. But how could she truly revel in the feeling if she couldn't share it with her best friend?

She'd asked Jenn to meet her for a bite at a seafood place near where she was working a job along the shore. They sat at the corner of the bar and ordered a couple of beers and a variety of shellfish appetizers to share. It was their thing because Maggie had a gag-inducing aversion to eating anything that she thought resembled a loogie.

"Did you finish the condo yet?" Cassie was dying to clear the air about meeting Deana for breakfast, but she didn't lead with that topic.

"Just about. A few touch-ups tomorrow, and I'll be done."

"Any hopes for the unit owner once you finish?"

Jenn chuckled as she squeezed a lime into her Corona. "Nah. She has a girlfriend. I know this because, apparently, I got a little too flirty with her one day, and by the next day, a bunch of pictures of her with the chick were arranged all over the place. She even had her come over to drop off some Dunkin, even though she had a coffeemaker right there on her counter."

Cassie chortled. "A woman who's clear about her boundaries. I like that."

"Yeah. This client was no Deana Godwin."

Ugh. Cassie stopped trying to dig an oyster out with her tiny fork and placed everything in her plate. Why had Jenn gone right to Deana from there? She had to say something about breakfast the other morning. If she didn't do it then, she'd miss the opportunity for the subject to flow naturally into the conversation.

"Yeah. I saw Deana the other morning. We had breakfast."

Jenn narrowed her eyes. "You did? Where?"

"This little place in Westport."

"What were you doing out there?"

"She invited me. She knows I work nights."

"She invited you but not Maggie or me?"

"Jenn, you guys work during the day. You would've lost half a day's pay just to meet us for breakfast? It's not like we went to a Broadway play without you."

Shit. Jenn recoiled a bit. Cassie was too defensive.

"No. I guess that would've been pretty stupid."

Cassie guzzled her beer to give them both a moment to regroup. Sweat beaded on her neck as she panicked at the extended silence.

"Was it a date?" Jenn finally asked.

"No. It was breakfast." She tapped her fingers against the beer bottle. "Then a pedicure." She'd planned to omit that last part and just stick with breakfast. But then she remembered her grandmother saying something about the devil being in the details, so she put it all out there, lest it come out later, at a less opportune time.

"That's either a date or you've found yourself a new best friend."

"Jenn, neither of those things is true. Look. If me hanging out with Deana occasionally is going to upset you—"

"No, no, no." Jenn waved away the suggestion. "I'm sorry. I over-reacted. I guess I'm just bitchy because the stretch between girlfriends has gone on longer than usual."

"Well, don't think for a second that old Jenn Ferrano magic is fading." She laughed, hoping the quip would deflect the tension. She hated the idea that Jenn might've thought she was trying to pull one over on her, but she was also a little ticked that she was giving her a hard time over Deana when they'd just had one hookup.

Jenn shrugged. "Whatever. When the right one comes along, I'll know."

"How?" Cassie dissected the meaning in the expression. "How does anyone truly know when they've met the right one?"

"They say it's something you feel. It's not the words the person says or the things they do necessarily. It's the way they make you feel when you're around them."

"Horny?"

Jenn chuckled. "Naturally. But it goes much deeper. You'll feel it at a cellular level."

"Like in your soul."

"Yes. That's exactly it."

"Have you felt it yet?"

Jenn shook her head. "Not yet. Did you feel it with Lorna?"

Cassie shook her head. "I suppose if I did, we'd still be together."

"Sometimes I envy those couples who meet young and spend their whole lives together. Imagine never having to worry late into the night that you'll end up alone forever."

"Jenn. Is that you in there?" Cassie playfully stuck her face in Jenn's.

Jenn pushed her away by the forehead as she sipped her beer. "Don't you ever wonder when or if you'll experience that one great love?"

Cassie downed the last sip of her beer and signaled for another round. How weird that what Jenn just described basically explained how she felt in Deana's presence. Impossible, though. Her emotional wires must still be crossed from Lorna.

Deana was the most unattainable woman she'd ever met. Why would Cassie feel comfortable enough with her to feel like she was the one?

CHAPTER ELEVEN

The first time Cassie and Deana had met up alone, it was merely by chance. Deana happened to be free for breakfast on a Friday while the other girls were working. No reason why Cassie shouldn't have accepted her invitation then.

This time, however, they were alone by design. A little impromptu, midweek lunch date. No big deal. It wasn't like Cassie had suggested a Saturday night on the town with Deana and excluded Jenn and Maggie. She simply wanted to learn more about Deana. She wanted the kind of conversation that happened only in a one-on-one dynamic, the kind in which small details were revealed, some inadvertently, when two people relaxed into each other's company.

"What did you want to be before you became a politician's wife?"

"Ugh. I used to love that title. Now it makes me cringe. It sounds so 1950s."

Cassie chuckled. "We're heading toward the twenty-first century. Guess you better update your identity."

"That's the goal." Deana nibbled at her veggie wrap. "After so many years with Jeffrey, my identity's become intertwined with his. And, of course, being Sean's mom. That will always be at the heart of who I am."

"What about when he grows up? Where do you see yourself then?"

The question seemed to stump her, as though she couldn't imagine her son being anything but a boy who needed her. "I don't know. I guess doing something helping people. I do love my charity work with the children's center."

"What was your major in college?"

"Liberal arts."

"Ooh. Okay."

Deana giggled. "Why does everyone react that way when I tell them?"

"I think because no one really knows what that degree means. To my knowledge, no career called a liberal artist exists, so..." She shrugged.

"To be honest, I didn't know what I wanted to study in college. I was modeling at the time and thought, hoped, I would have a career in that."

"How did that *not* happen? I mean, look at you."

Deana blushed. "I fell in love. The traveling got to be too much."

Cassie quelled her rising disgust. That stupid husband had been controlling her from the get-go. "You'd think a guy would be proud and supportive of his model girlfriend."

"It wasn't him. It was me," she said softly, seeming reluctant to admit fault. "I didn't want to be away from him so much—didn't want him to find someone else while I was gone. Posing for pictures in bikinis and walking the runway was fun and all, but at the end of the day, I was going to bed alone and missing the person I wanted to be with. It was the first of many times I overestimated Jeffrey."

"This is just one woman's opinion, but couldn't you get back into modeling? You're incredibly fit and don't even look your age."

"Do you even know my age?" Deana laughed. "I'm about twenty years past my prime. Besides, I'm not interested in doing that again."

"Seems like a waste. I can totally picture your mug in an ad for age-defying makeup. Older women would clear the shelves if they thought they could look like you."

"I know there's a compliment nestled somewhere in there, so thank you."

"The highest of compliments." Cassie suddenly grew self-conscious and realized she needed to reel it back. She was practically gushing over Deana's attractiveness, which wasn't what she wanted her to think she valued in her.

"What about you?" Deana said. "What did you major in to become a night-club owner, business?"

"Not at all. I was a communications major with a minor in political science at Georgetown. My dream was to stay in Washington and cover politics for the news. I'd worshipped Diane Sawyer, not to mention the major crush."

"You have her height, gorgeous blond hair, and I'm sure her intelligence. How did that not happen?"

"I fell in love."

Deana's lips melted into a grin. "Touché."

"It's so crazy how similar our choices were after graduation. We both deferred our potential by betting on another person."

"Love is a powerful thing, often blinding."

"Can we modify that to 'first love'? I'd like to think that when we grow up after experiencing love for the first time, we develop a more mature, rational approach to falling in love."

"Oh, I certainly hope that's true," Deana said. "I'm forty-one, and I've been in love only once."

"Me, too. I had a couple of relationships with people I loved before I met Lorna, but they weren't that full-on, knock-you-over-with-a-feather kind of romance."

"Is that what you had with Lorna?"

Cassie nodded. "Definitely in the beginning. Lorna made me feel the way I'd always wanted to—maybe because she was older, more experienced, more assertive. She was who I thought I wanted to become."

"I don't think I ever felt that way with Jeffrey. Don't get me wrong. We had passion and intimacy, and I loved his huge personality. He made me feel safe from the world and everything I thought love was about at the time."

"Then things change," Cassie said, referring to her own situation.

"Exactly. We grow further into adulthood and don't even realize we're growing apart."

"It sounds like you're telling my story."

"There is a certain interchangeability there." Deana sat back in her chair and waxed philosophical. "Maybe that's why our paths crossed when they did. Think about it. We had similar beginnings but at different times, me being a dozen years older than you. But we seem to be changing course in pretty much the same time and space."

"That is so deep for this early in the day."

"And corny, too, but I'm glad I met you, Cassie. Your friendship is like the beacon I've been searching for while I've been lost in these stormy seas."

"Wow. What's in that iced tea you're drinking?"

Deana looked down, her face rosy.

Cassie didn't mean to make light of her flowery remark because she was feeling it, too. She was feeling more than friendship for Deana, and it became more apparent each time they met. But when a woman exposed her emotional vulnerability, it wasn't the time to lay something like that on her.

Given both of their situations, it wasn't the time for anything more than friendship.

Deana grabbed the check again and handed the server her card despite Cassie's objections. "I promise I'll let you pay next time."

"You said that after breakfast last week."

"I mean it this time." Deana winked as she filled out the slip and handed it to back to the server.

As they walked toward the public parking lot, their shoulders kept touching. Again, the thought of leaving Cassie and driving home to Greenwich filled Deana with dread. She thought of stopping at one of the high-end boutiques or makeup stores to stall Cassie, but she didn't want to be a nuisance. Cassie probably had things she had to do back in New Haven before work, and she didn't want to come off as pushy.

Or that she had designs on her. Cassie had already joked about them flirting with each other. But what if she hadn't been joking? What if she'd enjoyed the flirtation as much as Deana had? She seemed to.

They stopped at their cars parked next to each other, and Deana spoke over the roof of Cassie's. "Would I be a bother if I asked you to come back this way for breakfast or lunch again…sooner rather than later?"

"A bother? Not at all. It's great to get out of New Haven County."

"Is that the only reason you meet me?"

"Absolutely not. Doesn't Paul Newman live here?" A wry smile formed on her lips.

That son of a gun. "Yes. I even saw his wife at the fabric store once. Sweet lady."

"I love Joanne Woodward. Another reason to meet you in Westport more often."

Deana loved Cassie's teasing, but part of her sought validation. She wanted Cassie to say that she wanted this friendship as much as she did. "Then should we say same time, same place next week?"

"Yes, but only if you really do agree that it's my turn to pick up the tab."

Deana flashed the okay sign, then paused. "Is it wrong of me to suggest it be just the two of us again?"

Cassie stretched her arms across the roof of her car and played with her keys. "Nope. I don't wanna have to pay for everyone."

"You could ask them to join us and just pay for me." Deana bit her bottom lip to prevent a devilish grin.

"I'll think about it." Cassie's talent for flirting was incredible.

"Call me when you get back to your area, so I know you made it home." Deana got in her car and let the air-conditioning blow at her overheated skin. She was concerned that it would soon give her away. How was she going to be able to control the way Cassie made her feel when they were together?

How was she going to make it an entire week before seeing her again?

❖

Cassie's quick phone call to let Deana know she'd arrived home turned into another half hour full of chitchat before she had to hang up and get ready to go to Pantheon. Now that softball season had begun, Wednesday nights were jamming with ladies who hung out after practice playing pool and tapping out her kegs.

She usually tended bar Wednesdays, and Jenn would pop in for a few beers and games of pool. As the guilt from deliberately neglecting to invite her to lunch today loomed, Cassie waited for her to finish her first beer before casually mentioning it.

"You met up with her again?" Jenn's face was scrunched with annoyance. "Why didn't you call me?"

Apparently, one beer wasn't enough to lessen the impact.

"I thought you were working…like last Friday."

"You still could've called. I finished early today. I would've met you guys."

Jenn was clearly hurt, and Cassie felt awful. She absolutely could've made a quick call to Jenn that morning, but she just didn't want to. She loved the vibe between her and Deana when it was just the two of them, but she couldn't keep making clandestine plans with her without controversy.

"I'm sorry. When, uh, *if* there's another time, I won't forget you. It was just a quick lunch." She felt the need to add that reassurance, but it seemed to have the opposite effect of what she'd intended.

"You don't have to get defensive."

"I wasn't. I just feel bad that you feel bad."

Jenn shrugged as she kept one eye on a pool game off to her right. "I don't feel bad. But if you were going with Maggie, you would've checked if I had a job."

This was getting weird. Cassie hadn't known the protocol in a situation like this. She'd never competed with a friend for the attention of the same girl—if that was actually happening. It was all still so murky.

"Jenn, are you into Deana? Do you guys still have a thing or what?"

"No. I've already told you we don't. She's married, and if she ever leaves her husband, it probably wouldn't be until the end of next year."

"Is that what you're waiting for?" Cassie held her breath, dreading the answer.

Jenn shook her head as she pressed the bottle of beer to her lips, seeming to eye a college-age brunette setting up her shot.

Although the headshake wasn't all that convincing, Cassie exhaled her angst like a tire with a slow leak. Despite her better judgment, she pursued the subject anyway. "If she'd been single when you met her, would you have wanted to go out with her?"

"If she was single, sure. Why not? You and I've already had this conversation. But we wouldn't work out in the long run."

"Are you confident of that?"

Jenn seemed to study her for a moment. "Cass, what's with this interrogation? Are you into her? Just tell me if you are."

"Pfft. Nooo." Cassie's protest was rather vehement, and she immediately regretted it. Was she into Deana? Yes, she was, but in the scope of the things, it was as futile for her as for Jenn. She didn't want a married woman who might or might not leave her husband someday any more than Jenn did. Furthermore, spurts of sadness and resentment toward Lorna still bedeviled her. Even though she was over the major emotional hump, it wouldn't be fair to start something with someone else until she'd fully processed the ripple effect of that upheaval.

Still, she was squandering a chance for full disclosure with her friend.

Jenn squinted at her. "Not even a little?"

"Look. Is she gorgeous and fun and intelligent? Yes. Who wouldn't want to be around that energy? And it's not my fault her situation leaves her available only during the day when you guys are at work."

"You got a point there." As Jenn finished off her beer, her posture seemed to soften. "Sorry I got all in-your-face about it. Maybe just a teensy part of me wishes I hadn't brushed her off so soon."

This conversation was not going in the right direction. What was up with Jenn? She'd never let a woman get her down unless it was into a sexual position. However, the fact that she was eyeing that cute young brunette was a good sign.

Cassie opened two bottles of beer in front of her. "Here. That hottie over there looks thirsty."

Jenn grinned and, in all her stunning audacity, walked over to the girl.

After that shameless diversionary tactic, Cassie promised herself she'd invite Jenn to lunch next week. And to any other future meeting with Deana. After all, they were an updated version of the Pantheon Girls, and she hated feeling like she was doing something sketchy, especially to a friend she'd considered a sister.

And now that the weather was getting warmer, they would have more opportunities to get out and do fun friend things as a group.

❖

The perks of being friends with a well-to-do politician's wife increased after Memorial Day weekend with an invitation to an exclusive Greenwich beach club. Five months after her breakup with Lorna, Cassie was finally starting to feel "normal" again, a sensation she defined as being comfortable in her own skin and wanting to surround herself with her core group of trusted friends. The witty banter and subtle flirtation she'd been enjoying with the newest member of the troupe was also helping her begin to resurrect her murdered self-esteem.

After a game of volleyball with Deana and her son in the pool, she made her way over to Maggie, who was lounging in the shade of an imported palm tree with a trashy novel and a cocktail in a hollowed-out pineapple.

"Elizabeth Taylor called," Cassie said as she plopped down on a chaise lounge next to her. "She wants her beach disguise back."

Maggie adjusted the tulle scarf around her head and lowered her sunglasses just enough to peer over them. "What's the matter? Getting tired of being chased around by Deana?"

"Don't look a gift host in the mouth. Besides, she's on her best behavior till the husband comes by and picks up Sean." She glanced around at the beach chairs lining the swimming pool and the people in them being tended to by good-looking cabana boys and girls. "Can you believe this place?"

Most of Maggie's attention was on her book. "Where's Jenn?"

"Probably inside on the phone with her new girlfriend, Renny."

"Where'd she meet this one?"

"I don't know. I'm just glad she's into her. The pressure of having to juggle her feelings with Deana's attention was getting me all balled up inside."

"What's going on with you and her, anyway? And don't say nothing. Nobody believes that anymore. Are you sleeping together?"

Cassie felt attacked. "No. I swear. I'd tell you if I was."

"Why not? Because you don't want Jenn's sloppy seconds?" Maggie chuckled to herself.

"Ugh. You're so weird." Cassie gave her a lazy slap on the arm. "I'm in a confusing space right now, and the last thing I need is to fall into some intense affair with a woman who can't give me what I need."

Maggie took off her sunglasses. "What do you need?"

Cassie opened her mouth to reply, then closed it. Maggie's question was way deeper than it sounded. "I'm not sure." She rewrapped the thick towel around her waist until the answer popped into her head. "Peace, maybe?"

"Makes total sense," Maggie said. "I get that the married part about Deana is off-putting, but why are you still confused? Lorna?"

Cassie sighed, suddenly uncomfortable with the topic. "Yes, Lorna. I guess. And I don't think I care for your tone."

"I'm not psychoanalyzing you, Cass. I'm just trying to talk with my friend."

"Okay, fine." Cassie pushed her locks back with her sunglasses. "I've just come out from under this oppressive pile of emotional garbage. I finally got my own apartment, and I'm starting to figure things out for my future. I'm absolutely not getting tangled up in Deana Godwin." She gazed across the pool and glimpsed Deana in a sheer beach coverup, her tanned body tantalizing in a black bikini. "No matter how incredibly sexy she is."

"Wipe your mouth. You're drooling."

Cassie pulled her sunglasses back down over her eyes. "How did your coffee date go the other day?"

"Not well."

Cassie leaned back to receive the late-afternoon sun on her face. "Care to elaborate?"

"Let's just say that when a person is waving more red flags than a high school color guard before you've finished your first mochaccino, you should pass on the second date."

"That's too bad. I was really rooting for this one."

"Why?"

"I don't know. Maybe because you're twenty-nine years old and have never had a relationship."

"I wish you could overcome your obsession with my status," she said before slurping the last of her drink. "Relationships are highly overrated. As evidenced by you and Jenn."

"Touché."

"Everyone eventually ends up single anyway," Maggie said, matter-of-factly. "I've just been able to avoid the untidy breakup that leads to it."

"But you've also avoided that amazing, magical endorphin rush and the physical pleasure of new love."

"You mean that fleeting blast of oxytocin that makes you lose all sense of logic and reason and do stupid things like stay inside a beach club on a gorgeous day so you can talk on the phone to your new girlfriend?"

"I'm finding it very hard to like you right now."

"It's the curse of having superior intelligence."

They both cracked up and then lay in their chairs until Jenn made her way out later for a casual club dinner.

After the sun set and the four of them had a few rounds of after-dinner drinks, Cassie was the first to get up and head to the cabana to change. Unaware she was being followed inside, she jumped when Deana closed the door behind them.

"I'm sorry. I didn't mean to scare you."

Cassie glanced down at Deana's bare feet. Her noisy Gucci sandals were conspicuously missing. "No problem. Thank you again for the invitation. We all had an amazing time."

Deana moved closer, her luscious glistening cleavage leading the way. "I wish you and the girls didn't have to leave."

"It's getting pretty late, and we certainly don't want to overstay our welcome."

"Don't be silly. I'm having the best time with you...all of you. Why don't you all come back to my house? I have two guest rooms."

Deana had been inching closer with each word, and now Cassie's back had finally reached the wall. As she glanced at Deana's tanned breasts, practically pressing into hers, her mouth watered. She was clearly buzzed, as she'd upped her wine intake after her husband picked up her son.

"I'm not sure that's a good idea," Cassie said. "Won't your husband object to all these strangers at his house?"

"He might if he were here. He took Sean fishing in upstate New York."

"So you're alone for the weekend?"

Deana bit her lip and nodded.

Cassie tingled at the plethora of sexy possibilities if she wasn't with Maggie and Jenn. But she was. "I, uh, I don't think I'm quite ready for a slumber party."

"I'm more of a slumber-party-for-two kind of woman anyway. Maybe another time."

Cassie nodded, expecting Deana to back away, but she continued staring seductively into Cassie's eyes.

Finally, she stepped back. "Okay. As long as you're all right to drive home."

"I'm not even buzzed." Locked in the pull of sexual energy between them, Cassie couldn't break eye contact. "Even though being this close to you is so intoxicating."

Deana placed her drink on the table next to them. "I love how you smell." She practically stuck her nose in Cassie's neck.

The warmth of Deana's breath and the softness of her lips as they grazed her ear heavily aroused her. She should've ushered Deana back, but she wasn't just being poetic before. She'd really felt intoxicated by Deana's intense sex appeal.

"You probably won't forgive me for this," Deana whispered. "But I can't help myself." She pressed her warm, salty lips against Cassie's and kissed her slowly.

Cassie inhaled her beachy, slightly sweaty scent as she pulled Deana's bikini-clad body against hers. The heat between them started between her legs and spread throughout her.

Deana clasped her hands behind Cassie's ears and plunged her tongue into her mouth, holding Cassie's head firmly in place. She whimpered as they flicked their tongues together and she ground into Cassie's thigh.

Cassie felt the heat of Deana's sex against her through her thin bikini bottom. She slid her fingers up the inside of Deana's thigh, but the door flew open and jolted them apart.

"Sorry," Maggie said. "I didn't know the room was *ocupado*."

Cassie licked the taste of Deana's mouth from her lips. "No problem. I was just about to rinse off before we hit the road." She grabbed her towel and jumped into the shower stall, closing the wooden door behind her.

Holy crap. What would've happened if Maggie hadn't had the worst sense of timing in the world?

"I was just telling Cass that you all can come and stay at my house if you don't want to drive home at this hour."

"What do you think, Cass?" Maggie said. "I'm sure Jenn won't mind either. It's a long ride back."

Cassie squeezed out some shampoo. "I really don't mind driving home."

"Oh, come on now," Deana said. "I'd feel better if you ladies weren't on the road this time of night."

"Okay. Fine," Cassie said. "Make sure it's okay with Jenn."

The next thing Cassie knew, the three of them were following Deana into a gated community.

Deana's backyard resembled the beach club minus Long Island Sound being only a few yards away. Cassie sat on an outdoor sofa in front of a fire in shorts and a hoodie, nursing a glass of wine she hadn't wanted after a day of drinking at the beach club. Deana had conveniently plopped down next to her, while Jenn and Maggie sat across the fire in chairs.

Cassie had been trying to get Jenn's attention while they talked, drank, and laughed, but she was too swept up in the revelry.

"Jenn," Cassie said assertively. "Can you come inside with me for a minute? I think I have something in my contact lens."

Jenn looked perplexed, so Cassie jerked her head toward the sliding-glass door for her to follow.

"When did you start wearing contacts?" Bleary-eyed, Jenn tried to poke at her eye.

"I don't." Cassie swatted her hand away from her face. "I've been trying to get your attention since we sat down."

"What are you so twitchy about?"

"Deana made a pass at me at the club," she said in whisper.

"She what?" Jenn shouted.

"Shut up." Cassie slapped a hand over her mouth and glanced over her shoulder. "You can't let me out of your sight tonight."

"Whoa, whoa. Let's back up for a second. What did she do?"

Cassie huffed. "She kissed me in the changing cabana. Thank God Maggie walked in when she did."

Jenn looked deflated. "I can't believe she came on to you."

"Are you offended for me or for you?"

"If anyone was going to have sex with Deana tonight while the husband's away, I thought it would be me."

"Don't you have a girlfriend?"

"Yes and no."

"Look. Nobody's having sex with anyone tonight. We're all supposed to be friends. Besides, the housekeeper is asleep somewhere in here."

"Is she hot? I don't mind if she joins." Jenn was slurring her words.

"Can we get back on topic here. Just make sure I'm not left alone in one of the guest rooms tonight. Okay? Can you manage that?"

"Do you and Deana have a thing go—"

Cassie cut her off as Deana opened the sliders.

"Everything okay in here?"

"Yes. Fine. Fantastic," Cassie said. "We were just coming out."

"Maggie was saying she's ready to call it a night," Deana said, looking at Cassie. "What do you gals think?"

Jenn stepped forward. "Cassie and Mags are ready, but I'll stay up and finish that bottle with you."

Was semi-single Jenn really trying to set the scene for seduction, knowing that Deana had just hit on Cassie earlier in the evening? Cassie despised feeling jealous over anything, especially when it involved her friends.

"Uh…" Deana's gaze darted between them. "Actually, I'm ready for bed myself. It's been a long, fun day." She gave Cassie what she'd felt was a reassuring smile.

Maggie opened the sliders carrying a couple of empty wineglasses and yawned.

"Come on, Mags. Looks like we're roomies tonight." Cassie accosted her, took the glasses from her, and placed them in the sink.

After Deana settled them in the guest rooms on the opposite side of the house, the turmoil inside Cassie had begun to fade. She brushed her teeth and scrubbed her face with some fancy facial cleanser, and then Cassie stared at her tan skin and disheveled, sun-bleached hair in the mirror. What a crazy night. She liked Deana. A lot. But the timing of their paths crossing couldn't have been worse.

She thought about Lorna, how she'd made her feel so worthless when she left her. Then along came this delightful, passionate, and blindingly gorgeous woman deluging her with attention. It was almost like the universe had plopped Deana into her world to prove to her that Lorna's approval was not the measure of her value. And that she should stop giving her that power.

She finished in the bathroom, and as soon as she approached the guest room, she heard the whisper.

"Cassie."

She whirled around to see Deana looking so innocent and naturally beautiful with no makeup and in silky summer pajamas.

"I just wanted to make sure you all have everything you need."

"Yes. Thank you," Cassie said. "Everything is perfect."

"Good, good." Deana looked down as though upset about something. "Listen. I just wanted to apologize to you for earlier at the beach club."

"Oh, no. It's fine."

"No. It isn't. I shouldn't have come on so strong. I assumed some things I shouldn't have and clearly made you uncomfortable. That was never my intention, and I'm sorry."

"It's okay. We were all drinking. It was a party atmosphere. We're cool."

"Are you sure? I'd hate to think I could've ruined such a promising friendship."

Cassie needed to lighten the mood. She certainly didn't want Deana to feel as badly as she seemed to about it. "Hey, it's not like you punched me in the face. What's a little kiss between friends?"

"Really? I didn't screw things up?"

"Absolutely not."

"I'm so glad to hear that." She pulled Cassie in for a hug, a close one.

Cassie couldn't help inhaling her freshly showered lavender scent. They were both holding on much longer than expected, so she forced herself to make the break.

"Good night, Deana. Thanks for putting us up for the night. I feel like I'm staying at the Four Seasons."

Deana chuckled. "Wait till you try Helga's eggs Benedict in the morning."

❖

As she was driving them home after breakfast, Cassie was quiet, ruminating about Deana while Jenn banged out a drum beat on her thigh to a Billy Idol song in the passenger seat.

"Hey," Maggie called out from the back. "You wanna turn that down a notch? You're blasting out my eardrums back here."

"Sorry," Jenn said. "You know my obsession with eighties music."

"Is anyone going to fill me in on what's going on with you two and Deana?"

That question finally hauled Cassie back to the present. "Huh?"

"Which one of you is having sex with her now?"

"Obviously not me," Cassie said. "I was in the room with you all night, not that you would've noticed if I'd slipped out with all that snoring."

"Sorry. It happens whenever I drink."

"It wasn't me either," Jenn said. "You know if it was, you would've heard about it the second we got in the car."

"True," Maggie said. "Well, Cass, she clearly has a thing for you."

"I guess it's pretty obvious."

"So is your attraction to her," Jenn said.

"Look. I admit I think she's smokin' hot," Cassie said. "But really, who doesn't? And I like her as a friend, a lot. That's all that's going on with us, friendship."

"Not if she has anything to say about it," Jenn said.

"Well, she doesn't. Not while she's married anyway."

"It might help if you stopped flirting so hard with her." Jenn's tone surprised her. It didn't have the slightest trace of facetiousness.

"Maybe we should both stop flirting with her. Then nobody will need to get an attitude every time we all hang out."

Jenn turned the radio volume way down. "I hope you're not suggesting that I'm the one with the attitude."

"Of course you are. I don't get all bent out of shape when you blast her with all that artist charisma."

"I can't help that she's drawn to that."

"*Was* drawn to that."

"Oh, right. Now she's into the sad little broken-hearted waif playing hard to get. Clearly, she's all about the chase."

"Um, is this turning into a full-blown fight?" Maggie asked. "If so, you may want to pull off the interstate."

"This isn't a full-blown fight," Cassie said. "What would we even be fighting over? The attention of a married, unavailable woman? Are we that petty?"

"You could just be honest and admit you like her and are pursuing her. Don't I deserve that as your friend?"

"You're only half right. I'm not the one doing the pursuing."

"You've slept with her already, haven't you?"

"I most certainly have not. I've already told you that. As your friend, I deserve your trust. If anything happened between us, I'd let you know."

Cassie's hands were getting sweaty from gripping the wheel. She turned the volume back up, as the silence in the car squeezed her like a vise.

"Look," she said after several miles. "If you want me to stop being friends with her, I will. It's not worth hurting someone I care about. But you should, too. She's a complicated woman, and her energy is throwing us all off."

"Not me," Maggie said from the back.

Cassie glared at her in the rearview mirror. "Oh, shut up."

"Whatever, Cass," Jenn said. "I don't want this stupid shit to interfere with our friendship either."

Cassie was relieved that they'd agreed to table the bickering even if it meant a quiet rest-of-the-ride home. The last thing she'd wanted was to allow anything to come between her and Jenn.

CHAPTER TWELVE

"I hope I didn't twist your arm to meet me." Deana said it playfully, sensing Cassie wasn't as carefree as usual. It had taken several phone calls over several weeks to get her to agree to go to lunch with her.

"Nah. I've just been busy with the club," Cassie said rather unconvincingly. "How have you been?"

"Fine. I've just missed your company. We always have such scintillating conversations. I especially love your take on politics."

Cassie giggled. "You don't go home and lay my opinions on your husband, do you?"

She shook her head. "We stopped talking politics as dinner conversation when I told him I hope George W. Bush doesn't win in November."

"You're a Gore woman? That must make for interesting pillow talk."

"Like I said, we don't talk politics anymore. It's his thing, and I just supported him. But he doesn't know what I do when I close the voting-booth curtain."

Cassie giggled again. Her icy exterior was starting to melt, and Deana basked in the warmth of her attention. At times emotive and at others aloof, Cassie Burke kept her guessing. A young woman full of maturity and intelligence beyond her years, she made Deana feel heard and understood in a way her husband had never been able to. Or had never tried to.

"I so respect a woman who has her own political beliefs and doesn't just go with what her husband tells her," Cassie said. "That's such an outdated custom."

"It's even more of a challenge when her husband makes a career out of it. But I'm glad I met you. You've opened my eyes to how women are so underserved in the political arena. We need to do a better job of making our voices heard."

"Well, I'm glad my minor in political science hasn't completely gone to waste."

"Do you think if you didn't own Pantheon, you'd be in a career where you'd utilize it more?"

"That was the original plan. Then when Lorna bought the club, I just fell into the role of manager." Cassie's demeanor brightened. "I definitely don't see myself being a nightclub owner that much longer."

"Are you still thinking of selling the club?"

Cassie nodded. "I've had inquiries from developers before. Someone wants to turn the building into high-end apartments. Someone else wanted to turn it into retail space."

"Sounds like you'll make a nice profit to get you started on your next venture, whatever it may be."

"I've been kicking around some ideas."

"I look forward to hearing about them."

Cassie smiled, but something was definitely off. Was she still upset about the kiss at the beach club? She thought they'd settled it that night. Whatever it was, Deana couldn't leave it hanging between them.

"Is everything okay, Cass?"

"Yeah. Do I not seem okay?"

"You don't seem yourself. You seem preoccupied." Deana's greatest fear was that Cassie's ex would sail back into her life and sweep her off her feet. It had been only six or seven months since they broke up. Maybe all they'd needed was some time apart.

"I have a few things on my mind, but I'll be fine."

She smiled, but the response didn't reassure Deana. If anything, the vagueness only made her think that Cassie's mood had something to do with Lorna.

"Feel free to share if it'll make you feel better." Deana braced herself for the confession.

Cassie shrugged and popped the last bite of her sandwich into her mouth. "It won't."

Deana ordered another glass of wine in an attempt to calm her racing heart. Cassie was about to end their friendship over Lorna, and she didn't know how to deal with it. But the ambiguity of it all was killing her.

"So, if you're getting back with Lorna and can't see me anymore, it's fine. I'd just like to know now so I'm not left wondering."

"What?" That remark finally snapped Cassie out of her monotone state. "What are you talking about?"

"Your mood. It's awful. It's like you wish you could be as far away from me as possible."

Cassie folded her arms across her chest. "You have it all wrong."

"You're not getting back with Lorna, or you don't want to be far away from me?"

"Both. Look. Something is bothering me, but it's *not* not wanting to be with you. In fact, it's the opposite." Cassie looked away, and her leg started bouncing under the table.

While Deana was relieved that it wasn't either of the scenarios she'd taunted herself with, the idea that Cassie was upset because they couldn't be closer hurt her even more.

"I'm sorry, Cass. I feel the same way. I'll try to get together with you more. I know I can make it happen."

"More breakfasts and lunches?" Her sarcasm was white hot.

"That's what friends do."

Cassie sighed. "How much longer are we going to pretend that's all we are? I have to admit it's not working that well for me anymore."

"It's not for me either, but I'm kind of stuck for now. You understand, don't you?"

"I know, and I do. It's the classic right-person-at-the-wrong-time scenario for both of us. I mean, I knew I liked you from the start. I just didn't know I was going to like you this much."

Deana took her hand in hers, happy that Cassie had thawed enough to open up. "I didn't either, but here we are."

"But I don't think the answer is seeing more of each other."

Deana sighed. "Are you saying you don't want to see me at all?"

Cassie seemed to be forcing her head to nod.

"For just a while or for good?"

"I don't think I can answer that at the moment."

This wasn't at all what Deana had expected or wanted, but she hadn't the stamina to try to convince Cassie otherwise.

Maybe they both needed a break.

❖

Halloween was Cassie's favorite of the special occasions celebrated at Pantheon, and Jenn and Maggie did not disappoint when it came to selecting costumes. Jenn showed up decked out in a purple suit, black curly wig, and pencil-thin mustache drawn on. Maggie was a zombie Girl Scout carrying a basket filled with boxed Girl Scout cookies and a few severed limbs.

Cassie dressed as an overdone news reporter in a tight suit carrying a microphone with a local news station's logo on it. She and some hired help for the evening were walking around the club, selling raffle tickets, giving away shots, and entering people for the costume contest at the end of the evening. She'd been so busy having fun and taking care of Halloween business, she'd barely noticed the woman in the pantsuit and rubber Hillary Clinton mask stalking her.

When she'd finally stopped to chat with Jenn and Maggie, the Hillary imposter approached her.

"I hope you're not going to hound me for an interview," the familiar voice said.

Jenn cracked up as though she were in on the joke.

"I'll have to get my Secret Service agent, Prince, to step in."

Jenn barged through Cassie and Maggie to get to Hillary. "I'm sorry, Ms. Burke," Jenn said. "You're going to have to step back and give Mrs. Clinton some room."

"Deana," Cassie said. "I know it's you in there. I recognize your eyes."

"Damn it." She pulled off the mask and attempted to fix her mussed hair. "There's no pulling one over on you, is there?"

"I told you she'd know it was you," Jenn said.

"Great costume," Cassie said. "Did you bring Bill with you tonight?" She walked toward the bar, and Deana followed.

"He was busy," she replied. "I think he said something about having a late meeting with an intern."

"Ooh." Cassie winced at the joke despite finding that she loved Deana's comedic timing. "Well, Hillary, I'm sure you'll have a much better time at a place like this without him."

Deana chuckled. "I guess it's a good sign if you haven't had the bouncer throw me out yet."

"I never throw anyone out on nights the cover charge is double." She winked, then ordered a Manhattan and a glass of pinot grigio.

"Your costume looks great on you," Deana said, then sipped her wine. "I can just picture you as a political correspondent for CNN or something."

Cassie giggled. "That'd be something all right. And what about you? Forget about the politician's wife. You totally look the part of a politician...minus the rubber face."

Deana held up the mask next to her face. "Don't people always accuse politicians of being two-faced anyway?" She tossed the mask onto the bar and leaned into the edge, twirling her glass by the stem.

"It's nice to see you again, Deana." Cassie sipped her Manhattan and studied Deana's profile. "It was very hard to keep telling Jenn no when she'd invite me along for dinner or a happy hour with you."

Deana finally turned her head toward her. "It was hard to keep hearing that you had. Oh, Jenn did her best to come up with all kinds of excuses as to why you couldn't make it. I'm sure she was relieved when I finally stopped asking."

"How are things going?"

She shrugged. "Status quo. Sean is doing well in middle school, and Jeffrey and I continue to do our dance to stay out of each other's way. One more year, and it'll be all over."

"You're really committed to divorcing him after the election."

"What do you think I'd been trying to tell you for months?"

"Win or lose?"

"Win or lose, I am moving out and finally having my own life. *Hasta la vista*, baby." She saluted the air. "Good-bye and good luck."

Cassie grinned. She'd missed Deana terribly in the months they hadn't seen each other. It seemed silly now that she'd needed to take such drastic measures to protect herself. They were having a drink together, laughing and chatting like their groove had never been interrupted.

"Maybe we can get together for dinner or something over the holidays. I'm sure the girls would enjoy a little reunion, too."

"I'd love that. You all are welcome to come out to my place and stay over again. Or I'll come here. Whatever you want."

Deana's smile was devastating. Cassie couldn't envision a time or a situation in which it wouldn't move her with the force of an earthquake. But this time, she vowed to be more mature about everything. Deana was a great woman, and Cassie's all-or-nothing approach hadn't served her well.

Later in the evening, the four of them had a corner to themselves where they savored that sense of sisterhood they'd felt when they first met, and everyone's stupid feelings weren't ruining everything.

CHAPTER THIRTEEN

New Year's Eve 1999

Cassie walked into Pantheon and sighed. The sight of sparse pockets of diehards there to ring in the new century with them warmed her heart, but the ghostly absence of so much of her past chilled the atmosphere. It wasn't just the memories of the crowds of feminine energy from a couple of years back or the widespread feeling of sisterhood when the LGBTQ community needed their own space for survival. The memories of Lorna that continued to resonate within the walls haunted her.

On that particular night, Lorna was not the woman in question when Cassie met up with Maggie, Jenn, and Jenn's girlfriend, Renny, at their table in the main bar area.

"Hey, girl," Jenn said as she wrapped Cassie in a hug. "Where's Deana?"

Cassie caught Maggie's smirk before responding. "We're on a break."

"I'm shocked," Maggie said.

Cassie huffed. "Come on, Mag. I told you how that bothers me."

"I'm sorry. I can't help myself—when I see my friend keep settling for less than she deserves."

"Ouch," Jenn said. "I thought we decided to be unconditionally supportive of our dear wayward friend on the last night of the century?"

"We did." Cassie glared at Maggie as she responded to Jenn. "And thank you for honoring our agreement. I mean it. We're really through this time, with whatever it is we had."

"It must've been so exhausting having the same argument all the time," Jenn said.

"Especially when you hadn't even slept together," Renny added. "That's dedication."

"Dedication?" Cassie said. "I was thinking more along the lines of mental instability."

"Don't be so hard on yourself," Jenn said. "The world is gonna end at midnight anyway when all the computers seize and explode. It's been a crazy year for all of us."

Maggie nodded as if she truly believed Jenn's prediction.

"I mean, I feel for Deana," Cassie said, "the position she's in, but that doesn't mean I have to remain tangled up in it. Are we friends? Are we more than friends? Is she leaving him? Is she staying? It's getting so old."

"She certainly deserves the World's Greatest Wife award for sticking by that jerk husband," Maggie said.

"Then I must deserve the World's Greatest Sort-of Side Piece award for making it on and off for all these months."

Jenn threw an arm around her shoulder. "Be proud of yourself that you didn't go all the way with her, Cass. You've got principles. I don't know how anyone in their right mind could've resisted Deana."

"I could've," Maggie said as she picked between her teeth with her cocktail straw.

"Case in point." Jenn rested a hand on Maggie's shoulder.

Cassie chuckled and thanked the server who brought over Cassie's favorite cocktail, a Manhattan, without needing to ask. "Isn't anyone else sad that I'm selling the space and soon Pantheon will be no more? Remember when Mr. Pike first called us the Pantheon Girls senior year?"

Maggie's face brightened. "That project was so much fun. It was the first time anyone seemed happy to work with me."

"And then when Lorna asked me what she should name this place, I jokingly said 'Pantheon,' and the next thing I knew, we were having a grand opening with these outrageously sexy women dressed like Greek goddesses."

"That night was the bomb," Jenn said as though reliving it in vivid imagery. "A gala event like no other."

"And now it's all coming to an end," Cassie said wistfully.

"The true end of an era," Maggie said.

Cassie imbibed the warmth of her friends as she sipped her drink. With the new century only hours away, she hoped her life would take a new turn for the better. No more drama, no more love-bombing narcissists, and no more emotional entanglements with married women. It was time to grow up and set out to build her own career and her independence from soul-sucking women who knew how to play right into her welcoming heart.

"You all can come and hang out with us anytime," Renny said, squeezing Jenn's shoulder. "We're going to be moving in together this year."

Cassie gave Maggie a side glance, then finally knocked loose a response. "Really?"

"Yeah, well," Jenn said. "We're almost thirty now. Gotta stop letting good ones get away, right?" While her words sounded convincing enough, her eyes conveyed a silent desperation that would likely send her into flight mode before Renny had the chance to lock it down.

Maggie looked around and shrugged. "I guess it's time we all move on. You're actually selling this place at a great time."

"Yeah," Jenn said. "The community doesn't seem to need gay bars as safe havens like we used to. We can thank *Will & Grace* for making us more socially acceptable."

"Those bastards," Cassie quipped.

"The rest of us are all slaves to nostalgia," Maggie said and pretended to run a hand through her hair. "Hence this stupendous mullet."

"Nobody rocks an eighties hairdo like you, my friend." Jenn clicked glasses with her.

"I can't believe it's been over a decade since we all met because of that brawl in the cafeteria," Cassie said.

Jenn's face lit up. "Whoever would've thought that a punk and a cheerleader would become best friends with each other and the nerd they both decided to defend?"

Maggie sucked in her cheeks. "I prefer to call myself studious."

"Hey, I may have been lumped in with the snotty cheerleaders, but I never called you a nerd or picked on anyone," Cassie said.

"You never talked to me either," Maggie said in a rare moment of authenticity.

That remark dinged Cassie's heart as she glanced reproachfully at Jenn.

"I never did either," Jenn said and touched Maggie's arm gently. "Not till I shoved a two-hundred-pound bully into a lunch table for you."

Cassie laughed at the memory. "You started a movement. I couldn't let you go at it alone."

Jenn laughed, too. "I don't know what was funnier, this lanky cheerleader jumping on Monster Malone's back or the looks on your fellow cheerleaders' faces when you brought her to the floor."

"We were like *The Breakfast Club*," Maggie said reminiscently. "Life imitating art. We forged a bond despite our differences."

Cassie raised her glass. "And we're closer than ever."

They leaned into each other in a silent gesture of solidarity. At that point, Renny wandered off.

"You know what the worst part of selling the bar will be?" Cassie said.

"Now you'll have to get a real job?" Jenn replied.

"Uh, no. Speaking of safe havens, this place is mine. Deana won't be popping in here anymore now that we're heading into the election year. She can't risk a scandal for the soon-to-be Senator Godwin." She punctuated her sentence with a pretend finger down her throat.

"He doesn't have a chance of winning in this state," Jenn said. "Deana should just pack it up right now."

"You can tell her that," Cassie said. "I'm trying to keep away from her."

"If we survive the new-century computer glitch, and the Farewell to Pantheon party is a go, you can tell her yourself," Jenn said. "I'm sure she won't miss it, election year or not."

"Well, it won't be for a few months yet. In the meantime, I'm gonna lay low around here just in case."

"Are you going to ignore her? What if she calls?"

"She has called a few times. Like the last time we went our separate ways, I just made polite excuses."

"Too bad you can't be like me and completely shut down your feelings," Jenn said. "You two could've had yourselves a wild night of hot sex before you never saw her again."

Cassie glared at her. "You're so full of shit. You don't shut your feelings down. You were so pissy when Deana started showing more interest in me."

Jenn clamped a hand over Cassie's mouth. "First of all, keep your voice down so my girlfriend doesn't hear you. Second, I wasn't pissy. I was woman enough and a loyal enough friend to admit to myself that she liked you better."

"I was a little worried there for a while," Cassie said. "This was the second major test in our friendship, but we pulled through it with flying colors."

Jenn threw an arm around Cassie's neck and squished her face against hers. "You're stuck with me forever, mutha-fucka."

"Don't threaten me with a good time," Cassie replied, and they both cackled.

Maggie stared at them. "You two are so dysfunctional."

"Hey, it's New Year's Eve," Cassie said as she raised her glass. "Let's start off the new century on a positive note. Here's to good friends, good times, and good decisions in 2000."

Despite Jenn's dire predictions of a millennial doomsday, 2000 had arrived safely, but as with most NYE resolutions, Cassie's did not. Against her better judgment, she agreed to meet Deana for dinner at the Westport café that had become their midway rendezvous point. They needed to talk face-to-face, as her avoidance tactics over the last several weeks hadn't yielded the desired results. Deana continued to call her, sometimes sounding distressed, further exacerbating Cassie's complicated feelings. The situation was bringing bad juju into her life, distracting her from what needed her attention.

She'd ordered a salad so she wouldn't be drinking on an empty stomach, but she wasn't at all hungry. She kept avoiding eye contact, because looking at Deana and hearing her voice was making her want to do the exact opposite of her intended mission.

"Thanks again for meeting me," Deana said. She picked at chicken salad nestled on a bed of watercress but hadn't eaten much herself. "I know you have a lot going on with Pantheon right now."

"A lot's going on in my head with you, too." She put her fork down and sipped her white wine.

"I can tell. You've hardly touched your dinner."

"Because I know we need to have the conversation we've been avoiding."

"Uh-oh. Is this the classic Hollywood breakup scene? You do it in a restaurant, so the other person won't freak out?" She was smirking, but Cassie saw the worry in her eyes.

"Why would I need a breakup strategy when we're not even a couple?"

"I know something's going on with you. You don't return my calls like you used to, and now suddenly you're busy on days you never used to be. Are we done being friends, too?"

She was right. Cassie had been doing all those things, but she hated that Deana was calling her out about it.

"We're not done being friends, Deana. I just need some space. We've been dancing on this line between friendship and more than friendship for too long. We need to forget about the line and be clear about boundaries."

Deana glanced out the window, then looked at her. "I'm trying, Cass. I love the friendship we've created. I'm really trying to keep my heart out of it, and I think I've been doing pretty well."

"You have. Better than me, apparently. I've tried to ignore my feelings, too, but I can't maintain this emotional back-and-forth anymore without it affecting other parts of my life."

"It's affecting me, too, but other than my son, having you in my life is the best thing about it. I don't want to lose you."

Cassie sighed. The thought of not talking to or spending time with Deana was eating away at her. She'd hated those few months at the end of summer when they hadn't seen each other. But so was desiring her and not being able to have her. "I'm really uncomfortable with where we are. I'm not ready for a relationship, and I sure as hell don't want one with a married woman, but that's all I think about lately, and it's driving me insane."

"I'm in a tough spot right now, and I've pulled you into it with me. I'm sorry for that."

"It wasn't against my will. I'm a big girl. I know how to accept responsibility for my actions."

"So where do we go from here?"

"I need a break, a real one this time." The words rolled out on their own. But once she heard herself say them, she was glad they were out there.

"Even as friends?"

As soon as Cassie nodded, Deana's eyes began to pool. *Shit. Not here in the restaurant.* Cassie's stomach started rolling over on itself.

"For how long?"

"I don't know." At that point, Cassie couldn't look at her, as she was on the verge herself. One teardrop from Deana, and she could burst open like a weakened levee. "Probably until you're divorced."

"Cassie. You don't mean that."

"I do. For now, anyway. Please be okay with that, Deana." Cassie stood up, feeling smothered from the conflict.

Deana stood, too, fire in her eyes. "You can't expect me to be okay with this. I have feelings, too."

"I'm sorry," Cassie said as she dropped a couple of twenties onto the table. "I just need a moment to breathe. Please try to understand that." She headed out to the parking lot, drained from the exchange.

Deana followed her to her car. "Cassie," she shouted. Her cheeks were wet as she approached. "Why are you doing this?"

Cassie was mortified. She glanced around, hoping nobody would overhear them. "Please don't, Deana. I told you why. It's not you. It's the situation."

"I'm sorry. I know I don't have the right to give you a hard time about it. Just please. Promise me you're not shutting me off completely. Tell me you'll give it some time and some thought, and we can talk more later."

"We don't have anything else to talk about as long as you're married."

"I'll be single by the end of the year."

"If that's true, we can talk then."

Deana scoffed, then dragged a hand under both eyes to dry her face. "That's great, Cassie. Fine. This is what you want? That's okay with me. I won't bother you anymore." She stormed off to her car.

"Deana, come on. Let's not end this on a bad note. I still care about you."

Deana stopped at her driver's-side door and produced two middle fingers that she jutted out to Cassie. "Here's what you can do with that." She slammed her door shut and peeled her Mercedes out of the parking lot.

Once in her car, Cassie leaned her head against the steering wheel and let her tears flow. As sad as it made her to watch Deana drive away so furious, she was relieved. She refused to allow anyone to imprison her in her own emotions again the way Lorna had. She'd spent too many hours in therapy to be dragged backward.

Maybe Deana would be true to her word and divorce her husband after he lost the election. But what if he did what nobody thought he'd do and won?

CHAPTER FOURTEEN

Cassie's boots clicked up and down the sidewalk outside Pantheon. Maggie had called her cell only moments ago warning her that Deana was back after a winter of silence and had already asked about her. She was seriously considering doing an about-face and scurrying off home. After wrestling with depression for a year, nursing wounds from the breakup of her relationship with Lorna, she was finally in a good place. Although she'd had no choice but to let go, it turned out to be the crucible she'd needed to evolve into a stronger woman, one more equipped to make healthy choices in all areas of her life. Giving in to her desire for a woman like Deana would undermine all the suffering and soul-searching that had led her here.

On the other hand, could she truly claim a victory if she couldn't even trust herself to meet her friends out for a drink?

"Like Roosevelt said, 'the only thing we have to fear,'" she said and yanked open Pantheon's heavy door.

With blinders on, she raced toward the bar where Maggie and Jenn were settled.

"What the hell kept you?" Maggie said. "We've been staking out the entrance for an hour."

"She looks really good, Cass," Jenn said without giving her a chance to answer Maggie.

Cassie allowed herself a side glance, chancing that she could catch Deana in her peripheral vision.

"She's been milling around us since we walked in," Maggie said.

"Great," Cassie announced with dread. But to be honest, she had to admit that the tingle crawling up her neck had Deana written all over it.

She ordered a dirty martini and positioned herself on a bar stool, ready, if necessary, to defend herself against the overpowering allure of Deana's pheromones.

Maggie assumed the voice of a film noir narrator. "Deana Godwin, a fortyish super-fem with gleaming lipstick tube of steel, rose to cult status at Pantheon since coming out and around months ago. She's a woman of formidable perseverance, determined to get what she wants—and what she wants is Cassie Burke."

Cassie stared at her in disbelief. "What is wrong with you?"

"You've gotta be the only one in here who won't do her," Jenn said. She scratched at her head through her spiky red hair. "I mean, she's a freakin' former model, for Christ's sake."

"Thanks for being so supportive," Cassie replied, drier than her martini.

"Not to mention she hails from the finest stock of Greenwich snobbery you can shake a Rolex at," Maggie added, rubbing her fingers together in the universal sign of money.

Cassie glared at them. "Who are you two, her publicists?"

"I don't know why you don't just give her what she wants," Maggie said. "You haven't been laid in ages, and it'll probably get her out of your hair." She casually swiped cat hair off Jenn's black oxford.

"Excuse you." Jenn slapped Maggie's hand away as she surveyed the crowd.

"I don't think fucking someone as a means to get rid of them is one of your most brilliant ideas," Cassie said. "That's something Jenn would do."

Jenn turned to face them, shifting a drink stirrer to the other side of her mouth. "Did I hear my name and 'fuck' in the same sentence?"

"I think you have that backward," Maggie said to Cassie under her breath. "Speaking of…"

The three braced themselves against the bar as Deana sauntered toward them with a grace and sensuality clearly held over from her days on the catwalk.

"Be still my heart." Deana smirked, staring into Cassie's eyes as if the other two were part of the decor.

"Hey, Deana," Cassie coolly replied. She sipped her drink, hoping her racing heart wasn't visible through her tight spandex shirt.

"Uh, excuse me, but didn't we fuck once?" Jenn asked.

Everyone turned to her, their faces decorated in various shades of horror.

"The perils of a lifetime of repressed bisexuality," Deana said with a curt grin.

Maggie elbowed Jenn. "Don't you know it's impolite to remind people of their highly regrettable mistakes?" Her laughter sounded forced and only exacerbated the awkwardness.

Cassie barely stifled hers as she glanced at Jenn.

"You weren't such a delicate flower then," Jenn said.

"I was just getting started." Deana directed a smoldering gaze at Cassie.

"Yeah. How'd that work out for you?" Jenn said.

Cassie glared at both of them. "How about you two take a time-out? I feel like a high school rumble is about to break out." She slid down the bar a bit, needing some space.

Deana immediately filled in the empty spot. "Are you still pretending you're not ready for a relationship?"

"Are you still married?" Cassie's reply was louder than she'd intended.

Maggie's face stretched oblong in awe. "Ooh, shots fired."

Cassie and Deana stared each other down.

"Ugh, lesbians. Let's go do a lap around," Jenn said to Maggie.

"And miss what happens next?" Maggie replied.

"Bye, ladies," Cassie said through clenched teeth.

"How about you and I take a walk?" Deana laced her arm through Cassie's and led her away toward the corner arranged with comfy furniture. "I told you months ago my marriage is long over. Why won't you believe me?" Impatience pooled in her eyes.

"Mainly because you're still married," Cassie said. "Or have you been in Mexico getting one of those quickie divorces?"

Deana pulled her onto a sectional sofa near the pool table. "I thought you'd be just a little excited to see me," she said in a pout.

Cassie sighed and fluffed out her straggly curls. "What exactly am I supposed to do with you, Deana?" She looked away as she sipped her cocktail.

"You know there's still something between us," Deana said. "And you also know my situation."

"I do. Why do you think I try so hard to avoid you?"

"Don't try so hard. Things won't always be like they are now."

After another sip, Cassie leaned forward on her elbows, steering clear of any semblance of intimacy. "Where's your son?"

"Home." Deana's voice was rich, cool velvet, but her shaking leg was giving her away.

Cassie stared blankly at a group of young girls playing pool. What was she doing even sitting here entertaining her?

"It's so simple for you, isn't it?" Deana's tone was decidedly less playful.

"What are you talking about?"

Deana shook her head in obvious frustration. "Not everything can be so clearly defined. Just because you came out when you were *two* doesn't mean everyone's transition is as smooth or as obvious." She looked up at an old drip stain on the wall, and Cassie sensed that the unwavering cool Deana was known for was, in fact, wavering.

"Whatever," Cassie said and sucked at the last drop of her martini.

"Cassie, I can't stop thinking about you, and God knows I've tried," Deana said. "Why do you think I've been MIA for over two months?"

"Wifely duties? Motherly obligations?" Even Cassie heard the overkill in her sarcasm.

Hurt flashed across Deana's porcelain face. "I may regret giving Jeffrey more than he deserved from me, but I'll never regret having Sean."

"I'm sorry," Cassie said. "Sometimes this situation really brings out my inner bitch."

"So you do still have feelings for me." Deana grinned with irresistible innocence as her hand drifted over Cassie's thigh.

Cassie picked up her arm and gently placed it back into her own lap.

"Look, I know it's really complicated right now, but in November—"

"No, you look, Deana." The crack of the pool balls breaking startled her. "You know I don't do drama and dysfunction—especially in relationships. I got off that train with Lorna, and I don't intend to board another one."

Deana leaned back into the sofa and grew sullen. Cassie sat motionless, fighting the urge to look at her, to throw her arms around her and confess how badly she wanted her. But the reality of Deana's world swiftly rescued her from the fantasy.

"So now you're going to sit there and pout all night?" Cassie said.

"You didn't let me finish," Deana said.

"I'm sorry. Go ahead."

"Things will be different in November."

Cassie nodded, but she wasn't falling for empty promises.

"When he loses, I'm filing for divorce. The day after, in fact. My lawyer's just waiting on the retainer."

Cassie snorted. "And if he wins?"

"Oh, please. A Republican US Senate candidate in Connecticut has very little chance of winning now."

"That's not what I asked you."

"Cass, I'm filing in November either way. I'm done playing the role for Jeff, my family, for everyone."

"Doesn't that clown have his eyes on the White House some day?"

Deana giggled. "What mediocre, wealthy white man in politics doesn't? But it's irrelevant. Our deal concerns his run for the senate, and when that's over, so are we."

The determination in Deana's tone impressed Cassie and finally allowed her to simmer down. "Believe it or not, I am glad to see you again."

"So am I. Of all things, I miss our friendship. I miss just talking about anything."

"Why did we have to muck it all up?"

Deana chuckled. "I don't know." She turned to look her in the eye. "Do you still find me attractive?"

Cassie's defenses were weakening, but she played it off. "Who doesn't?" She twirled the olive around her empty glass.

"Apparently, you." She narrowed her hungry eyes. "The way you back away from me, you'd think I have an STD."

"Worse. You have a husband."

"Touché."

"Deana, you're stunning," Cassie said. "You know you can have any woman you want. But you and I are looking for very different things."

"Do you even know what I'm looking for?"

"To sow your wild lesbian oats," Cassie said. "To escape an unhappy marriage. I don't know. Whatever you want, I hope you find it. But you won't find it with me—not now anyway. You still have a long way to go on your journey."

"You're being condescending," Deana said with a frown.

"I'm sorry." Cassie gave her hand a quick squeeze. "I don't mean to be. But we really are orbiting in two separate universes right now."

"I know. Sometimes I feel so lost. I think that's one of the things I find so attractive about you—you're so grounded, so stable."

Cassie almost guffawed. "Me? You clearly are lost in space. But thanks for the compliment."

Deana's lip quivered slightly. "Can't we go back to being friends?"

Cassie studied her face, her impassioned eyes pleading for acceptance, her glossy lips begging to be kissed. It was the most candid Deana had ever been since they'd met, and she seemed genuine and vulnerable and...human.

Notwithstanding the irritating sexual tension between them, Cassie had enjoyed hanging out with Deana in the past—lunches, shopping, and at Pantheon playing pool, darts, their push-and-pull tango on the dance floor toward the end of the night. It was supposed to have been innocent fun—until the feelings started their bullshit, and they both pulled away.

Now here Deana was revealing a part of herself that Cassie couldn't dismiss. Forget all the bravado, all the posturing. Deana needed a friend. But was Cassie finally strong and stable enough to be truly just friends?

"We are friends," she said with a comforting smile. "We simply need to start acting like it."

Deana smiled. "I got the next round." She motioned Cassie to follow her to the bar.

For the rest of evening, all four of them played several friendly games of pool, exchanging partners throughout, and all seemed to be genuinely enjoying each other's company. When the lights flashed for last call, Cassie informed Jenn and Maggie that she was leaving before the final song. She pulled Deana aside. "I'm glad you came tonight, and we were able to clear the air. You're a special person, and I'd really like to keep you as a friend no matter what the future holds."

They started walking out to the parking lot together.

"I'm so happy you feel that way," Deana said. "I was really nervous driving here tonight. I honestly expected the worst. But I should've known you'd be cool. You're a special person, too, Cass."

They stopped at Cassie's car and stood for an awkward moment.

"I know it's late, and my house is so far from here, but would you mind terribly giving me a lift home?"

"You don't have your car?"

"I do, but I'm not sure I'm totally okay to drive. You can sleep over. On my couch. This isn't a trap to get you alone. I swear."

Cassie held her gaze as she unlocked the doors. "I believe you're a woman of your word."

"Thanks," Deana said as she slipped into the passenger seat. "I really owe you for this."

"No, you don't. This is my first brand-new car ever, so I'll take any excuse to get her out on the highway."

"It's an exquisite machine, sleek and sexy…like it was built just for you."

Cassie pulled onto the entrance ramp to the highway, trying to focus on the road, but the weight of Deana's gaze kept pulling at her.

Why was she resisting her? So what if Deana was married to a guy and came on like an Avon saleswoman on speed? Maybe Jenn was on to something. Maybe one night of unbridled, no-strings-attached sex was exactly what Cassie needed.

But she knew herself too well. Husband aside, Deana was the kind of woman she could fall hard for, and despite her doubts about her present mental state, she could never be crazy enough to dive into an inferno like Deana Godwin. The timing, for one thing, was positively hideous.

❖

Cassie pulled her fresh-off-the-lot Lexus sedan in front of the sprawling mansion Deana unassumingly called her digs. It was after two a.m., and you could hear a money clip drop on the immaculately manicured street. As Cassie cracked the window, inhaling the enticing smell of obscene wealth, Deana grabbed the car keys out of the ignition, a strictly amateur move, but one Cassie never saw coming.

"What are you doing?" Her antics amused Cassie.

"I didn't want you shoving me out of the car before it stopped completely." Deana teased her as she fingered the clinking keys.

"You know I wouldn't do that," Cassie replied, scanning the neighborhood to avoid eye contact. After a moment Cassie heard the keys hit the floor and felt a hand slowly creeping up her thigh. "Deana, we're right in front of your house."

"My husband is in New York, and my housekeeper and son are sound asleep," Deana reassured her in a breathy whisper while kissing her neck.

The window thwarted Cassie's attempt to pull back from her. "Ouch." She rubbed the left side of her head.

"Are you all right?" Deana was practically in Cassie's lap now.

"Well, I—" was all Cassie got out as Deana clutched the back of her neck and started kissing her hard, so hard she couldn't stop her if she'd wanted to.

Deana was a poisoned drink, but Cassie also craved her. It had been nothing short of a miracle that she'd been able to restrain herself this long. Especially after experiencing the heaven of Deana's soft, wet lips.

Cassie had all but forgotten what it felt like to be desired intensely. It had been years since Lorna grabbed her with such pure sexual greediness.

Deana straddled her, slowly snaking her tongue into her mouth, and Cassie tasted the minty residue of an Altoid she had sucked through most of Fairfield County. The car windows turned steamy from their heavy panting, an unplanned benefit because if that old security guard spied them from his booth, he'd surely succumb to a coronary.

"Deana, we shouldn't do this," Cassie whispered, compelled by an annoyingly strong moral compass that always popped up at the worst time.

Though preoccupied with maneuvering her hands under Cassie's shirt to unhook her bra, Deana said, "Yes, we should, baby," her warm breath dampening Cassie's ear. "God, you feel so good." She caressed Cassie's stomach and slowly made her way upward.

Cassie attempted to control the ten or so hands of a mythological creature Deana seemed to have sprouted, but she wasn't succeeding, and it wasn't because Deana was stronger. She'd wanted this as much as Deana, but she lingered in the moment, scared to move forward yet aware she couldn't turn back.

Deana fumbled with Cassie's button-fly jeans, tearing at them like they housed the only fire hose in a burning building.

"Deana," Cassie gasped as she slid her hands up Deana's velvety sides.

"What?" She flicked her tongue around Cassie's ear.

"Never mind." Cassie moaned and cranked her seat all the way back, allowing Deana an all-access pass.

"If I knew all it takes is a tongue in your ear, I would've slipped it to you months ago."

Cassie giggled as Deana pulled her shirt off over her head. She leaned back, swept into the torrent of passion that seemed to unleash both of their inner nymphomaniacs.

Their sensual kisses exploded into madness. Cassie slid Deana's pants down to her ankles and quickly unbuttoned her blouse, revealing her silky bra. Deana fell against the steering column, making the horn blare.

After regrouping from their giggle, Deana placed Cassie's hand on her firm stomach, her eyes seeming to beg for her touch.

Cassie slid her fingertips down and inside Deana's panties, sending a shudder of pleasure through her as she thumbed her swollen sex. Deana's uninhibited moans engulfed the car's interior, and Cassie drank in the primal sounds of her escalating pleasure, the mixture of her perfume and sweet perspiration glistening on her stomach. Cassie pulled her toward her mouth and finished her with her tongue, sending her collapsing into Cassie's lap.

"Oh my God, Cass." Deana gasped for breath. "I never knew my body could do that," she said, then broke into a chuckle.

"You could seriously make a fortune in porn." Cassie stroked Deana's back with her fingers as she caught her breath.

"Only if I'm costarring with you." She lunged at Cassie's mouth, kissing her hungrily. She pulled Cassie on top of her across the front seat as she worked Cassie's jeans down enough to manipulate her fingers into her wetness.

Cassie ground into her fingers, working away at months of built-up sexual desire for Deana. "God. I hope your neighbors are asleep," she said in a strained whisper as her climax grew to an intensity impossible to keep silent.

After a lengthy crescendo of *Oh God*s, more than a year's worth of complicated emotions burst out of Cassie and into the tight, sweaty air of her brand-new Lexus.

So much for new-car smell.

❖

The alarm clock jolted Cassie out of a fitful sleep at seven thirty a.m., even though she'd crawled into her bed less than three hours ago. She lay wrapped in the sheet for a moment, staring at the dormant ceiling fan, trying to determine whether last night with Deana had actually happened or it was just a wonderfully vivid erotic dream. It had to be a dream. Cassie Burke was a woman of irreproachable moral character, and having passionate sex in a car after two in the morning with someone she wasn't in a relationship with was a high crime indeed.

Not to mention a serious threat to the sluggish progress her heart had made trying to get past her breakup.

She allowed herself a thorough torso stretch before rolling out of bed and slipping into a pair of worn purple slippers. She tugged her cat's tail as it swirled in through one of her legs and around the other and padded down the hall toward the bathroom, recalling snippets of torrid details from her sexy dream about Deana.

She was just about convinced that it was only a dream when she walked up to the mirror over the sink and discovered to her horror the glaringly obvious raspberry blotch staring back at her from the left side of her neck.

"Holy shit." Cassie rubbed at Deana's enormous insignia as though that would make it disappear.

She stared at her reflection, shame bubbling in the pit of her stomach. Okay, so they got hot and heavy in her new Lexus last night, but she didn't have any reason to feel ashamed about it. It wasn't as though she'd picked her up at a truck stop. They'd known each other for several months. And even though Cassie persisted in the delusion that they were just friends, they were unequivocally much more. The attraction between them was tangible, a crackling current of electricity running from one to the other, certain to scorch any interloper fool enough to try to come between them.

She poured a cup of coffee and sat at her kitchen table. Now that she and Deana had consummated their connection, regardless of how crass the situation, what was she supposed to do next? What was the behavior protocol after having sex with someone who was supposed to be only a friend? Jenn would know. The reigning queen of turnstile lovers could surely offer a few words of wisdom to a nervous newcomer to the seedy world of one-nighters.

Long live the Queen.

❖

Saturday night Cassie was going to dinner with the girls and then on to the last Techno Saturday dance party ever at Pantheon. It was also the night of the week that Cassie and Jenn faced their most harrowing challenge, getting Maggie presentable for the occasion, a task not suited for the faint of heart. Poor Maggie. One might've wondered if the convent wouldn't have been a better life choice. No pressure to date, and no such thing as wearing too much black.

Driven to exasperation, Cassie and Jenn hovered around her in her cluttered bedroom, begging her to comb through her ratty hair, iron her shirt, or, at the very least, remove yesterday's black eyeliner so her eyes didn't look like they were being consumed in twin lunar eclipses.

"You're never going to meet anyone, Mags," Jenn said, yanking on the tail of Maggie's faded shirt.

"Who says I want to?" Maggie defended herself as she yanked the shirttail out of Jenn's grip.

"Everyone wants to meet someone, Margaret Ann, even a misanthrope like you," Jenn replied.

"What's wrong with the way I look anyway?" She did a half-twirl in front of the mirror.

"You look like you're homeless," Cassie said politely as she tried to pull her fingers through a knot in the back of Maggie's hair.

"The homeless look is what's in now," Maggie said, shooing Cassie's hand away like a fly on a picnic table.

"Only among the homeless, doll," Cassie said and turned her attention to the jumble of garments hanging in Maggie's disheveled closet.

"Why are you wearing a mock neck in this weather?" Maggie said.

"Don't try to change the subject," Cassie replied, giving her a gentle push. "Now come on. We're going to be late."

"Oh, all right," Maggie mumbled. She snatched a pink shower scrunchy from Cassie's hand, its price tag still dangling, and stomped into the bathroom, slamming the door for effect.

"We'll get her laid yet." Jenn fell onto Maggie's bed and snagged the latest issue of *Out* magazine off the nightstand.

"Are you sure you want to do that?" Cassie said.

Jenn smiled. "If you see anything moving on me, just flick it off."

Cassie plopped down on a beanbag chair, pulling a long tube sock from under her and flinging it across the room. She was dying to blab about what had happened with Deana last night but preferred to have it dragged out of her. She began whistling loudly and out of tune in an effort to garner Jenn's attention.

Without looking up, Jenn said, "Do you mind? I'm reading."

Annoyed, Cassie grabbed an empty tissue box from the floor and winged it at her.

Jenn looked annoyed. "What up, beyotch?"

"I have to talk to you."

"So talk." She continued thumbing through the magazine.

"It's important." Cassie sang the phrase.

"I'm listening," Jenn sang back, still thumbing.

"I hooked up with Deana last night."

The magazine slid off Jenn and flopped to the floor. "You what?" She hurled herself into an upright position on the edge of the bed. "I can't believe you didn't call me first thing this morning."

Cassie sprang upright and played with a strand of her hair. "I'm still kind of freaking about it, okay?" She then yelled, "I must be out of my effing mind," before falling backward into the beanbag.

Jenn leapt off the bed. "This is a momentous occasion, one that demands a veritable oodle of martinis."

Cassie smiled, then buried her face in her hands.

"Cassie Burke has had intimate contact with another human being." Jenn carried on. "And they said it couldn't happen." She danced around like a fool. "Take that, Lorna. The mighty Deana has broken your hold."

"Will you shut up," Cassie said through convulsive laughter.

"Oh, this is big, Cass." Jenn looked serious as she knelt on the floor next to her. "I swear, man. We were convinced you'd never get over Lorna." She huffed, having bounced herself into a froth.

Cassie was surprised. "But you guys kept promising me I'd do it eventually."

"That's just shit friends say when it's totally hopeless," Jenn said. "But hey. Turns out we were right." She flipped her palms up with a cheeky grin.

❖

The girls were assembled around Pantheon's last functioning pinball machine as Maggie worked it into a pinging, flashing frenzy. She shot Jenn the stink eye for placing her beer bottle on its glass top.

"Nice mock neck." Jenn was teasing her. "Very subtle." She sipped her beer as Cassie squinted with a disapproving smile.

"Stop fidgeting, Cass," Maggie said. "You're gonna make me tilt."

"I feel funny being here." Cassie splashed the olive up and down in her martini. "Like should I have called her and told her we were hanging out here tonight?"

"Quit worrying," Jenn said. "Now that she's finally gotten into your pants, you'll probably never see her again. And if you do, just tell her you were drunk or some shit. Or better yet, tell her you're getting back together with Lorna."

"You should choke when you say that," Cassie said. "No, I'm cool, really. You're right. We had our fling, got it out of our systems, and now she's out of my hair." She turned to Maggie, beaming with pride. "See, I took your advice after all."

Turning back toward Jenn, Cassie was smashed in the face with the vision of Deana leaning against a corner less than fifteen feet away, arms folded across her low-cut blouse, a sexy smirk blossoming on her lips. The three pinball wizards paused, offering Mrs. Godwin the homage of awestruck gawking she had so earned standing there all looking like that.

"Like I said before…" Maggie was deadpan. "Game on."

"Oh yeah," Jenn added.

CHAPTER FIFTEEN

"Jeffrey, I want a divorce." Deana made her declaration that Sunday afternoon as she shifted rice pilaf around her plate, trying to decipher her husband's reaction through the kitchen's low lighting.

"Not this again." Jeffrey chewed a forkful of filet mignon while still perusing a folded edition of *The Wall Street Journal.*

"Jeffrey, why are we living like this? We both know it's over." She gulped down the rest of her merlot to quell her rising frustration.

"Deana, I'm not giving you a divorce now. The election is six months away. We agreed to this a long time ago, and you said you'd stand by me. Divorces and elections just don't mix."

She fired back. "But mistresses and elections do? Oh, that's right. It is the US Senate."

"I don't know what you're talking about," he said evasively, slicing through his filet.

"Jeffrey, please don't insult me. We haven't had sex in, what, two years now? Not that I'm complaining, believe me, but I know damn well if you're not getting it from me, you're getting it somewhere else."

A condescending smile illuminated his handsome face. "I can take you upstairs after dinner, for old time's sake." He leered. "Or how about I just sweep the china off the table, and we'll do it right here."

She sneered. "I'm eating, if you don't mind. Besides, maybe you're not the only one getting it somewhere else."

He dropped his fork onto his plate. She tried to gauge what was clouding over him. A twinge of jealousy? Anger at her audacity to be just like him? Suddenly, he gave a chilling grin. "Oh, really. Well, you just better make sure you conceal him as well I do Beth."

Deana felt her smile spreading out to her ears.

"Did I say something funny?"

"Nowadays, Jeffrey, I find everything you say funny." She got up from the table and placed her barely touched plate of food on the counter. "By the way, she's not a *him*. She's a *her*." She tried not to smirk as she dabbed the corners of her mouth with a napkin.

He laid the folded paper on the table. "You've got to be kidding me."

"I have to go pick up Sean from practice now." She headed toward the foyer.

Jeffrey was close behind. "So what are you, some kind of lesbo now?"

"It's lesbian, Jeffrey, and yes. I believe 'lipstick' is the kind they call me." She was finding far more pleasure in this exchange than she'd imagined.

"That's terrific." He rubbed his firm abs over his shirt in defeat. "You're still not getting the divorce until after I'm elected." His tone grew threatening. "That's a promise."

She grabbed her keys off the credenza and slammed the door behind her. One of the things she liked least about Jeffrey was that he was as single-minded as she was. Playing by his rules for now was the logical thing to do, but what harm would a call to her lawyer do?

As Deana drove her Mercedes SUV out of the circular driveway and down the street, she wondered how Cassie would take this latest news.

❖

The setting sun cast a bronze glow on the deck of the bustling seafood restaurant. Seated around an umbrella table on the deck overlooking Long Island Sound, the four of them were enjoying the cascade of a gentle breeze on an early spring day, screechy songs of seagulls above, and a playful banter that would've given strangers the impression they'd been friends forever.

"Cassie, you two are making me sick. Will you stop grinning?" Jenn teased them. "When was the last time you saw them without these grins?" she asked Maggie.

"A month ago," Maggie said, sucking through her straw.

Cassie and Deana shrugged, offering no defense. They'd be the first to admit that it was hard not to grin since finding in each other a kind of happiness neither could ever have anticipated.

"So, how's the online dating going?" Cassie asked Jenn while buttering a piece of bread.

"Well, if my first experience was any indication, I should pull my profile immediately." Jenn sighed as the other girls smiled with piqued interest.

"I haven't found any trouble with it," Maggie casually offered.

"You haven't had any responses either," Jenn replied.

"I wonder why that is." Deana pondered sincerely as Jenn and Cassie exchanged knowing smirks.

"You obviously haven't seen the picture she put up," Jenn said.

"What's wrong with my picture?" Maggie asked innocently.

"Christ, Maggie, you look like a ghost," Jenn said as Cassie nearly spewed chardonnay all over the table. "All pasty and washed out. I'm surprised the Paranormal Society hasn't contacted you to see if you're a real, living person."

"That's rather harsh," Deana said, patting Maggie's forearm sympathetically.

"Honey," Cassie said, taking Deana's hand. "In Jenn's defense, we have at least a dozen photos of Maggie in which she looks lovely, and she chose *that* one." She gave Maggie an admonishing glare. "She posted that one on purpose, just to be ironic."

Maggie tried not to smile as she slurped her clam chowder.

"What was so bad about your date, Jenn?" Deana asked.

"Nothing till I realized I was at the movies with Typhoid Mary." She became wildly animated. "She sat there sneezing through the entire film. By the end, she had a pile of snot rags in her lap so high, I wished I was wearing a biohazard suit." They all collapsed into each other in laughter as she explained, sprinkling in groans of disgust. "And then she had the nerve to hold my hand in the car afterward." That information elicited the loudest groans from the table. "Turns out she's allergic to hair gel."

"I don't suppose you'd consider forgoing the hair gel," Deana inquired with a smile.

"Baby, there ain't a woman alive worth the dry, fly-away look." Jenn poured the rest of her beer into a glass. "I'll turn celibate first."

As the girls' rowdiness carried out to sea, Cassie looked at Deana, so comfortable among her friends. It was clear that Maggie and Jenn loved her, too. How could they not? The woman could charm the scratchy skirt off a Sunday school teacher.

Cassie let her smile fade as she wondered how much deeper she would allow herself to go with a woman living a double life. What if Deana was just stringing her along on some try-sexual adventure she should've gotten out of her system in college? The heavy reality that she was in love with a woman who still went home to a husband every night was wearing on her. And growing increasingly difficult to ignore.

Cassie and Deana said their good-byes privately at Deana's car. After Deana drove off, Cassie nudged Maggie out of the way and climbed into the back seat of Jenn's car, hoping to avoid the ambush of questions she knew they would already have locked and loaded.

"So, Cass…" Jenn made eye contact with her in the rearview mirror.

"Yes?"

"You know what we're going to ask, don't you?"

"Yeah, and after thinking long and hard about it, I realized that if I'm not happy with her situation but more unhappy without her, it just makes sense to stick it out with her until she fixes her problem."

"You thought long and hard about it, and that's the best solution you came up with?"

Cassie huffed. "You know what, Maggie? You should sit this one out since you've never had a relationship. Ever."

"Whoa, Cass. Easy," Jenn said. "She's only trying to help."

"Condescension has never helped anything."

"Look. You know we love Deana, but we don't want you to get hurt. She says she's leaving her husband after the election, but that's a while from now. You'll have an awful lot of time to become emotionally invested. And then what happens if she doesn't leave him in the fall?"

"What if she does?" Cassie hated the desperation in her voice.

Jenn sighed. "We love seeing you happy with Deana. And you clearly are when you're together, but you're also miserable when you go long stretches without seeing her."

"We're afraid this is Lorna the Sequel," Maggie added. "We're not trying to tell you what to do, but…"

Cassie knocked her head into the headrest and closed her eyes. She'd absolutely hated this intervention but couldn't argue against anything they were saying. Deana was a crazy, uncalculated risk, especially to a heart not fully healed.

"I hear what you're saying, guys," she said. "I'm just taking it day by day."

But freeing herself from the hold Deana already had on her wouldn't happen just because it was the wise thing to do.

CHAPTER SIXTEEN

Pantheon's farewell party started out well enough. The club was again at capacity as many of the former regulars made the pilgrimage from all over Connecticut and even beyond to say good-bye to a tri-state institution.

After a bumpy night of failed negotiations, Deana stormed out of Pantheon in a rage. She'd screamed the obligatory "How could you do this?" when Cassie said she wanted to cool it for a while and bristled at how nonchalant she was about cooling it after their two intense months together. But in reality, Cassie wasn't nonchalant about anything involving Deana. The waiting game had just become too much with the torture of having to settle for stolen moments, the pain and longing of constantly missing her, the promise that felt so far off in the future it almost didn't seem possible.

Cassie hadn't liked who she'd become waiting on Deana's promise to divorce Jeffrey.

"Damn it." She stood at the pool table, already seized with pangs of regret. The hurt radiating in Deana's face when she told her they couldn't see each other anymore was surprising, alarming even. Deana was one tough cookie, and frankly, Cassie had never considered it possible to hurt her. For months Cassie had rebuffed her, which seemed to only fuel her fire. And now this? Seeing Deana charge out of Pantheon through the oblivious dancing mob was for Cassie eerily reminiscent of the nights she was in those same shoes, desperate to escape the crush of Lorna's callous insensitivity.

"I should go after her." Cassie absently banged her pool cue on the scuffed wood floor.

"Don't do it unless you mean it," Jenn said as she took her shot, closing an eye for sharper aim.

"Better yet, do it," Maggie said. "Let's make this a real disaster." She widened her eyes like a ghoul as she tore at a hangnail on her thumb.

Cassie glared at her. "Who are you, Bizarro Maggie? Since when do you dispense advice for the sociopath?"

"I think she has a point," Jenn said.

Cassie put a hand on her hip. "Oh, and what might that be, pray tell?"

"What you're experiencing is classic bad-breakup fallout," Maggie said, taking off her sneaker to scratch the bottom of her foot.

"Go," Jenn yelled.

"Which is?" Cassie said as she eyeballed her next shot.

"You're still all twisted up from Lorna," she replied.

Jenn nodded. "Totally."

"You two are out of your melons," Cassie said. "I'm *totally* over Lorna."

"I doubt it's totally," Maggie said. "And you're certainly not over the trauma of the breakup. It still haunts you, on a subconscious level of course." She removed her sock for a deeper scratch. "It taunts you, teases you. Every time you're with Deana having one of your big old orgasm parties, in the back of your mind, your fractured psyche is screaming, 'She's gonna dump you, she's gonna dump you,' so you've moved into self-protect mode."

Cassie and Jenn stood there, leaning on their cues, mesmerized by Maggie's fascinating dissertation.

"You're in love with Deana, Cass," Maggie said. "That's a fact, but you see, the head is always one step behind the heart, so you still foolishly believe there's time to save yourself. The husband thing is just a really handy excuse."

A semicircle of other lesbians gathered around Jenn and Cassie, drinking in Maggie's sage words along with their Heinekens.

"And your point is?" Cassie felt her face heating with frustration.

"*My point is,*" Maggie said, "you can continue this asinine charade for as long as you want. But the sad fact is you want Deana, and you're still gonna want her tomorrow and the next day, and long after she's decided to blow this pickle stand for parts unknown." Maggie's grin grew so obnoxious it took Cassie all she was made of not to clobber her over the head with the pool cue.

After a round of applause from the onlookers, Maggie announced that she had to pee and exited the poolroom.

Jenn burst into laughter. "Boy, did she nail you or what?"

"Bite me," Cassie said.

"Are you gonna call Deana?"

"Where do you think I'm going?" Cassie took out her cell phone and headed outside, scanning for Deana's number with her thumb.

❖

Deana had parked in the garage several blocks away from the bar, an uneventful walk in the daytime but considerably more exciting alone at night. Her pace was slow as her eyes were welling up faster than she could wipe them clear. The sound of pebbles crunching under slowly creeping tires alerted her to the beat-up black van behind her without headlights.

When she picked up her pace, the driver accelerated. She bolted toward the garage entrance as the van's side door slid open with a thunder. She looked over her just as her assailant grabbed her around the neck and the stomach. She managed to belt out half a scream before the man cupped his hand over her mouth and pulled her into the van.

In a matter of seconds, the door slammed shut, and the van screeched off down the street.

"Let me go," she shouted. Still restrained by the man who'd snatched her off the street, she kicked at another man in a ski mask kneeling in front of her.

"Shut up, dyke." He slapped her across the face and knelt down on her legs to stop their wild flailing.

The pain of her crushed shins caused her to scream again. This time a closed right fist to her mouth silenced her. The beefy man holding her from behind shoved a rag into her mouth.

"What's the matter? Not so butch after all, are you?"

The two men cackled.

Deana's attempts to scream and kick were purely reflexive, as she saw little hope of escaping until they were good and ready for her to.

"I said shut up." He delivered another blow to her face, breaking her nose and finally subduing her fierce struggle.

Her overloaded senses created chaos in her mind. The physical pain dazed and weakened her, the taste of the blood-stained rag nauseated her, and the flood of tears clouding her eyes blinded her. She couldn't even rely on her sense of hearing as the noise from the clunky van and the ringing in her right ear from an earlier blow turned ordinarily discernible sounds into a cacophony.

"What's a sexy lady like you doing in a place like that?" The man holding her legs reached for her black dress pants.

"Yo, man. What are you doing?" said the man restraining her as the van turned a corner. "Cool it."

"Mind your fucking business," he said.

Deana let out a final, guttural groan into the night before the next punch rendered her in a state of semi-consciousness.

❖

Cassie rocketed down the hallway toward the nurses' station, nearly crashing into it as her boots screeched to a halt.

"Deana Godwin's room, please," she said in a huff.

"I'm sorry. Only family can see her now," the nurse replied like a recording. She never even looked up from the chart she was examining.

"Please." Cassie's voice cracked. "Please let me see her." She blotted an errant tear as she pleaded.

The nurse finally looked up. "I know you." She smiled. "You own Pantheon."

Cassie nodded, relieved by her expression of familiarity. "Yeah, Deana's my…"

"Go ahead," she said. "She's three doors down on the right."

As Cassie was about to bolt, the nurse called out to her in a covert whisper. "She's not alone…just so you know."

"Thanks," she replied and sailed off down the hall. Her heart pounded as she approached the room. How badly hurt was she? Was she even conscious? In all her flashes of expectations, she hadn't expected Deana's husband to appear in the doorway.

They paused and inspected each other from head to toe.

"She's sleeping," he said after a moment, his face a pillar of stone.

Cassie held her ground. "That's fine. I just want to see her quick."

He refused to step aside so she could pass. "You didn't win, you know," he said with a scowl.

"Looks like none of us did." She mumbled "asshole" as she nudged past him to get to Deana.

He was right. She was sleeping, or more like drugged up with painkillers. She stood frozen, appalled by the sight of Deana, her beautiful face a battered tapestry of bruises and gauze. What kind of fucking monster could do this to a person? She pulled a chair next to her bed and gently cupped Deana's hand in hers, careful not to disturb the oxygen clip on her finger but unable to avoid soaking it with a downpour of tears.

Outside, she heard the doctor greet Jeffrey, so she got up to eavesdrop.

"Physically, your wife should rebound fine," he said. "Her brain scans showed no signs of permanent damage, and I can recommend an excellent cosmetic surgeon for her nose."

"Thank God," he said.

"The rape is another matter."

"Rape?" Jeffrey said. "No, no."

"We have a trauma counseling team if you'd—"

"Rape?"

Cassie winced as Jeffrey repeated that horrible word.

"No. That can't be," he said.

"Why can't it?" the doctor replied.

CHAPTER SEVENTEEN

Two weeks later Deana still wasn't answering her calls, and Cassie was climbing the walls, unable to sleep, fueled by caffeine and regret. Each day she'd scoured the newspaper hoping to learn something more about the crime and, more importantly, how Deana was doing since she was released from the hospital. Early that morning she'd stopped at a convenience store for two coffees and a paper before heading to Jenn's apartment.

They sat on the terrace with bagels and coffee before Jenn had to leave to appraise a prospective painting job. Cassie opened the paper as Jenn spread the cream cheese.

"Holy shit," Cassie said. "He's copping a plea."

"Who? The husband?"

Cassie nodded as she read. "He said those bastards were only supposed to rough her up a little to scare her away from Pantheon."

"Did they say your name in the story?"

"No. Just the bar," Cassie said. "I'm out of it. I was very cooperative when they questioned me."

Jenn shook her head as she chewed. "Nice husband. He hired those lowlifes to scare her, and they end up raping her."

"Only one did. That's how Jeffrey was able to plea to lesser charges. It says the other scumbag agreed to testify against the rapist and that the rape wasn't part of the prearranged plot."

"Ugh. What the fuck was he thinking?"

"I mean, the arrogance of these rich, powerful men." Cassie folded the paper and picked up her coffee. "Karma got him, though. His career and the next ten to fifteen years of his life are over."

"Small consolation for Deana. Have you heard from her yet?"

Cassie shook her head. "She still hasn't returned my calls or texts. I'm wondering if I should just go to her house."

"I don't know about that."

"Do you think she's angry at me? Like she blames me for this happening? I guess it is partly my fault. If we hadn't had that fight that night, she never would've stormed off."

"No. I can understand you feeling that way, but this attack had nothing to do with you. Those guys were stalking her. If they hadn't gotten her that night, they would've some other time."

"Not leaving Pantheon." Cassie's eyes started to pool.

"Don't you dare blame yourself for this, Cass. Deana made her own choices, and it's not your fault she married a sociopath."

"It's hard not to feel a little responsible when she made all those choices to see me."

"I know you're hurting for a lot of reasons. Just don't add to it by thinking you could've done something to prevent this."

"I guess. But why won't she talk to me or even text me back just to let me know she's all right?"

"She's not all right. She's been traumatized."

"And she won't let me help her."

Jenn looked like it was killing her not to have the right answers. "I'm sorry, so sorry." She got up and wrapped Cassie in a hug that released the deluge of emotion she'd been holding in for weeks.

She couldn't even imagine the burden of this nightmare Deana would have to carry with her forever.

❖

Squeezing her eyes closed to block out the sun, Cassie reminded herself to give Jenn or Maggie a ring just to let them know she wasn't lying dead somewhere. They were good friends and deserved that courtesy.

Adrift, she gazed out at the water and the lone fisherman in his canoe from the scenic overlook as she rested her hands on the steering wheel. With no bar to run anymore and Deana gone from her life, she'd been struggling to find a reason to get out of bed each day. She thought again about the voice mail Deana had left her from the airport before boarding her flight. Although she'd deleted it days ago, in her mind it played over and over.

"Hi, Cass, it's me." Her voice sounded nasal from crying. "I know you must be worried, but don't be. Sean and I are going away to stay with my brother. We'll be there for a while…I don't know how long." She paused, her anguish palpable. "I didn't mean to run out on you, but I just…I just needed to get away from everyone and everything that reminded me of…" Completing that thought would've been redundant. "Anyway, I don't know where we're going from here, but, um, take care of yourself, okay, and, uh…shit, I'm sorry."

The finality in her tone seared deeper into Cassie's heart with each recollection. Deana had sighed and said, "I love you, Cass," her voice a delicate quiver.

End of message.

Cassie took off, too, bound for anywhere; no place existed where she'd have been able to escape the haunting memories of Deana and the tragic hand fate had dealt her.

On the upside, yesterday was Cassie and Lorna's anniversary… and it had never even crossed her mind.

CHAPTER EIGHTEEN

Cassie had been staring at the section of the bistro that used to be Pantheon's video room while she was stuck in a loop of memories of Deana. They'd known each other only a short time, and it had been over twenty years since she'd seen her, but obviously her mark on Cassie's life had been indelible.

Jenn snapped her fingers in front of her face. "Our server keeps staring at us."

"She wants the table," Maggie said. "This place clearly kills it at Sunday brunch."

Cassie took a long sip of ice water as she reoriented herself. "We still didn't decide on a destination for our birthdays. How the hell did we get so off-track talking about the past?"

"That's what you do when you're old," Jenn said with a chuckle. "Talk about the past and have brunch."

"Although we had some great times over the years," Cassie said, "I'm quite happy leaving some of them there and enjoying the present. I say we wrap this up and just go on one of those lesbian cruises."

Jenn grimaced. "Amelia is not going to let me do that without her. Let's stick with Vegas."

"Eww. No." Maggie shook her head vigorously. "All the heat and hookers. I'm staunchly supporting a condo on the beach in P-Town."

"Boring," Jenn said. "We've all been there a million times."

Cassie grabbed the check binder and dropped her credit card in it as soon as the server put it down. "I'm gonna make an executive decision right now. Mykonos."

"Greece?" Jenn asked.

"Duh," Cassie replied. "It makes perfect sense. We're the fucking Pantheon Girls, for Christ's sake. Mr. Pike would be so proud to know we all finally made it there together. God rest Mr. Pike," she added, and the three of them made the sign of the cross.

"I like it," Maggie said.

Jenn nodded. "I like it, too. I just have to make sure everything checks out okay on my scan." She tried to hand Cassie some cash, but she pushed it away.

"Absolutely," Cassie said. "We're going to entertain only positive thoughts about that."

"Right." Jenn crossed both sets of fingers. "And speaking of positive, we have Maggie's thing this week."

"Yes, Wednesday." Cassie grabbed Maggie's hand excitedly.

Maggie rolled her eyes. "Don't remind me."

"Well, if you didn't want to be honored like a hero, you shouldn't have acted like one," Cassie said as they all stood and stretched.

"An old woman collapsed right in front of me in the clearance aisle of TJ Maxx. What was I supposed to do? Step over her?"

"Only after dialing 9-1-1," Jenn said.

Cassie threw an arm around Maggie's shoulder as they headed out the door. "Maggie would never do that. She has the heart of a true hero."

"Yeah. Something like that," Maggie mumbled.

Jenn's car was parked on the street closest to the entrance, so they all stopped there to say good-bye.

When Maggie walked away, Jenn grabbed Cassie by the sleeve of her jacket. "Hey. Can I ask a favor?"

❖

The morning of Jenn's biopsy appointment, Cassie picked her up early so they could stop for coffee at their favorite coffeehouse. Even though she was playing it cool, Cassie knew Jenn was scared. Cassie was, too, but if ever there was a time to believe in the power of positive thinking, it was now.

She tested the temperature of her latte with her top lip before going in for the sip. "Are you planning to tell me the real reason I'm taking you to this appointment and not Amelia?"

"Cass, you know this isn't my first cancer rodeo. I told her she didn't need to rearrange her whole business trip just to take me to an appointment that I could've gone to alone."

"And she was okay with that?"

"Not the alone part, but she was fine when I said you'd take me."

"I'm glad she can be so cavalier about it," Cassie said. "I mean, not that you have anything to worry about yet. I didn't mean 'yet.' I meant maybe not at all. Not maybe, but I'm definitely sure nothing's—"

"Cass." Jenn grabbed her hand to stop her spiral. "I'm well aware there could be other reasons for my symptoms and the scan could come back negative. Relax."

"Right, right. Let's go with that." She crossed her fingers. "So, what's going on with Amelia besides her business trip?"

Jenn hesitated as she tapped the side of her mug. "We need some time apart."

Cassie took a frothy sip and nibbled at a giant cinnamon biscotti they were supposed to be splitting. It was obviously much more involved than that, but now wasn't the time to start peeling back layers. "You guys have a fight?"

"We're beyond having anything to fight about. I'm taking these few days she'll be gone to contemplate a major decision."

"Is this about her wanting to move to Florida?"

Jenn nodded as she sipped her black coffee.

"Are you going?" Cassie had to force down her mouthful of biscotti as she awaited the answer.

Jenn shook her head and sighed. "I have no interest in moving to some backward red state just to keep our roommate situation afloat, lower taxes or not."

"Roommate?"

"You know that's what we are. We've had conversations."

"Yeah, but all long-term relationships slow down, and sometimes you do feel like roommates. I mean, that's what I've read. I don't know. I've never been with anyone long-term other than Lorna."

"It isn't sometimes. It's all the time. It's been like that for several years, but you get stuck in the habit of things, you know?"

Cassie nodded, but she didn't know. After Lorna and her truncated relationship with Deana, she'd never managed to stay with anyone much longer than a couple of years, the mark where partners usually expect some sort of permanent commitment. When pressed, Cassie would find some excuse to hightail it out before anyone had a chance to roll up on her in a U-Haul.

"Then your major decision is divorce?"

"That seems to be the direction the universe is pushing me. Amelia's going to retire sooner than later, and she says Connecticut is too expensive."

"She's not wrong." Cassie was running out of things to say. She'd thought back to her later years with Lorna, and they weren't happy ones. She'd just convinced herself they were. But still, she didn't want to throw negative energy on Jenn's situation. "Maybe you just need a tune-up in couples' counseling."

Jenn shrugged. "I don't know. I honestly feel like the train has left the station for good."

Cassie watched her face as she gazed out the window and sipped her coffee. She hated watching her best friend go through such a tough time and feeling so powerless to help her.

Jenn turned back as if sensing Cassie's concern. "And, Cass, what if this is cancer again? And this time I don't beat it?"

"Jenn. Don't say that. Please. Say what if you do beat it…"

"Exactly. How many more chances am I gonna get in this life? I don't want to just exist. I want to live. I have more things to experience and people to meet."

"Does Amelia know you're at this point?"

"She won't be shocked if she comes home and I tell her I'm going to file. She'll probably suggest counseling again, but…" She didn't need to finish her sentence.

"Seems like you've made up your mind. You know Maggie and I are here for you no matter what you need."

Jenn's expression finally brightened. "If Amelia and I do split, this will be the first time we're all single again since the summer before college."

Cassie laughed. "Technically, even then you and I weren't single."

"Ooh, yeah. Our summer of love."

"Imagine how different our lives would be if we'd stayed together."

"I'm glad we didn't," Jenn replied. "I would've hated it if we stayed together for a while, then broke up and never spoke again like you and Lorna."

"Why are you saying the name of She-Who-Must-Not-Be-Named? You know the proper way to pronounce it is 'Lornamorte.'"

They fell into hysterics.

"Oh my God. I forgot that's what we called her."

"A name most fitting," Cassie said.

Jenn looked at her sincerely. "What's next on the horizon for you?"

"Me?" The question genuinely took her by surprise. "I'm all about our big fiftieth vacation to Mykonos. As soon as you get the all-clear from your doc, I'm booking it."

Jenn smiled. "I mean after that. You have your dream career in political consulting and a beautiful home. Isn't something missing?"

"Oh, barf. You mean that whole 'someone to share it with' propaganda?"

"Well, yeah. If you're asexual like Maggie, that's one thing, but…"

"I'm not asexual, but I also don't need a relationship to complete me. I'm totally fine being single."

"That's where you and I differ the most. I love having someone to share my life with. Part of me thinks I should stay with Amelia for the companionship. We still get along and enjoy a lot of the same things. I mean, we're not kids anymore."

"We're also not seventy-five. I'd rethink that if I were you. You have too much passion to be satisfied with any situation simply because it's convenient."

"Same goes for you, my friend. Don't let your passion go to waste just because true love's eluded you."

"What do you suggest? I invest in one of those high-tech, lifelike, synthetic women?"

Jenn narrowed her eyes. "Maybe we can get a discount if we order two."

Cassie laughed. "That would actually be funnier if part of me didn't think you're serious."

"Only partly serious." Jenn winked as she finished her coffee.

Cassie checked her watch. "Let's get you to your appointment. Maybe they can fit you in for a brain scan, too, while you're there."

CHAPTER NINETEEN

The auditorium bustled with voices and camera flashes, and Cassie and Jenn were more excited than anyone as they sat flanking Maggie in the audience at the State of Connecticut's annual Good Samaritan Awards ceremony. This year Maggie was being honored for her selfless and heroic effort in performing CPR on an elderly woman who'd suffered a heart attack while shopping at TJ Maxx. Given her lifelong propensity to avoid all human contact, the decision not to bolt away was the heroic part.

Cassie laid her hand on Maggie's knee to stop it from shaking. "Have I mentioned how proud I am of you?"

"Incessantly," Maggie replied. Her eyes were fixed on the stage as the ceremony began. "I don't want to go up there when they call me, Cass. You go."

"Are you nuts? I'm not getting the award. You are."

Jenn leaned forward. "Mags, what is the matter with you? This is huge. We're both so proud of you. We can't wait to see you receive it."

"How long have you both known me? Since when do I ever feel comfortable getting an ounce of attention?"

"Well, never," Cassie said. "But you need to make an exception in this case. You should be so excited. Your state is honoring your heroism. Think of how impressed your students will be."

Maggie shook her head, clearly unmoved. "I still don't understand how my name was even put into the running."

"Obviously, it was either the woman you saved or the store," Jenn said.

"Jenn, please pretend you're me and accept it. I'm having a serious anxiety attack. I honestly don't think my legs will carry me up there."

"How about we go up there with you?" Jenn said.

"Absolutely," Cassie said. "We've got you, girl."

"Uh, I'd just rather not show my face up there at all, if it's okay with you guys." Maggie started to get up, but Cassie and Jenn each grabbed an arm and lowered her into her seat.

"Come on, Mags. Pull yourself together here," Cassie said, starting to lose patience. "It's not that big a deal. Just walk up there, take the fucking plaque, and walk back."

"Look, there's something I never told you guys about that day I saved that woman." Maggie continued to stare straight ahead, her face breaking out in blotches.

Cassie eyed Jenn. "We're listening."

"I can't go up there because…"

"Our next recipient of the Good Samaritan award is from New Haven County and is being honored for her selfless act of saving the life of Mrs. Zelda Spallone the day she went into cardiac arrest while shopping in a department store."

"That's you they're talking about," Jenn said.

"Why can't you go up there?" Cassie asked tersely.

"I was stopped for shoplifting right before the woman keeled over. And the security guard who nabbed me is right up there on stage."

"Ms. Margaret Lavery," the emcee said. The crowd broke into applause. "Come on up here, Ms. Lavery."

Cassie's jaw remained practically unhinged as she watched Jenn push Maggie out of the row and Maggie slink her way up to the stage. It finally unlocked when Jenn broke out in hysterical laughter.

"I don't even know what to say about any of this," Cassie whispered as they clapped.

Jenn was still giggling. "If this isn't the fucking Maggiest moment of Maggie's life, I don't know what is. I'm so stoked we're here to witness it."

After the ceremony, the recipients gathered in the lobby to have their photos taken and comment for the local online paper. As they watched Maggie pose and speak to the reporter with a pained expression, they were still giggling over the absurdity of it all.

"You must be proud of your friend."

Cassie whipped her head around to the tall, attractive transwoman looking on with them. "I'm sorry. Have we met?"

"No, but I'm acquainted with your friend." She extended her hand. "Marybeth Winkler. Loss-prevention specialist at TJ Maxx."

Jenn's face blanched. "Are you here to arrest her?"

Cassie elbowed her.

"No," Marybeth said with a chuckle. "I nominated her for the award."

"And a more selfless, caring individual you'll never find," Cassie said, trying to cover for Jenn's arrest remark.

"I know. Despite the fact that she knew I was tailing her for pocketing a little ceramic boiled-egg holder, she still stopped and gave that old woman CPR until the paramedics arrived. I really think she would've died if she hadn't."

"And then what, she escaped in all the chaos?" Cassie asked.

Marybeth shook her head. "I pretended to look away. I couldn't take her into custody after what she'd done for that poor thing." Her eyes twinkled. "Besides, she's just so meek and adorable. She'd never stand a chance in a women's prison."

"True that," Jenn said, and Cassie nodded.

"So, is she single?" Marybeth asked.

"Who, Maggie?" Cassie asked.

Marybeth nodded like Cassie was dim. "I'd like to ask her out to dinner. What do you think?"

"I think that's a spectacular idea," Jenn said.

"You do?" Cassie said, then caught herself. "She does. And I do, too."

Marybeth beamed as she sighed with apparent relief. "I was attracted to her the minute I saw her in kitchenware, touching all the tiny merchandise until she slipped that one item into her coat pocket. I wanted to ask her out then, but I thought taking her into custody wasn't the right time to suggest dinner."

"Good call there, Marybeth," Jenn said. "Why don't you let us prime her for you. She's a bit shy."

"Yes, yes. Stay right there." Cassie grabbed Jenn, and they approached Maggie.

"Are you two done fraternizing with the enemy?" Maggie said. "Let's get out of here. I've had enough of people for the week."

"Hold on," Cassie said. "You got it all wrong. She's not the enemy. She's the one who nominated you for this award."

"Then, yes, she is the enemy." Maggie tried to move away, but Jenn pulled her arm.

"Wait. Did you see how pretty she is? She told us she'd like to take you to dinner."

Maggie stared at both of them. "Is this some kind of joke?"

"It's not a joke," Jenn said excitedly. "It's serendipity. A small-time klepto meets a loss-prevention officer? Are you kidding me? This is the shit they make horrible lesbian movies about."

"Come on. Let's go talk to her," Cassie said. "She's super nice. You can thank her for the nomination."

"And for not pressing charges," Jenn added. They both took an arm and led Maggie over to Marybeth, who was standing in the foyer talking with a group.

When she saw Maggie coming, she broke away from her conversation. "Well, hello again, Ms. Lavery. Congratulations."

"Thanks," Maggie replied softly.

Cassie was ready for the awkward silence. "We're heading out to grab some lunch downtown. Would you like to join us?"

"Aren't you sweet," Marybeth said. "I have to get back to work now, but thank you. Some other time."

"You bet," Jenn said.

Cassie sighed as Maggie led them toward the exit before anything else could be suggested. If that was how serendipity worked, then it sucked.

"Oh, Maggie," the throaty voice called seductively.

All three of them stopped just shy of the revolving door. They swung Maggie around to Marybeth standing behind them.

"I was wondering if you liked Audrey Hepburn."

"Who doesn't?" Maggie projected herself with a slight edge of confidence.

"There's a film retrospective on her at the Kate next weekend. Would you like to join me?"

Maggie's face lit up. When they stepped away from the door to talk more, Cassie and Jenn slipped outside and waited on the steps.

"Audrey Hepburn?" Cassie said. "How random."

"Not really. Maggie also had an Audrey Hepburn T-shirt stuffed in her jacket at the store when that woman dropped."

"Serendipity," Cassie said with a smile.

"Indeed," Jenn replied.

❖

By early Friday afternoon, Cassie was already in weekend mode. After running out for a sandwich and an iced coffee, she sat back in her office chair with a leg on her desk as she sipped her drink. What a week it had been. Maggie's star had shone with her fifteen minutes of fame, and she had made plans to go out with the lovely, empathetic Marybeth. Jenn, on the other hand, had about the worst week ever with another cancer diagnosis. At that point, Cassie wasn't sure what emotion was going to take hold of her, so she went middle-of-the-road and chose gratitude.

One more appointment with a potential new client, and her week was finished. Bring on a weekend of relaxation that would feature a little day drinking and a lot of TV binge-watching. Hopefully, this woman wouldn't be late.

She opened the file she'd started on her and scanned through it. A simple public relations plan for a woman beginning a campaign for state senate. Shouldn't take too long. She'd done this before many times for local politicians and already had a template in place. She'd start with a review of the candidate's social media, discuss an official website, an exploratory online survey, and mass-emailing from the local democratic committee lead list. Political candidates were her favorite to help market, especially females, since women were still so under-represented in government at all levels.

When the office door opened, she sprang from behind her desk to greet her appointment in the small waiting room. She rounded the corner, her cool professionalism at the ready, but the woman's face rendered her silent, frozen, nearly catatonic as her brain processed the familiarity.

The woman stared back before speaking. Then with a slight breath, "Hi, Cassie."

"Deana." It came out in a whisper before she pulled it back together. "You're Deana Warner?"

"Warner's my maiden name." She seemed to be studying Cassie with a matching level of curiosity. "How…how are you?"

"I honestly don't know at the moment." Cassie willed her limbs to move, to do something so she didn't appear as numb and dumb as she felt.

"Can I sit?" Deana asked.

"Oh, uh, I'm sorry. Yeah. Please." Cassie finally broke free from the spell and sat across from her, fumbling with the new-client folder.

"I can see how surprised you must be." Deana sat upright in the chair, her hands shaking in her lap. "Maybe I should've told you it was me over the phone."

"And blown that entrance?"

The quip seemed to put Deana a little at ease. "To be honest, I thought you'd refuse the appointment if you knew it was me."

"Normally, I would've googled you prior to the meeting, but it's been a crazy week."

"If you want me to leave, I'll understand."

"No, no. Not at all." She cleared her throat to catch her breath. "I mean, it's been, what, twenty years?"

Deana nodded. "It feels like an entire lifetime."

Cassie opened the folder, but the words on the page looked like lines of dead ants. She couldn't process anything except that Deana fucking Godwin was sitting before her like a statue of an ancient goddess, her classic beauty weathered but timeless.

"I'm glad to see there's no hard feelings," Deana said gently. "At least none that'll stand in the way of a professional relationship."

Cassie sat back and crossed her legs, relaxing into the audacity of this woman she'd once been so deeply in love with. "No. Of course not. But you do realize I'm not the only public relations firm in Connecticut. In fact, I'm probably the smallest."

Deana grinned through a blush. "I know that, but when I saw that you ran this firm, you were the only one I considered."

"I'm assuming that since you're planning a state senate run here that Connecticut is your primary state of residence again."

"Yes. I moved back about two years ago after my son got married."

"What? Little Sean is married? Wow. It has been a lifetime." While letting that fact sink in, Cassie smiled, but her heart deflated a little knowing Deana had been in the state for two years and hadn't tried to contact her till now.

"And I'm about to be the grandmother of twins."

Cassie leaned forward, resting her elbows on her desk. "That's fantastic, Deana. Congrats. I'm so happy to see that your life has turned out so well. I've wondered about you over the years."

"Thank you. It was touch-and-go there for a while, but I found an amazing therapist who helped me process and come to terms with so much in my life. I went back to college to become a social worker specializing in rape crisis counseling."

Cassie leaned back again, speechless. Her stomach twisted as she recalled what had happened to Deana as a result of their affair. Her feelings must've shown on her face.

"I've been doing that for about fifteen years now," Deana added. "It's been transformational. As odd as it sounds, I wouldn't be in this wonderful place in my life had I not experienced that trauma. Not that I'd recommend it to anyone, but it's just how I choose to view it."

"You're amazing. I just...I have no words to talk about your strength and courage."

Deana had that old, familiar, warm glow that always clutched Cassie's heart. "The last step in my journey is an apology to you. It's long overdue."

"Me? What could you possibly have to apologize to me for?"

"For cutting you off when I left the state. I was such a mess. I was barely holding it together for my son."

Cassie offered a genuine smile, but inside she was going under in a flash flood of emotion as she recalled what Deana's swift departure and ghosting did to her. She'd floundered in guilt and a web of unresolved questions. It took her years to trust someone again in a relationship, and even then, it wasn't complete trust, the kind found in a healthy, safe emotional connection.

"Well, thank you for that. So, anyway, what can I do for you... professionally?"

The abruptness of Cassie's subject-changing question seemed to throw Deana off her game. "I, uh, well, to start, I'd like to get a social media package together and strategize about incorporating my past into my campaign platform. The rest will be up to you."

Cassie's brain slowly returned to active functioning. She could do this. Though having this magnificent phantom emerge from her past and plop down in front of her wildly unsettled her, this was business. "We should start with a family-first approach. A focus on your women-and-children advocacy work."

"Exactly. Parts of New Haven County are underserved and could use more programs for battered women and their children." She pulled a folder from her attaché case. "I've done some research in towns in the 12th district, where I live. Opportunities for job training and mental health for mothers and their kids aren't what they should be, based on comparisons with other areas."

Cassie stared at every inch of Deana as she spoke so passionately about the topic. Now in her early sixties, Deana had a natural beauty and sex appeal that had unquestionably endured through the decades. But she now had an air of strength and purpose that was even more attractive.

Was taking her on as a client wise? Her head and heart were still spinning from the vortex of emotions stirred up by Deana's sudden, surprise appearance. If she didn't settle down immediately, she wouldn't be able to provide her with the effective consulting and public relations she deserved. Should she refer her to somebody else? Pretend this encounter was just another dream like she used to have for months after Deana disappeared?

"What do you think?" Deana asked, but Cassie had completely zoned out while she was talking. "I can email you this data if you'd like."

"Uh, yeah." Cassie stood, and Deana followed. "Yes, please. That sounds good. Send it over, and I'll review it this weekend. I can call you Monday."

"Great. Thank you." Deana's gaze lingered for a moment before she extended her hand.

Cassie shook it, but when she tried to pull her hand away, Deana held on. Her lips parted as though she was about to say something crucial. Instead, she released her grip and thanked her again as she walked out.

Cassie sat back down and waited for the intoxicating scent of Deana to fade. After a moment, she felt like she'd just experienced a mirage, some wild apparition from a past life that had floated in through an open window, then evaporated. She remembered hearing the name Deana Warner in a casual political chat or two among professional acquaintances, but never would she have made the connection that it could be Deana Godwin, former wife of disgraced politician Jeffrey Godwin.

And the woman who had forever changed the shape and scope of Cassie's heart.

Two whole decades. Like Deana had said, it seemed like a lifetime. And Cassie still had never found a love like she'd experienced with her—as star-crossed as it was.

Her stomach sank at the notion that she'd seemingly agreed to take Deana on as a client without thoroughly weighing the implications. No matter how much professional integrity Cassie possessed, emotions were a force all their own.

She needed to spend some time this weekend considering them before she got back to Deana with a contract.

❖

That Saturday afternoon, Cassie had conscripted Jenn for an emergency happy hour on Maggie's back patio. Unannounced pop-ins were the only way to ensure Maggie's attendance. Cassie filled her and Maggie's glasses with chilled pinot grigio as they sat around Maggie's gas-fueled fire pit.

Cassie relaxed into the patio-chair cushions, sipped her wine, and let out a breathy, "Holy fuck."

Jenn glared over her glass of lemon water as she sipped. "Can you please tell us what's so urgent?"

"Okay." Cassie took some deep breaths. "So, remember the meeting I had yesterday with a potential new client?"

Jenn and Maggie both shook their heads.

Cassie scoffed. "Don't you two listen when I talk?"

"Anyway," Jenn said with an eye roll.

"Anyway, you will never guess in a million years who it was."

"Hillary Clinton," Maggie said.

"AOC," Jenn said.

"Can you fucking be serious for a minute?"

"Just tell us," Jenn said.

"Deana." Cassie felt her eyes widen in anticipation of their reactions.

"Are you fucking kidding me?" Jenn said. "You're just now telling us?"

"This was not something I could text," Cassie said. "I couldn't miss the looks on your faces."

"What does she need a campaign consultant for?" Maggie asked. "Or was that just a ruse to contact you?"

"I think a little of both. She's running for state senate."

"No shit," Jenn said. "Deana Godwin is back from the edge and wants to become a politician just like her creep ex-husband. She did divorce him after all that conspiracy business, didn't she?"

Cassie sneered at the stupidity of her remark. "What do you think? And she's Deana Warner now. She took back her maiden name."

"Wow." Jenn seemed to let the idea settle in her brain. Then, "How does she look?"

Cassie exhaled slowly. "Amazing. You will not believe just how amazing she looks. I'm certain I was staring at her like a weirdo the whole time she was sitting across from me."

"Are you taking her on as a client?" Maggie asked.

"Yeah. I mean I'd like to. She's a social worker now, a women's domestic violence advocate. Personal feelings aside, I've no doubt she'll make a great state senator."

"Is she married again or with anyone?"

"I have no idea. We didn't get that far in the conversation. It was just a preliminary interview. I'll set up a meeting with her next week to put the whole plan together."

"She must be back on guys if she's running for office," Maggie said.

"That's a rather silly assumption in this state and in this day and age," Cassie said. "Besides, she's running as a Democrat."

"Twenty bucks says she's with a woman," Jenn said.

"What if she's single?" Maggie asked.

"Ooh, yeah, Cass. What if she's single?"

"Good question," she said pensively. "You hardly ever see single people, especially females, run for office. I've never represented one."

"That's not why I was asking," Jenn said. "You think you'd hook up with her if she is?"

"Are you nuts? I'm still getting over the shock of seeing her standing in front of me twenty-four hours ago. I can't wrap my head around anything like that."

"I'm not suggesting jumping back in where you left off."

"That would be impossible," Cassie said.

"Well, duh. I meant like starting from scratch as two single women. Have a few dates and see where it goes from there."

Cassie looked at Maggie, who was always eager to shoot down a ridiculous idea.

"Valid," Maggie said with a shrug.

"What do you mean, 'valid'?" Cassie was aghast. "The last time we were together it was fucking disastrous. Common sense indicates that we conclude our business arrangement and run far, far away from each other."

Maggie dug through the potato-chip bowl. "I disagree. That was decades ago. You're both different people now with entirely different circumstances. I think the universe brought you back together after so many years for a reason."

"See?" Jenn said with a proud grin. "Thanks, Mags. And save some of the folded chips for me."

"Whatever," Cassie said. "We can sit here and speculate all night, but who's to say Deana's interested in anything more than business? Our meeting was totally professional, with a little bit of catching up.

Her apology made it feel more like an attempt to tie up loose ends than the start of anything new…other than business."

"What did you spend, like fifteen minutes together? I'm sure it was pretty unnerving for both of you. You'll just have to see how it goes during your next meeting."

Cassie nodded as she sipped her wine. "The big takeaway here is that I finally know that she's okay after all that went down. In fact, she's more than okay. She's never looked better, and it seems like she's never been happier."

"I don't think that's the big takeaway at all," Jenn said.

Maggie whipped out her phone. "Let's google her."

"Did you look for her on social media?" Jenn asked.

Cassie rolled her eyes. "You know I find social media a distasteful but necessary evil that I use only for professional reasons."

Jenn looked at Maggie. "That means she checked and couldn't find her."

"I did not check." Cassie downed her drink. "This conversation is starting to upset my stomach. Jenn, how are you doing?"

"Oh, no." She shook her head. "You're not using my illness to pussy out of a conversation you don't want to have."

"You were just informed that you may have to start chemo. We wanna know how you're doing with that."

"I had my moment, but then I decided to be proactive. I'm gonna shave my head before my hair starts falling out."

"Wanna do it here?" Maggie said.

While Cassie was grateful the focus was off her and Deana, she suddenly felt winded at the thought of her friend on chemo. Then shaving her head because she knew she was going to lose her hair. She marveled at Jenn's strength.

"Jenn might want privacy for that," she said. "Maybe she wants Amelia to be with her for it."

Jenn sighed. "I think I'd rather have you guys here for it. You got a shaver, Mags?"

Maggie sprang from her seat and headed toward the sliders.

"Not the one you use to shave your box," Jenn yelled out.

Cassie sprayed out the sip of pinot grigio she'd just taken. "What makes you think she shaves?"

Jenn joined the laughter. "She's seeing Marybeth," she said softly. "I just assumed."

"Do you think they've had sex yet?"

"I don't know. But Marybeth is the first person she's ever been on a second date with, so if anyone had a prayer with Maggie, it's her."

"Oh my God." Cassie giggled like a kid. "Let's see if we can get it out of her when she comes back."

"Okay." Jenn's eyes twinkled.

"But we have to be subtle and respectful," Cassie said. "You know how she is. She'll clam right up if we make her feel uncomfortable."

Jenn was nodding as Cassie spoke. "I get it."

"She's coming. Let me handle it."

Maggie stepped out onto the patio with a shaver in hand. "Ready?"

Jenn stripped off her shirt and sat upright in her sports bra. "Ready."

Cassie leapt up, sat on the armrest of Jenn's chair, and held her hand.

"Here we go." Maggie clicked on the shaver.

Jenn closed her eyes, and Cassie tightened her grip.

Maggie ran the shaver down the middle of Jenn's head, leaving a path in her already short hair. Cassie cringed as tufts of hair cascaded to the patio.

"So, Mags," Cassie said casually. "How are things with Marybeth?"

"Yeah. Did you have sex with her yet?"

Maggie pulled the shaver away, leaving Jenn half bald. Cassie bit her lip to hide the smile forming at the sight.

"What do you mean 'yet'?" Maggie propped a hand on her hip. "What part of asexual don't you understand?"

"Don't get upset," Cassie said. "We weren't trying to be rude."

"You know I'm an Ace. So is Marybeth. We had this conversation on our first date. That's why we're still seeing each other."

"That's great," Jenn said. "So it's going well then."

"Yes," Maggie said, still sounding annoyed. "She's a lovely person."

"I'm so happy for you," Cassie said.

"Me, too." Jenn smiled and stared expectantly at Maggie. "Think you can finish me off now?"

Maggie's eyes flashed with a devilish glimmer. "That's what she said."

"I can't with you two." Cassie laughed in spite of herself as she jumped up to get her phone after it buzzed with a text.

It was from Deana. For some reason she felt the need to walk to the other side of the patio to read it.

Just wanted to say thank you for your time yesterday and that it was so nice to see you again. Glad you're doing so well.

She stared at Deana's simple words and her name at the top of the text, recalling the sound of her voice in her office Friday. Also how good she smelled, and how the mere mention of her name still made Cassie's heart flutter.

She then reminded herself that it wasn't too late to back out.

CHAPTER TWENTY

A s Cassie approached the café, her palms were sweating like a whistleblower testifying before Congress. Deana had made her invitation seem purely business, a follow-up to their initial meeting, but Cassie's heart had insisted that, at some point, they wouldn't be able to keep their conversation from veering personal. How could it not?

Everything had been left hanging from a cliff's edge after Deana's assault—no closure, no good-byes, no check-ins over the years saying, "Hey, how's it going? How've you been? How long did it take for you to forget me?" Cassie had never forgotten Deana. She'd just learned to live without her.

She shook those anxiety-inducing thoughts from her mind as she pulled the café door open. As she rounded the corner into the bar area, the sight of Deana perched at a high-top table backlit by the setting sun nearly turned her to stone like Medusa's glare. Something in the way she carried herself had changed, like her confidence was authentic now with none of the bravado of a woman who'd been struggling to figure out her identity.

Deana stood and surprised her with a hug—a warm, tight one. "Thank you for meeting me here. I'm sure your schedule is already full."

"No problem," Cassie said as they sat. "I'm happy to accommodate the future state senator for the 12th district in Connecticut."

Deana glanced around as though searching for that person. "I still can't believe I'm doing this. And at my age, no less."

"Sixty's the new forty, isn't it?" Cassie wanted to add that she'd only grown more striking in the twenty-plus years since she'd seen her, but that wasn't how one kept everything professional.

"That's what my son and daughter-in-law say, but…" Deana shrugged.

"I still can't believe Sean is married and you're about to be a grandmother."

Deana rolled her eyes in amusement. "Right? Maybe I don't look sixty, but nothing can make you feel more ancient than the word 'grandmother.'" She produced a photo on her phone of a happy couple, half of which was enormously pregnant.

"Oh my God. That poor girl." Cassie giggled as she studied the photo. "Sean is so handsome and most definitely took after you."

"Thank you. And he's the sweetest guy, too."

"I'm so happy to see that you're doing well." Without thinking, Cassie placed her hand on Deana's, then quickly pulled it back. "Well, so far, I can say your image is nice and shiny for a political career. What's your marital status? Husband? Wife?"

"Single. Does that tarnish my *perfect* image?"

Cassie chuckled. "Not for state politics. Are you seeing anyone? I'm only asking from the perspective of crafting your public profile."

Deana shook her head. "Single in every sense of the word."

Cassie was surprised at how delighted that news made her feel, and not from a professional standpoint. "How is that even possible? You're the entire package."

The blush across Deana's face said it all.

"I'm sorry," Cassie said. "That was a really dumb thing to say." She picked up the menu and used it as a sort of a force field to shield herself from Deana's magnetism, which was as strong as it always was…if not stronger.

"That was cute," Deana said with a sly smile. "I feel better about this now that I have a skilled strategist to coach me."

"At the risk of screwing myself out of consulting fees, honestly, you don't need much in the way of coaching. Just be yourself, share your story, and tell the people what you can do for them."

"That's it? Why does it seem so much more involved than that?"

"It is on a national level, where so much more is at stake. It's a total power game. At the state level, citizens are more concerned with competent, well-meaning politicians working together to better the lives of everyone living here."

"Shouldn't that be the goal at the federal level as well?"

Cassie snorted into her water glass. "You'd think so, but look how well the desire to do what's best for everyone worked out for Liz Cheney after January sixth."

Deana smirked knowingly with a slow head nod. "I guess I'll just focus on getting elected to our general assembly."

"Let's not abandon the idea of you making it to Congress someday. But right now, baby steps. Come by my office by the end of the week, and I'll have a full plan in place. We can fill in the blanks together."

Deana raised her water glass in agreement. "Does that mean we can officially celebrate our new business partnership with a drink?"

So moved by Deana's selfless idealism, Cassie's answer wandered out on its own. "How about a drink and some dinner? I'm starving, and I hear the penne alla vodka here is phenomenal."

Surprisingly, Deana's smile penetrated her heart the way it had twenty years earlier. Or maybe it shouldn't have been surprising at all, given how Cassie had felt about her when things had ended so tragically and abruptly.

She smiled back and reminded herself that this was a professional partnership like any other. For a decade, she'd cultivated a reputation as a shrewd, effective image consultant and political strategist for local politicians and other leaders. She wasn't about to let her past with Deana dim the glow of that accomplishment.

The next day at work Cassie had been occupied with a media package for the new CEO of an aerospace corporation, one of Connecticut's largest employers. While she'd detested how the climate in corporate America made these men seem like gods, she occasionally did their bidding and reaped the handsome rewards. She hadn't had much mental space to reflect on her dinner with Deana the night before, until Jenn checked in with her later in the afternoon.

"How are you feeling?" Cassie spoke through the speaker on her cell. "I'm sorry I haven't asked lately."

"I'm fine," Jenn replied. "And you asked me two days ago. How are you? How did your meeting with Deana go? Did she say anything about me?"

Cassie chuckled at Jenn's comic timing. "It was good. And yes, of course, she asked about you and Maggie."

"I'm assuming it stayed professional and you didn't end up having car sex in front of her house again." Dramatic pause. "Or did you?"

"Jenn," Cassie shrieked. "Can you not right now? You know the answer to that."

"A girl can dream, can't she?"

"We had a great talk, delicious food, and I've decided to take her on as a client."

"Seriously?" Suddenly, the lightness disappeared from Jenn's tone.

"Yes, I'm serious. She has an amazing message, a solid platform, and a level of enthusiasm I've never seen in a candidate running for anything. I truly believe she's got a shot at winning, a strong one."

"Cool. Okay. Yeah. Hitch your wagon to a star."

"What the fuck are you trying to say?"

"Do you think this is a good idea? For you, not your career. I mean, Jesus, Cass. Anyone but Deana Godwin."

"It's Deana Warner."

"Whatever," Jenn snapped.

"Look. Don't start this shit with me."

"Whoa. Take it easy. I'm just watching out for you, my friend. I still remember what it was like for you when things—"

"I know. I know. I'm sorry. I totally get where you're coming from. You bore the brunt of my breakdown, and I understand you not wanting to go through it again."

"Cass, this is not about what I went through with you, and you know it. I just want to know you'll be okay when the business arrangement is over."

Cassie sighed. Why was she getting so defensive with Jenn? The woman was in the throes of a major health crisis, and there she was worrying about her. "Jenn, I appreciate your instinct to protect me. I love you for it, but I got this. I am not the same woman I was twenty years ago, and neither is Deana. Shit. I'm still giddy as fuck that she's done such amazing things with her life since the attack. I'm so excited she chose me to partner with her in her election bid."

"You're fucking amazing," Jenn replied. "I feel stupid for even bringing this up in the first place. I should've known you had it all under control."

Cassie laughed. "Don't ever stop looking out for me. I'm bound to fuck up again sooner or later."

Jenn returned a giggle. "Same, sista. Same."

They ended the call seemingly in good spirits, but when Cassie leaned back in her chair, she realized Jenn had gotten into her head. Careerwise, this was a no-brainer. But was allowing Deana Warner back into her world emotional suicide?

She rubbed her eyes under her reading glasses and decided to call it a day at work.

❖

Cassie's car seemed on autopilot as she turned onto Maggie's street. When she pulled into the driveway, she hadn't paid attention to the car parked in front of her house. Maggie had two friends. Literally two friends. So the thought that she already had company hadn't even occurred to Cassie.

"Hi, Cass," Maggie said as she stood in her open doorway holding a bottle.

Cassie looked around her and saw a tall woman with a glass of wine sitting on the arm of Maggie's sectional sofa. Her double take must've been less than subtle.

"Aren't you coming in?" Maggie asked.

"Are you inviting me in? It looks like I'm interrupting something."

Maggie shook her head. "You're not. I'm just making stir-fry for dinner. Come in and join us."

Cassie's feet wouldn't move. "You have someone here," she whispered. "Marybeth. That's Marybeth, isn't it?"

"Yeah. Come on in." She opened the door wider as if that was why Cassie hadn't moved.

"Hi, Cassie," Marybeth called out in her sweet tenor voice.

"Hi, Marybeth," she replied just as amiably, then lowered her volume. "Mags, you're clearly having a date. I'm not gonna crash it. I'll talk to you tomorrow."

"Please don't leave," Marybeth said as she approached Maggie from behind. "I'd love for us to get to know each other better over this lovely dinner Maggie's preparing."

Cassie looked at Maggie, who smiled and nodded. "Well, it's a good thing I stopped at the package store first." She brought her bottle of wine into the kitchen where Maggie had resumed prepping for her stir-fry.

"Maggie tells me you've recently had an encounter with a woman from your past who meant a lot to you. I hope it's going as you want it to." Marybeth poured Cassie some wine.

"To be honest, I don't know how I want it to go. I mean, obviously, it's a business relationship, and I would like for it to be successful, but other than that…" She was starting to ramble.

"Well, I wish you and your client all the success." Marybeth smiled and sipped her wine.

"Thank you." Cassie sat on a bar stool at the countertop at the edge of the kitchen. She was captivated as she watched Maggie do her little domestic thing and interact with Marybeth, who was acting as her sous-chef. She'd lost count as to what number date this was, but they'd clearly become an item since she received her Good Samaritan award.

"Jenn's still feeling okay?" Maggie asked.

"She must be. She's in Brooklyn working on a mural project. Her surgery's in two weeks, so I think she wanted to get away from everything while she mentally prepares. And by everything, I mean Amelia."

Maggie shook her head. "I can't believe she's going ahead with the divorce in the middle of dealing with cancer."

"Might as well take care of every shitty thing in life at once and get it over with." Cassie shrugged.

"I admire her courage," Marybeth said. "And I certainly relate to the pressures of making a life-changing decision."

"You're both pretty courageous," Cassie said. "You, too, Mags. I'm surrounded by a bunch of badasses, and it's thoroughly inspiring."

Maggie's subtle smile indicated she knew what Cassie was referring to. "We're all shining examples that it's never too late to take a leap of faith."

"Aww. Am I your leap of faith?" Marybeth asked.

Maggie's shy smile at her was adorable. They were adorable, and Cassie couldn't stop staring at them.

She stood up. "I've never felt more like a third wheel in my entire life than I do right now. Thanks for the wine and the inspiration, but I'm gonna head out."

"No. Please don't leave," Marybeth said.

"Cass, dinner's ready," Maggie added. "Just have something to eat with us, and then you can go any way the wind blows."

"You two were about to have such beautiful quality time, and I—"

Marybeth clasped her hand. "Anytime a friend shows up, it's

quality time. Besides, Maggie and I will have plenty more opportunities to enjoy dinner for two."

Cassie looked up at Marybeth and smiled. If she was any sweeter, Cassie might fall for her, too.

❖

Cassie sat at a high-top table for two at a local wine bar people-watching as she waited for Deana to arrive. She'd chosen a public place for their meeting, knowing she'd be a bundle of nerves for a number of reasons. Although a locale that served alcohol came with inherent risks, it was still a safer bet than the quiet oasis of her office.

When Deana walked in, the sight of her affably greeting the hostess and then breezing over to her left her semi-breathless. Accepting her as a client would probably be a big mistake, one she'd already decided she'd look back on someday with no regrets.

"Hey," Deana said and remained standing.

Cassie got up and glided into a brief, awkward hug. "I hope you didn't mind meeting in person." She motioned for Deana to join her at the table.

"Not at all. I'm glad you were able to. I thought it would just be on the phone or Zoom after our initial meeting."

"I'll be honest. The curiosity was killing me. I know that was totally unprofessional to say, but please don't hold it against me."

Deana smiled. "I won't. I'm almost certain you don't do this with all your clients."

Cassie relaxed somewhat. "Yes. I usually don't have history with any of them."

"I can imagine you'd be curious, considering how things ended. As I said the other day, I'm sorry for my abrupt—"

"No, please." Cassie held up a hand. "You don't need to apologize."

"I feel like I do," She tapped her middle finger lightly on the menu. "I know how deeply it hurt you. I read your letter."

The letter. Cassie had long forgotten about sending it. She licked her dry lips as she recalled the intense anguish that had inspired that letter. After discovering that Deana had fled the state without so much as a "see ya," Cassie had used the internet to find an address for her and dashed off a lengthy, rambling plea saturated in desperation.

"Look, Deana. It's been forever. I understand now that you did what you had to do to process your trauma. It wasn't my place to tell you how to accomplish that or to assert my own needs on you. Our whole relationship was pretty much a shit show from the start."

"Oh." Deana retreated as though Cassie's words were a shiv slicing into her gut.

Cassie sighed and leaned toward her across the table. "I didn't mean it like that. I just meant…"

"I get it. I was married, and I was wrong to pursue you. And your biggest regret in life was letting me."

"No." Cassie looked out the window, then directly at her. "My biggest regret was that you were hurt because I let you. It took me so long to work through that guilt."

Deana placed her hand on top of Cassie's. "That had nothing to do with you. That was Jeffrey's misguided attempt to keep control over me. That was a sexual predator who recognized an opportunity to violate a woman and took it."

"I know who the real perpetrators were. It just killed me that the opportunity arose because you wanted to be with me. Worst of all, I couldn't even be there to comfort and support you afterward." Cassie leaned back as the painful memories came slicing through, but it was clearly too late to mask them.

Deana clasped her fingers together and rested her elbows on the table. Her words slipped out softly, almost intimately. "I came to realize it was a mistake to run out on you. As I began the road to healing, I could've used your support and your friendship."

"I blamed you for a long time for taking that away from me. I didn't know much about coping mechanisms back then or that sometimes the kindest thing you can do for someone you care about is give them space."

Deana shrugged. "That made two of us. And it wasn't only about me. I freaked out about Sean. I just didn't feel like I could keep him safe here anymore. Even though Jeffrey was going to prison, I didn't know what he was still capable of. That's why I chose to move down South."

"And left no forwarding address."

"Mistakes were made."

Cassie nodded as she glanced out the window again.

"I'll understand if you want to rescind your offer to take me on as a client," Deana said. "While I know, based on my research, that you're excellent at what you do, I contacted you first and foremost to apologize, to try to set things right between us." She leaned back and folded her arms across her chest in resignation. "I mean, is that even possible?"

Cassie relaxed into a cautious smile. "First, you don't ever have to apologize for what you did while you were in survival mode. And second, I appreciate you contacting me after all this time. It means a lot."

"Enough to stay past one drink? Now that we have all that other stuff out of the way, I'd love to just have dinner with an old friend."

"An idea that's long overdue." Cassie smiled and signaled the server over to them.

By the end of dinner, Cassie knew she was in trouble. Just as Jenn had predicted, or had cursed her, she was feeling things she shouldn't have toward a client. The physical attraction was one thing. It was inevitable, given Deana's natural beauty and how gracefully she'd aged. But Cassie was a mature adult now and could control what was left of her hormones.

The emotional part was a different story. Her love for Deana had never died. It just went dormant—for a couple of decades. If Deana was to stay in her life at least through her campaign, it was destined to come raging back like an inexorable wave with the potential to destroy everything in its path.

The only reasonable course of action to take from here on was to avoid in-person meetings and handle everything through text or email unless absolutely necessary.

Funny how once again everything relating to Deana hung in the balance until Election Day.

❖

After Deana had gone over to her son and daughter-in-law's house to cook dinner for them, she realized in the two years she'd been back in Connecticut, she hadn't really made any friends. Other than an occasional after-work drink with coworkers at the Department of Children and Families, she'd kept to herself and spent most of her time with Sean and Nicole, and her schnauzer. This realization hit her when she'd wanted to talk about Cassie, her former love interest, not her new professional colleague.

She finished her glass of red wine and began clearing the dinner dishes, much to the obvious relief of Nicole, who went to sit down.

Sean got up to help. "Hey. I thought we were going to talk about how your meeting went with that campaign consultant."

Nicole was now relaxing in the recliner in the family room but could see and hear them, thanks to the open floor plan. "I may not be able to move at this point, but I'm happy to help out any way I can with your social media platforms."

"Thanks, sweetie," Deana said. "I will take you up on that. Cassie, the consultant, said that will be key to getting visibility and my message out before we start running TV and radio spots."

"Sounds like you're in capable hands," Sean said. "How did you find her?"

She contemplated finally telling her son the full, unedited story about her past now that he was a grown man. She'd learned through her therapy years earlier that she didn't need to, nor should she, keep her trauma a secret. But even though he was in his early thirties, she still saw him as her baby—her only baby. What if she told him that her affair with Cassie had started the avalanche of trouble that robbed him of his relationship with his own father? He'd be devastated. And probably furious with her. She couldn't jeopardize her bond with her only family, especially when he was about to become a parent.

"I asked around at work, and coincidentally, the name Cassie Burke came up." The lie didn't sit well with her.

"Why is that a coincidence?" Sean asked.

"Oh, well, she was an acquaintance from years ago before we moved down South. You met her when you were a kid."

He shrugged as though he hadn't recalled, and Deana took that as a good thing.

"Anyway, she's super nice and has an extensive background in public relations and politics."

"Awesome," he said. "I look forward to meeting her again at your victory party."

"Victory party." She chuckled. "Wouldn't it be mind-blowing if I actually win?"

"Prepare your mind to be blown," Nicole said. "You're winning this. And then on to the US presidency."

"Sure. Why not? Just let me get used to state government first."

The more Deana helped people, the more she wanted to continue that work on a larger scale. First, volunteering in a women's shelter in Charleston, then working as a social worker there and in Hartford, and soon, hopefully, trying to improve women's lives and conditions statewide. Other than having a child, Deana couldn't remember a time in her life when she'd wanted anything more than this. Except maybe Cassie. She remembered loving Cassie so deeply. She'd built so many dreams on the prospect of what could've been with her after she'd divorced Jeffrey.

Then the assault happened, and the trajectories of all their lives changed forever.

She and Cassie had had a nice dinner together the other night after finally talking about all the things they'd both been carrying for too long. The word "cathartic" would've been an understatement. Deana hoped to rekindle their friendship, but after so long, would Cassie want that?

Or would her victory celebration be the last time she'd ever see her?

CHAPTER TWENTY-ONE

Deana was pleased to see that as soon as she had signed the agreement, Cassie hit the ground running on her campaign. First was a series of campaign fund-raisers at different locations in the district, ranging from a spaghetti dinner at a community center to that night's event, a wine-and-cheese happy hour at a beach club in Madison.

She'd watched Cassie move casually in and out of conversations as though she were a donor herself, sipping, smiling, and mesmerizing everyone in the room while she'd gathered bits of info about what their concerns were in the state and their district.

After chatting with a local business owner who was hoping to expand, Deana caught a quick chill when Cassie rolled up behind her and whispered, "What a great turnout," in her ear.

"I can't believe you filled the place at seventy-five dollars a head," she replied, studying the nuances time had added to the face she'd so adored twenty years earlier.

"I just did what I usually do. These people are coming out for you and your message."

Deana sipped a chardonnay. "I recognize a few faces from my days as a politician's wife. I wonder what they're doing out this way."

"It's been over twenty years. People move. Especially exceptionally wealthy people."

"Or maybe they're just curious to see how Jeffrey Godwin's victim wife turned her life around."

"You're a survivor, not a victim," Cassie said sternly. "That's the message. And they know that. That's why they're here, to back a winner."

Deana giggled. "You really are the Queen of Spin."

"That's why they pay me the big bucks," Cassie said. "Excuse me for a minute."

This was the second time the same attractive woman in a small group of older women had summoned Cassie. They'd already presented themselves as supporters, but Deana noticed right off that this particular woman was more interested in Cassie than in Deana's platform.

As she worked the room, glimpsing Cassie and the woman laugh distracted her. Maybe it was just a friend of Cassie coming out for support. She was dying to know, but she had to be subtle.

The minute she caught Cassie's eye, she nodded her over.

"Hey. What's up?" she asked.

"How do you think things are going?"

Cassie arched an eyebrow. "Look around. We couldn't have expected a better crowd if we paid for it. How are people responding when you talk with them?"

"Great. I'm not sure if it's me or the wine, but they seem enthusiastic."

Cassie chuckled. "I'm certain it's you. Don't start losing confidence already. We've only just begun."

"Me? Never. I guess I just want this so bad that I want to make sure I do everything to the highest standard."

Cassie smiled and patted her arm. "Be yourself and speak your truth. That's the winning combination right there."

Staring into Cassie's eyes, Deana let her attention drift off a bit. She remembered her as a twenty-something, fair-haired beauty when they first met, a wounded starling that wanted to be free. Now at fifty, she'd evolved into a beautiful, elegant woman with an undeniably commanding presence.

That woman gawking in their direction was clearly under her spell and was aiming to steal Cassie's attention away.

"Your friends want you again," Deana said with a slight sneer.

"Who?" Cassie looked over her shoulder.

"Your friends over there." She indicated the group.

"I just met them tonight," she replied. "Very nice women. They even mentioned volunteering."

"All of them or just the one drooling over you?"

Cassie whipped her head back at her with an unassuming smile. "What are you talking about?"

Deana wanted to kick herself. What had gotten into her? She sounded like a jealous girlfriend. Then, like any good politician, she immediately switched into damage control. "Just kidding." She spewed out a phony laugh, which only made things more awkward. "That's wonderful. I'll gladly accept all the volunteers I can get."

"Absolutely," Cassie said. "Let me see if I can go get them locked in."

Deana took that opportunity to run to the ladies' room and pull herself together. While she'd used her campaign as an excuse to contact Cassie, she'd intended to achieve the closure she'd assumed they both needed. A way to make amends for past wrongs and to have a cordial business relationship.

At least that's what she'd felt in the beginning.

After dabbing her cheeks with a cool, damp paper towel, she resumed her rounds chatting with her supporters and vowed to dismiss any personal thoughts of Cassie and the woman who had her in her crosshairs.

❖

Cassie hadn't noticed anything unusual about the woman, Helena, until Deana had put her on blast. When she'd approached the group of women who owned a prestigious salon in Madison, Helena had stepped forward and done all the talking. She was attractive, in her fifties, adorned with lots of chunky jewelry and a wild jumble of auburn curls. She definitely would've caught Cassie's eye had she sauntered into Pantheon years ago.

But those days were over in more than one sense. This was a professional outing for Cassie, and she never mixed business with pleasure.

Helena clearly didn't know that. "Will you be there at headquarters while I'm making the campaign calls?"

"Actually, the first round you can make from the comfort of your own home," Cassie said. "We'll email you a list of numbers to cold-call and a script to follow. Easy-peasy."

"That's no fun," she said. "I was hoping we'd all get to hang out together."

"You and your friends can certainly get together and make a party of it. Lots of folks do that these days."

As they all headed toward the door to leave, Helena herded Cassie to walk a step behind her friends. "Do you think you and I can meet for coffee or something to review what I'm supposed to do? I've never been a campaign volunteer before."

"Oh, it's easy. Everything you need to know will be in the email."

She grinned. "I guess I'm being too subtle with my hints."

On the contrary, Cassie wanted to say.

"If you're free sometime, I'd like to take you out for a drink, a little networking. You know, one businesswoman to another."

Cassie felt an awkward smile appear on her face. "Um, that might be nice," she said. "How about after the election? I'm swamped with work this time of year, like an accountant during tax season."

A small laugh emanated from Helena's throat. She wasn't buying it, but Cassie hoped she hadn't just cost Deana a group of volunteers.

"I guess that could work," she said with a sly grin. "Then you'll be in touch? I mean, about the campaign calls?"

"Yes. Absolutely. And thank you again for your interest…in volunteering. Your interest in volunteering."

As she watched Helena and her friends pile into a car, she let out her breath. First campaign crisis averted.

"I told you so."

Cassie turned around to Deana's playfully smug face. "How long were you standing there?"

"Not long, but I didn't need to hear what I already knew. Did she manage to charm your phone number out of you?"

They started walking to their cars parked side by side. "I don't know if I'd use the word 'charm.'" A jolt of nerves ran through her, but she rebounded with a cool, "As a matter of fact, I got all of their numbers and emails out of them so they can start cold-calling potential voters immediately."

"Oh, my." Deana tapped her face. "I hope you're not going to have to sacrifice your virtue to win me a local election."

Cassie chuckled. "I might if I had to."

"That's going to cost me extra, huh?"

"It'll cost you big-time."

"Is that expenditure allowed under the campaign finance regulations?"

"Who said anything about money?"

Cassie's heart was pounding, and Deana's giggle proved that she'd out-flirted her. It was fun, and titillating, and Cassie knew better than to go there with a client, but Deana wasn't just any client.

"Thanks again for tonight," Deana said. "I'm so glad you're on my team."

"Me, too." Cassie smiled and opened her car door.

"So, uh…" Deana said. "If you think you'd all be for it, maybe we, I mean you and I and Maggie and Jenn could get together for a bite sometime. I'd love to see them again. That is, if it's not some type of business ethics violation."

Cassie laughed. "No. I think we're good on that. And I'm sure they'd love to see you, too." Her knees nearly gave out at the realization that she loved seeing Deana, too. Not just that first time they'd reconnected, but every time. Every single time they'd met since they began their political partnership. "I'll check with them, and we can pick a day."

"Sounds great," Deana said and disappeared inside her car.

When Cassie first invited her to join them at Maggie's house on a Saturday afternoon for college football, Deana recoiled at the thought of reuniting in such an intimate setting. Someone's house? Surely a neutral zone like a restaurant or bar would've been better. But when she learned that Cassie's alma mater, Georgetown, was playing Maggie's, it seemed an ideal setting for a casual reunion. With the action happening on the football field, they would be able to work out the kinks from their past together and perhaps fall into a new friendship dynamic.

She rang the doorbell and, while waiting for someone to answer, switched the wine bottle to her less sweaty hand and readjusted the tray of buffalo wings.

"I'm so glad you were able to make it." Cassie greeted her with a light kiss on the cheek as she relieved her of the heavy foil tray. "These smell delicious."

"Thank you so much for inviting me." She followed Cassie into the living room.

"It's so great to see you again," Jenn said as she ambushed her with an embrace that transcended their years of separation.

Maggie waved at her from behind Jenn.

"Let's go sit down," Cassie said. "They're about to kick off. What would you like to drink?"

"Wine, please. Whatever you have open is fine." Deana sat on the sectional sofa off-side of the huge TV mounted on the wall.

"Congrats on your senate run," Jenn said. "I only wish I lived in your district so I could vote for you."

Maggie tore into a buffalo wing. "I do live there. You have mine."

"Thank you both. I appreciate the encouragement. I have my work cut out for me to try to unseat an incumbent, especially at the local level."

"From what Cassie says about your platform, you're gonna give him a run for his money."

"I hope so." She smiled and thanked Cassie when she handed her a glass of wine. "You guys look adorable in your team jerseys."

"This old thing?" Cassie tugged at her jersey as she sat in the large space between Deana and Maggie. "Pass that chili dip."

Cassie was acting differently than she had been during their last few meetings. She was almost like a dude at a Buffalo Wild Wings on Super Bowl Sunday. Was she putting on this cool, unaffected act in front of the girls, or was this really her demeanor outside a professional setting? Maybe Cassie regarded all her clients with a level of intimacy that made them feel supported and confident, and Deana had just read too deeply into it.

"Chips?" Cassie casually stretched her arm to offer her the bowl, barely dragging her eyes away from the TV.

"No, thanks," Deana said politely even though Cassie was being slightly annoying.

After they all sat back into the sofa cushions for kickoff, Deana observed their profiled faces, three sets of eyes fixed on the TV screen. She couldn't relax. It was surreal being in their group presence again after so many years. Even though they'd welcomed her into the group years ago and were just as welcoming today, she still felt like the odd woman out. Maybe she'd be more comfortable after a little conversation. "So, Jenn, Maggie, tell me what you're up to these days."

Jenn turned to her as though she'd forgotten Deana was there. "Well, as you know," Jenn said. "Thanks to your generous patronage many years ago, I make a fine living as a commissioned artist here and sometimes abroad. And I've been married to my wife, Amelia, for over fifteen years."

"That's fantastic," Deana said. "So you were the marrying kind after all."

Jenn leaned back and clasped her hands behind her head, letting Deana know she still had that sassy mojo that had once attracted her. "Eh, you know. Once you get deep into your thirties, it's tiring being chased all the time. I finally let one catch me."

Cassie shook her head. "Can you believe her? Some things never change."

Deana grinned, finally able to exhale now that Cassie was engaged in the conversation. "How about you, Maggie?"

Maggie turned her head toward her. "I was recently caught—"

"Caught the attention," Cassie said, leaning in front of her. "She recently caught the attention of a lovely store security guard named Marybeth. They're dating now."

"Fabulous," Deana said. She nudged Cassie with her elbow. "Looks like you and I are the only confirmed bachelorettes in this bunch."

Cassie glanced at her but couldn't seem to hold eye contact. "You have so many great things happening in your life, how would you fit a girlfriend in?" She turned to the other girls. "Did you know she's about to be a grandmother to twins any day now?"

Jenn and Maggie gushed at the announcement.

Their round of catching up on each other's lives had helped quell Deana's nervousness, except for when Cassie would change positions on the couch and brush up against her. Was she doing it on purpose? Or had Deana been reading way too much into everything?

At the end of the first quarter, Cassie stood, stretched, and went to the kitchen for the rest of the food.

"Let me help you," Deana said and trailed her. She watched Cassie's shoulder-length, wavy blond hair bounce above the number on the back of her jersey. How much more appealing her beauty was now that she was fifty. That old cliché "aging like fine wine" could've been coined just for her.

"Are you having fun so far?" Cassie asked as she took plastic wrap off a charcuterie board.

"So much fun. I was a little apprehensive at first about how the chemistry would be with all of us after so long, but now I feel right at home." That wasn't entirely true, but she was pleased at how sincere it had sounded.

"I'm glad. And I'm sure they'll be on board to help your campaign any way they can."

Deana's enthusiasm sank. Once again Cassie brought their

connection back to her campaign. Even in a purely social setting. Was that really what all this was about?

"Are you okay?"

"Yeah." Deana brushed off the perfect opening for an honest conversation about what she was feeling. Now just wasn't the right time. "So do you think we'll still hang out as friends when you're not working for me anymore?"

"I hope you'll still have time to hang out with us bums when you're state senator." She looked her directly in the eyes as she licked a blob of dip from her fingers. "You don't believe you're going to win, do you?"

"I wanna believe it. Let's just call it cautious optimism."

"That must be one of the things people are responding to in you, complete lack of arrogance."

Deana smiled, but she didn't want to talk to Cassie the campaign consultant. She was searching for her new old friend.

"Let's go in. The second quarter's started."

When she turned to leave, Deana pulled at the back of her jersey. "Cass, wait."

"Yeah?"

"You don't have to do this, you know."

"Do what?"

"Invite me to things, make me feel like a part of something just because you're working for me."

"Deana, that's crazy. First of all, Maggie told me to invite you here, and I was thrilled at the suggestion. Even more thrilled that you actually showed up. I thought we decided from the start of your campaign that we would be friends regardless of what happens in the election."

Deana rested her hip against the counter. "Well, don't I feel silly now. Thank you for reassuring this insecure old broad."

"C'mon. Open that bottle of red and get in here." Cassie smiled, and for the first time since they'd reunited, Deana recognized the warmth and safety in Cassie's eyes that had drawn her in so many years ago.

CHAPTER TWENTY-TWO

One of Cassie's most well-received campaign strategies in the months leading up to Election Day was hosting a series of town hall–like events to introduce Deana to the various groups of constituents she'd be serving if elected. On this day, she'd organized a pancake breakfast held at a community center frequented by seniors.

By this point in the campaign, Deana had needed little coaching. She was a natural at speaking with people, making them feel heard and comfortable in her presence. She had a level of sincerity that Cassie hadn't experienced with any other client, and she felt exceptionally proud to attach her name to Deana's team.

"Good morning, everyone." Deana's voice came over the PA system. "Please don't stop enjoying your breakfast. I just wanted to say a few words. As most of you know, I'm Deana Warner, and I'm excited to be running for the state senate. I wanted to thank you all for coming this morning and give special thanks to those who've approached Cassie Burke about volunteering for our campaign. With only six weeks till Election Day, we appreciate all the help we can get. I'm so looking forward to serving you and the entire 12th district in our state senate if I'm lucky enough to earn your votes."

She paused as the crowd offered robust applause.

"I'll be walking around the room getting to know all of you and, most importantly, hearing your concerns. I want to be aware of what you need so I can do all I can up at the Capitol to improve your lives and your families' here in our beautiful state of Connecticut."

She thanked them again, stepped away from the mic stand, and headed toward Cassie. "How did I do?"

"Nailed it, like always," Cassie said. "I don't know why you continue to ask me after every public speech. You're a boss."

"I'm still a little insecure. This is the big time. I just want to make sure I'm projecting myself in a natural, sincere manner and that I'm saying enough."

"We all know the days of the long-winded politician are over. You instinctively realize how much to say and how to say it. You did great."

"Really?"

Cassie stole a second to imbibe the adorableness of Deana's worried eyes and pouty lips before responding. "Honest to God. I get more confident in your victory after every appearance. If you don't win, it certainly won't be due to an image problem."

"You're a little biased on your assessment, given that we're friends."

"Well, I've never represented a friend before, but I'd like to think that I'd give my friend as much honest, useful feedback as I would any client."

Deana brushed her fingers down the side of Cassie's arm with a warm smile. "Of course you would. Anyway, let me start making the rounds."

She walked off, and Cassie couldn't help noticing how incredible her calves looked in her skirt and heels. How could she be even hotter at sixty than at forty?

Cassie admonished herself for crossing the professional boundary in her mind yet again and went to the large percolator to refill her coffee cup. She leaned against the wall with a hand in her pocket, sipping her coffee and watching Deana listen intently and engage with voters as she worked her way around each table.

When Deana's phone started vibrating in Cassie's pocket, she pulled it from her blazer to check it. It was Sean.

"Hey, Sean, it's Cassie," she said as she walked out into the hall.

"Hey, Cass. I know my mom's busy now, but we're at the hospital. Nicole's in labor."

"Already? Is everything okay with Nicole and the babies?"

"Yeah. Yeah. Her doc says she's ready to go at any minute."

"Oh my God, yay! I'll tell your mom." She ended the call and had to decide if she should let her client finish her public engagement or run over and tell her friend that her only child was about to become a father at any second.

She chugged her coffee and flew over to Deana, who was mid-sentence. Sliding her hand under Deana's arm, she whispered, "Sean just called. We have to go. Now."

"What?" She appeared thrown by the interruption at first, but then it struck her. "Oh. I'm so sorry," she said to the table. "But I have to—"

"The future senator is about to be a grandma," Cassie yelled, and they ran out of the community center amid cheers.

"I'm so glad you were with me when the call came in." Deana's shaking knee was rattling the console. "I don't think I could drive. I'm too nervous."

"I'm so happy and excited for you, Deana. And I'm glad I'm with you, too, for this momentous event."

Deana placed her hand on top of Cassie's as it rested on the gear shift and absently caressed it. She was obviously a wreck, but still the touch felt romantic. *Come on, Cassie.* She silently chided herself. What was the matter with her, thinking such things at a time like that?

"I hope everything's going to be okay," Deana said. "They're coming three weeks early. My poor Seany must be beside himself."

"He's gonna be fine. She's gonna be fine. Everyone's gonna be fine. You're gonna be there for Sean in five minutes." Cassie pressed her foot down harder as they neared the exit for the hospital.

When she pulled up in front of the entrance, she stopped so abruptly, they both lurched forward.

Her hand on the door handle, Deana turned to her. "Cassie, I can't thank you enough for—"

"Go," she shouted. "Go see about your babies."

Deana grabbed her head with both hands and laid the hardest kiss possible on Cassie's lips. "Thank you." She jumped out of the car and bolted into the hospital.

Shocked, Cassie stared straight ahead as she tried to process what had just happened. Until the car behind her blared its horn.

She drove off, running her tongue over lips, savoring the taste of Deana.

❖

The next morning, Cassie was still radiating from Deana's absent-minded kiss. She stood at the sink, looking out the window, and sipped her coffee, periodically touching a finger to her lips where Deana's had made contact. Was she supposed to say anything to her about it? Or should she just pass it off as the exuberant delirium of a first-time grandma?

The kiss, as vexing as it was, provided a welcome distraction as the stress building up to Jenn's surgery that morning had been about to crush her. Her stomach in knots, she poured the rest of her coffee down the drain and headed to the hospital to wait for word.

As she sat in the waiting room, she tried to subdue her anxious imagination. Jenn's prognosis was excellent—if the surgeon determined the cancer hadn't spread beyond her thyroid.

If. Such a small word, yet so often people clung to it like a life raft in a tsunami.

Maggie walked in with a tray of three coffees. She hugged Cassie, then sat next to her. "I brought one for Amelia. Where is she?"

"She'll be coming."

"Strange, huh? Imagine your partner is having cancer surgery, and you have that 'I'll get there when I get there' attitude."

"I'm sure that's not what she's thinking, Mags. You know they haven't been doing well."

"All marriages go through rough patches, so I've been told. But times like these are usually the make-or-break. I can't imagine she'd just drop her off and leave."

"I definitely think they're broken. This health crisis has just put everything on hold."

Maggie unzipped her jacket and sipped her coffee. "No word from anyone yet?"

Cassie shook her head as she cradled her cup in her lap. "I'm scared," she said without looking up.

"Cancer's a scary thing. Luckily, they caught it early enough, and Jenn takes good care of her body these days. She's gonna beat this."

"Only if it hasn't spread."

Maggie was quiet for a moment, which only amplified Cassie's apprehension. "Let's just assume that it hasn't," she finally said.

"What's going to happen if she gets it for a third time?" Cassie's volume was rising as she spiraled. "I mean, why did it come back in a different area this time? We're all fifty now. People don't get healthier as they grow older."

"Cass, take a few breaths. Let's just focus our energy on things that are actually happening. Don't catastrophize. Use your words to express what's going on inside you."

Cassie guffawed. "Did you seriously just use your middle-school-psychologist spiel on me?"

Maggie nodded. "It's not the first time. Did it work?"

Cassie's chest was more open to take in a deep, cleansing breath. "It actually did. You fuck. You could've just talked to me like an adult, you know."

"I always do…when you're acting like one."

She shouldered Maggie, grateful for the levity. When her phone vibrated, she yanked it from her pocket. It was a text from Deana with a photo of the new babies, a boy and a girl, both asleep in their proud father's arms, along with a slew of corresponding emojis.

She texted back, *Omg, I'm about to die from all this cuteness. Good thing I'm in the hospital now.*

Oh, sorry. I forgot that today was Jenn's surgery. How is she?

Cassie got up and walked into a nearby hall to phone her. For some reason, she wanted to hear Deana's voice instead of texting. "No word yet. Maggie and I are hanging out in the waiting room."

"Would you like me to take a ride down? I could bring you guys something to eat."

Cassie nearly melted inside from her generosity. "No. Thank you. We're fine here. Besides, don't you have your hands full right now? Those babies are gorgeous."

"Thanks, and yes. I promised to be on auxiliary duty for a while until their parents get their bearings."

Cassie peeked into the waiting room and saw Maggie talking with Amelia. She wondered if that meant Jenn was coming out of surgery. After ending the call, Cassie returned to the waiting room and rejoined the seemingly endless wait.

❖

That night Cassie made herself a quick lemon-chicken-and-chickpea salad for dinner. She wanted to eat light to make sure she'd have room for the bottle of wine she planned to demolish throughout the evening. With Jenn resting comfortably in her post-surgery, overnight hospital stay, and the news that no additional cancer had been detected during the thyroidectomy, she could breathe again. Cassie just wanted to sink into her recliner with some type of disturbing Netflix documentary and top off her wineglass till the bottle was empty.

She'd just poured her second glass and was searching the program menu when someone knocked at the door. She rolled her eyes at the thought of an uninvited guest or, worse, some solicitor asking if he could talk to her about their Lord and savior, Jesus Christ.

She jumped up, remembering she'd recently placed a wine order and perhaps it was FedEx requiring a signature. Without looking out the peephole, she pulled the door open.

"Hi." Deana stood there displaying a bottle of red and a small bakery box. "The man at the package store said you simply can't drink this wine without a chocolate pairing."

Cassie laughed and stepped aside to let her in.

"I'm sorry I came by without texting first, but I just wanted to drop this off for you. I'm not staying."

The greatest pop-in of all time, and she wasn't staying? "What? You have to. I can't eat and drink all this myself. Well, I can, but my doctor would strongly advise against it."

"I didn't want to intrude on your privacy. It just seemed like you were having a rough day."

"I was, and you're not intruding at all. Please. Have a seat." She showed her to the sofa.

"Oh. I see that the party's started without me," Deana said playfully.

"I was determined to have a party tonight whether anyone showed up or not. This is awfully thoughtful of you." She brought over another wineglass and some napkins and sat beside her on the sofa.

"Hope you like lava cake."

"Um, what kind of freak doesn't?" Cassie handed her a fork.

"I should've brought two," Deana said.

Cassie glared at her. "You shouldn't have brought one, but I'm glad you did."

They both leaned back and dug their forks into the cake Cassie held up for them. Despite her desperate desire to indulge in a solitary bottle of wine that night, she couldn't subdue the smile fighting its way onto her face. She just hoped Deana wouldn't notice.

Luckily, the cake had her full attention. "What are we watching?"

"Haven't decided yet," Cassie said. "Any thoughts?"

She didn't immediately answer, but oh, the way she was licking the fudge off her fork...

"Well, uh, we can have dessert first and then decide."

"Put on whatever you want to watch," Deana replied. "I didn't mean to disrupt your plans."

"What plans? I was gonna drink alone until I passed out in my recliner."

"Sign me up."

Cassie giggled and blotted her mouth with a napkin. "Okay. How about something with Kristin Wiig?"

"Who?"

She giggled again. "Sorry. I forgot you're in your early sixties."

"That was rather aggressive. Please don't remind me."

Cassie chuckled. "Hey, if I look even half as good as you do when I'm in my sixties, I'll be reminding everyone I know all the time."

Deana laughed as she sipped her wine. "Oh, I could always count on you for an uplifting compliment in a moment of vulnerability."

"I'm only speaking the truth," she said as she topped off Deana's glass. "I'm pretty confident you will never not be beautiful."

Deana gazed at her as though a switch had been flipped. She hadn't meant to go that far, but as she'd just said, she was only speaking the truth.

"Thank you. You're very sweet." She stared straight ahead as she sipped her wine, and the atmosphere around them suddenly got tight.

Cassie hoped she hadn't assumed she was trying to come on to her. That was the last thing on her mind. Well, not the last thing, but she was enjoying her company and sincerely meant for her compliments to be uplifting.

Now she was nervous. She closed the cake box, drained what was in her glass, and gave herself a refill well beyond the standard restaurant pour.

"I, uh, I hope I didn't make you feel uncomfortable."

Deana finally turned her head toward her. "You kinda did, but not in the way you think."

Cassie stiffened, and she spoke robotically. "In case it isn't obvious, I don't know what I'm thinking at the moment."

Deana licked her bottom lip as she stared at Cassie's mouth. "I'm a bit mixed up at the moment myself." She placed her glass on the coffee table, and Cassie copied her.

"Can I make a confession?" Cassie asked.

She nodded.

"I still have to pinch myself to believe you're back in my life."

Deana smiled. "In the spirit of full disclosure...same. So much has changed over the years. But not everything."

"What's included in the 'not everything' category, if you don't mind me asking?"

Deana leaned back and stretched her arm across the back of the couch. "Abstract things. Thoughts, feelings. You know. Or maybe you don't. I shouldn't presume."

Cassie grinned at her coy sensuality. "You can presume. You have wine license to do so."

Deana chuckled. "I've never heard of wine license before. Is it similar to artistic license?"

"Very. Both provide uninhibited freedom."

The way Deana lightly tongued her own bottom lip as she gazed at her showed Cassie she was catching on. "To do what?"

"Anything that feels right…"

Cassie gave in to the magnetism drawing them closer. The sounds of their breathing came together in a sensuous symphony, and as Deana's lips parted, Cassie closed her eyes and anticipated their lusciousness.

Just as they were about to make contact, her ringing cell phone jolted her back. "Shit. It's Amelia." She stood up and darted into the kitchen. "Is everything okay?"

"Yes. Sorry. I didn't mean to startle you," Amelia said. "Jenn just wanted me to call to let you know she's feeling okay and is going to bed early, so don't feel obligated…"

As Amelia trailed off, Cassie watched Deana gather herself and her purse and head toward the door. Cassie tried to signal her to stay, but she just waved and backed herself out.

Shit. Shit. Shit.

Cassie went to the window as Amelia droned on. Once inside her car, Deana hesitated before driving away. Would she come back inside? Was she chastising herself for what happened between them? What had just happened between them?

What more would've happened if Amelia hadn't called?

Cassie shook her head and went back to her recliner and lonely bottle of wine.

CHAPTER TWENTY-THREE

After over a week of her and Cassie completely avoiding the topic of their wine-and-chocolate-lava-cake near-miss, Deana felt safe enough to reach out and invite her over to Sean and Nicole's house to meet the babies.

Surprisingly, Cassie had agreed. And as a bonus, she seemed just as unwilling to broach the topic as her. It had been a close call, and thankfully, Jenn's wife had intervened with an update on her before they'd done something they might've regretted.

However, as she sat there staring at Cassie's soulful eyes and sparkling smile while she held her grandson, she would've gladly traded a hot make-out session with her for a little regret.

"You're a natural at this grandmother thing," she said as she adjusted her granddaughter in her arms.

"Nothing to it when they're this age," Cassie said. "If you can hold an overstuffed burrito, you can handle an infant."

"Speaking of overstuffed, these guys are ready for a diaper change. I'll take her first, then come back for him."

"That's silly." Cassie got up. "I'll come with you and take care of him."

"Are you sure? Infant diapers can be pretty scary."

"I have nieces. I've changed a diaper before."

"When? Twenty years ago?"

"What does it matter? Has baby poop changed since then?"

Deana giggled. "Okay, hotshot. Have at it." She placed her granddaughter on the changing table and watched as Cassie got to work on her grandson.

"Whoa," Cassie yelled. "Mother of God."

Deana looked over, and Cassie's face was buried in the crook of her elbow as she railed against her gag reflex. "Hang on. I'll be right there," she said, trying to stay serious.

"No, no," Cassie replied. "I got this."

"Okay, but you really should—"

Cassie held up a hand. "Chill. I said I got this."

A stream of pee shot up from the undiapered baby and squirted Cassie on the chin. "Oh, damn. Your grandson's sprung a leak."

This time Deana couldn't contain her laughter. "That's what I was trying to tell you. You have to keep boys covered. Their little winkies are like fountains."

"I only ever changed baby girls," Cassie said. "I should've consulted the manual for him."

By this point, they were both losing themselves in silliness. Deana had to wipe the tears from her eyes, and Cassie was merciless in making her laugh even more with her witty remarks. Deana finally made a sincere attempt to pull herself together. "C'mon. Let's wrap this up before my daughter-in-law gets back from the store and fires us."

They got the babies cleaned up and dressed, and after Deana prepared their bottles, they returned to their positions side by side on the sofa and began feeding them.

Moments later, Nicole came in and stopped immediately. "Oh em gee." She dropped her shopping bags, whipped out her cell phone, and aimed it at them. "Wait till you guys see this picture. Adorbs."

Deana looked at her granddaughter sucking away at her bottle, then at Cassie holding her grandson. It was ridiculously cute. "Send it to me, please."

Nicole moved closer to snap more shots of the babies. "Not for nothing, but you'd make the hottest lesbian-grandparent couple in the universe."

"Nicole!" Deana cringed and immediately glanced over at Cassie, who was smiling as she blushed.

"I know you're just friends," Nicole said. "I'm just saying I can see this as the best *AARP* cover story ever."

"I just turned fifty this year, and I'm already making the cover of *AARP*?" Cassie said.

Deana and Nicole laughed as Sean came in from the backyard.

"Whoa. What's going on here?"

"Nothing," Deana said. "We were just leaving."

Sean and Nicole each picked up a baby. "You're not staying for dinner?" he asked.

"We have dinner reservations," Deana said.

"An early victory celebration," Cassie added.

"Have fun, ladies." Nicole waved her daughter's arm at them. "And please, do something I wouldn't do."

"Your daughter-in-law has quite a sense of humor," Cassie said as they walked to her car.

"I'm so sorry about that." Deana cringed again. "I'll talk to her about making those kinds of comments."

"No. I'm just kidding. Don't make her feel bad."

"I don't want her to make you feel uncomfortable. We're in a business relationship, and those comments are kind of like sexual harassment."

Cassie chuckled. "She's not harassing me. She's a cute kid. Leave her alone."

Deana smiled and relaxed in the passenger seat. She was relieved that Cassie had taken it all in the spirit in which it was meant, especially after that night she'd popped in at her house. In her younger days when they'd first met, she'd been too assertive with Cassie, even bordering on aggressive at times.

She wasn't that woman anymore—that uncertain, restless, scared woman. She'd evolved into a person she loved being. Love and sex and romance were nice, but she was in a different place in her life, where those things were no longer the be-all and end-all.

If all Cassie wanted was a business relationship that could maybe remain a friendship once the election was over, Deana would be fine with that.

❖

At the restaurant, once the wine was decided upon and poured, Cassie kept thinking about the words Deana had chosen to assert that she and Cassie were not a hot GILF couple. Not even friends. Deana referred to them as colleagues. A business relationship. Was that just for the benefit of her daughter-in-law? Because the other night on her couch what was simmering between them was anything but collegial.

She watched Deana sip her wine as she perused the dinner menu. Should she bring up her word choice for further clarification or just let it be? It wasn't the best time to go picking at scabs since she still had over a month left of professional consultation with Deana on the campaign.

As they finished their first course of soup and salad, Cassie had had enough time to work in the topic in a non-inflammatory manner.

"So after you win, do you think you'll still want to get together occasionally for dinner?"

Deana blotted the corners of her mouth. "Absolutely. I've brought that up to you in the past. I mean, I'd love to be part of the Pantheon Girls again." She offered an ironic smile. "How's Jenn feeling, by the way?"

"She's doing great. Turns out the cancer hadn't spread, so she doesn't need chemo. They're giving her rounds of radiation and some follow-up medication for a while."

"Thank God for that." Then the news seemed to register with her. "Wait. Do you mean Jenn shaved her head bald for nothing?"

"Seems that way." Cassie chuckled. "That was such a Jenn thing to do."

"That poor woman." Deana couldn't help but laugh. "Although she is rocking that purple dye on her peach fuzz."

"I'm just so relieved for her. She's gone through a lot. And now she has to deal with her marriage and the possibility of uprooting her whole life."

Deana shivered at the memory of her years of purgatory with Jeffrey. Sometimes the memories were alarmingly vivid. "Been there. Done that. Not fun."

"Right?" Cassie said. "We all make it through somehow."

"And usually are much better off in the end."

"When I think of all the energy I expended worrying about things I never had control over, all the self-doubt that plagued me through my twenties." Cassie shook her head. "In the end all those treacherous paths led me right to where I am today. Literally, there's nowhere I'd rather be."

"I don't mean to keep copying your answers, but same. Campaign aside, it's so nice to be in your company again."

Cassie smiled over the rim of her drink but didn't offer a response. Hmm. Was she still feeling strange about that night at her place? Nothing had happened. Almost didn't count, especially when it was so out of nowhere. It would probably be best if they'd just forgotten about it.

After arguing over who was going to pay the tab, they agreed to split it, and both tossed their cards in the binder. Once Cassie experienced the first yawn, Deana knew the night was over.

As they drove in Cassie's car back to Sean's house to get hers, Deana let out a long sigh.

Cassie glanced over at her. "Are you okay?"

"Yeah." Deana's feathery reply didn't sound convincing. Knowing Cassie, she wasn't going to let it slide.

"So…" she said as though on cue.

Deana trembled inside. Were they finally going to talk about the near-kiss? And then maybe have another?

"I was thinking…" She turned down the radio.

"Yeah?" Deana's heart began drumming in double time.

Cassie sucked in a deep breath, parted her lips, and then exhaled.

Deana swallowed hard, fully bracing for Cassie to offer some grand admission of love, or lust, or secret longing…

"How would the kids feel about us putting the twins in your TV ad with you?"

That was what she was thinking? She deflated back down into her seat, sort of relieved and disappointed that Cassie hadn't seemed to give what had almost gone down between them any additional thought. After all, she'd been worried about Jenn and a little tipsy from the wine that night. Deana now felt silly. She'd clearly been overthinking it. And perhaps overestimating Cassie's interest.

"Thoughts?"

"You don't think that might come off as a little cheesy or gratuitous?"

"Neither. You're a children's and family advocate by profession. You want the voters in your district to know that family is your priority. It'll still be effective without the babies, but they're so dang cute, it would be an irresistible touch."

"I'll ask the kids."

"Great. I'll have to let the director know ASAP so she can rework the scenes for the shoot next week."

Deana said good night and got into her car. On the ride home, her brain volleyed conflicting thoughts back and forth like it was in a Wimbledon final. In the positive column, Cassie was unperturbed by the low-grade sexual tension that had arisen since they began spending time together again. Same for Deana. She was mature enough and professional enough to navigate around it so that it didn't affect their business arrangement.

On the negative side, her feelings for Cassie were growing, like it or not. And they seemed to be outpacing Cassie's. After that night, she was left wondering if Cassie had any feelings at all beyond those of friendship.

Deana needed to just take the win and forget about feelings.

❖

Cassie spent the Saturday before Election Day with boots on the ground, canvassing neighborhoods door-to-door in Deana's district. She'd maintained a slight lead over her opponent on and off for most of the race, so with only a few days remaining, it was crunch time. While Deana and her son covered one area in Madison, Cassie had Maggie and Jenn on her team in another.

"Are you okay?" Cassie asked Jenn when she'd met up with them around a corner.

"Why don't we break for lunch or something?" Jenn replied.

Cassie rolled her eyes. "I told you that you shouldn't have come with us. You're tired because you're still recovering."

"I'm not tired. I'm just hungry. It'll still be light out when we finish eating."

"I'd rather just get it done," Maggie said. "Getting all these doors slammed in my face is hurting my self-esteem."

Cassie huffed. "I can finish up myself. Why don't you two just go get something to eat. I'll see you during the week." She plucked the "Warner for State Senate" flyers out of their hands.

Jenn plucked them back. "Don't be dense. We don't have many pamphlets left. Let's just go until they're gone."

"Fine," Cassie said. "Let's branch out in three different directions, and we'll meet back at the car in an hour. Can your stomach wait that long?"

"Yes, ma'am," Jenn said with a military salute and spun away from her on her heel.

Cassie turned and headed in the opposite direction but soon heard sneakers shuffling to catch up to her.

"Are you crabby because you're not gonna have an excuse to spend time with Deana after Tuesday?"

Cassie wheeled around on Jenn, who stood there on the sidewalk looking goofy in her double-sided alpaca hat with tasseled side flaps. "Why would I need an excuse to hang out with a friend?"

"When that friend is more than a friend."

Cassie continued walking. "There is nothing going on between us other than friendship. We've both been completely professional with each other during the entire campaign."

"And I bet it's been killing you both."

This was not a conversation Cassie was going to let happen. "We'll get this done a lot faster if we separate." She increased her stride, but Jenn scurried alongside her.

"What are you doing, Cass? Are you waiting for the election to be over?"

"For what?"

"To ask Deana out. To tell her you're still in love with her. To sweep her up in your arms and whisk her off to the nearest wedding chapel."

She chuckled. "Grow up, Jenn."

"For fuck's sake. If you lose her again, I'll never for—"

Cassie stopped, causing Jenn to bump into her. "Deana and I are friends. We live three towns apart. I'm not losing her, and she's not losing me no matter how the election goes."

When she continued her stride, Jenn mumbled, "Chickenshit."

"What?"

"I said you're a chickenshit. You're keeping Deana in the friend zone because you're afraid to let yourself be vulnerable again."

"And?"

"What do you mean, *And*? You're supposed to argue with me and deny being in love with her. Deny being scared. Say shit like it's too late or our chance has passed, so I can convince you you're wrong and be the hero of your love story."

"Jenn." She paused to rub the beginnings of a headache in her temple. "Look. I can't deny I'm in love with Deana because I still am. But that doesn't mean we should try to repeat the past. I'm so grateful for the chance to have her back in my life as a friend, like I am with you and Mags. Our lives are so much different than they used to be, and frankly, so are we."

Jenn studied her with an almost pitying gaze. "You're not even gonna try?"

Before Cassie answered, she thought briefly about the night she and Deana had the perfect chance to take their relationship to the next level, but Deana ran out of her house in the split second she was given to reconsider.

Cassie shook her head and forced a smile. "It's working out for both of us this way."

"Okay," Jenn said. "I won't badger you about it anymore."

"Thank you," she replied and bumped her in the shoulder.

"Wait till she's elected governor. Then make your move." Jenn cackled and skipped off, waving her pamphlets back at Cassie.

CHAPTER TWENTY-FOUR

Several hours after the polls closed on Election Day, the cacophony of excited voices in Deana's campaign headquarters fell to a steady buzz once Cassie turned up the volume on the TV. The local news was running a ticker tape of preliminary precinct reports at the bottom of the screen as field reporters stationed at various candidates' headquarters gave live reports.

Cassie watched from the sidelines as Deana participated in a live TV interview.

"How does it feel to know you've maintained a steady lead over your incumbent opponent since the returns started coming in?"

"Part of me can't believe any of this is happening, let alone that I'm in the lead." She came across as so sweet and humble. "The other part of me, the eternal optimist, can't wait to get to the capitol and start to work making life better for Connecticut residents."

"If you're elected, what will your first order of business be?"

"To serve on the Human Services Committee. I want to emphasize my commitment to advocacy and social justice for women and children and victims of domestic violence."

"You're a survivor of domestic violence yourself."

Deana seemed to stand taller at the statement. "Yes. I am. And that's why I've dedicated my career to helping other women and children who may not have the resources that were available to me at the time. Survival and recovery must never be luxuries afforded to only some."

Deana hadn't even officially won yet, but Cassie swooned at the charisma, sincerity, and confidence she'd exuded throughout the interview.

"Thank you and good luck," the reporter said. "Kiesha, Gerry, back to you."

After Deana thanked the reporter, she beelined it right for Cassie, seeming propelled by an unseen force. "Thank God that's over."

When she pretended to collapse into her arms, Cassie took full advantage and hung onto her longer than necessary. "You were stellar. Seasoned politicians only wish they had the finesse you have."

"I'll let you in on a secret. I'm faking it."

They shared an easy, light-hearted moment that seemed to culminate the essence of their months of working together toward this one significant goal.

"You better not be faking anything." Cassie glanced up at the TV. "You're four percentage points ahead. That covers the margin of error."

Deana exhaled. "That means I'm winning."

Cassie nodded slowly as she allowed a cautious smile to spread across her face. They stared into each other's eyes as though they were ready to conquer the world together.

"Mom," Sean called out. He and Nicole came into the headquarters, each carrying a twin in its carrier.

Cassie wandered off so Deana could have some family time as they waited for the all-but-inevitable conclusion to become official. She opened a bottle of water and chugged it as a small wave of letdown washed over her.

While she'd done consulting for political candidates before, she'd never actually worked so closely with one from start to finish. The challenge of shaping, packaging, and implementing the Deana Warner political brand had been the most exhilarating experience of her career. As were these final moments counting down to victory.

She glanced over at Deana holding her grandson as she chatted with her family. Her dazzling smile was impossible to ignore. So she didn't. She just stared and stared and stared...

Until Deana turned toward her and waved her over to them.

As she approached them and Deana's gaze lingered on hers, she realized she was going to miss more than the thrill of campaign life.

Sean gave Cassie another hug. "We're heading out now to put these guys to bed." He sort of herded her off to the side with his baby carrier. "I just wanted to thank you for all this."

Cassie was surprised. "I was merely the consultant. She did everything."

"I mean for your friendship and support while she was campaigning. I've never seen her happier or more vibrant. The transformation is incredible. She has to win. This is what she was meant to do."

She consulted the TV again. "We've already heard from the three smaller towns. It's just a matter of waiting for Madison's polling places to call in their official results."

He smiled. "State Senator Deana Warner. Goddamn, I like the sound of that."

"Me, too," Cassie said as she brushed his arm. "You both have so much to be proud of each other for."

"Deana, Cassie," Helena shouted, holding up a phone. "It's Madison's last polling location."

Practically the entire room followed Deana to the desk to take the call, no one uttering so much as a murmur.

"This is Deana Warner." As she listened, her eyes grew as bright and as wild as a forest fire. "Yes. Yes, thank you so much." She ended the call and blurted, "I won!"

The entire room erupted into cheers and applause, with Cassie yelling the loudest. After hugging and kissing her family, Deana wheeled around and pulled Cassie in for a long hug and a fast kiss that landed full on her lips.

She licked and blotted the smear of gloss Deana left on her before she began whirling through the room hugging everyone else.

Everyone's eyes were riveted on Deana at that moment. Everyone's except Helena's.

❖

By elevenish the party was over, and only a couple of local college students and Helena remained to help clean up and straighten out Deana's campaign headquarters. The fact that Helena was still more focused on Cassie than anything else throughout all the magnificent chaos that night wasn't lost on Deana. She wasn't fooling anyone out there till the very end, sidling up next to Cassie…her intentions were obvious. How tacky.

Cassie, on the other hand, was much harder to read. Was she into Helena as well, or was that just her public relations talent on full display?

"I think we're all set here," Deana said. "Thank you again for your hard work. You must be exhausted. Head home and get some sleep."

She gave the students quick mom hugs, thanked them again for their dedicated volunteerism, and then extended her hand to Helena.

"Are you sure you don't need help?" Helena said with a counterfeit smile. "You deserve to go home and savor your victory. I can help Cassie. I'm off tomorrow, so I don't mind staying late."

The fuck you will. She glanced in Cassie's direction. After closing a trash bag full of recyclables, Cassie began folding up chairs. Deana put her arm around Helena and moved her toward the exit as she spoke. "I wouldn't hear of it, Helena. You've done so much for us already. Cassie and I have it from here."

"Well, if you're su—"

"I'm positive. Good night."

Once Helena was out the door, Deana helped Cassie fold the remaining chairs.

"Did Helena leave?" Cassie asked.

"Yes. She had to run," Deana lied and began stacking the folding chairs on a cart. "Are you upset she didn't say good-bye?"

Cassie cocked an eyebrow. "No."

Deana sucked at her teeth. She was hoping to get more out of Cassie than just a "no." "I can tell she's into you. Now that the campaign's over, you can go out with her."

"So can you."

"Me?" Deana chuckled. "That makes no sense. Besides, I'm picky. I have a thing only for blondes."

"I'm sure she'd change her hair color for you." Cassie made a face and went for the last group of chairs in the far corner of the room.

Deana sighed with relief. It was pretty clear Cassie wasn't into Helena, but her curiously timed aloofness was throwing her. Was Cassie planning to be done with her now that the election was over? She couldn't imagine that their closeness during the campaign was all part of the Cassie experience she'd paid for. Her heart began to race as Cassie had just about finished with the last of the chairs. What if they left here tonight and never spoke again? What if that was what Cassie assumed she'd wanted?

She swallowed against the sick feeling brewing in her stomach and slowly approached her with no clue about what she was going to say. "Can I talk to you a minute?"

Cassie stopped folding and looked at her.

"This night's been so surreal, hasn't it? I still can't believe I won."

"I can," she replied. "You ran an impeccable campaign."

"I never could've without you. This win is for both of us."

"You did most of the work leading up to this point. And now you'll have to do it all yourself."

"I'm ready for it," Deana said.

Cassie smiled as she seemed to wonder what to do with her hands. She settled on shoving them in her pockets. "You must be exhausted. Why don't you head home, and I'll finish the rest of this crap tomorrow?" She moved toward the small collection of trash.

"No. Not yet." Deana rubbed her hands together as her nerves kicked in. "I uh, I still have more to say."

Cassie made a goofy face. "Jeez. How many different ways can you find to thank me?"

"It's not about that." After a night of nonstop talking, she struggled for a transition into expressing what had stirred in her for months.

"What is it?"

She took a deep breath. "Look. I know you think that when I moved out of state, I'd forgotten about you. That I'd run away from you. I get that. I understand about optics. But I want you to know something." She grasped Cassie by both hands and pulled her closer. "I want you to know the truth. That not long after I'd left, I made a promise to myself that I held onto throughout the years."

"Which is…"

"I promised myself that if I ever had the good fortune to cross paths with you again, this time, I'd never let you get away."

Cassie's mouth hung open.

"If you feel it's too late for us or that you can't see me as anything more than a friend, I'll understand. And I'll be happy just being your friend. But I couldn't let you walk out the door one more time without telling you how I've felt, how I feel about you right this minute."

Deana sighed in frustration as Cassie seemed to have gone mute. "Can you please just say something? Say no, forget it, piss off, anything, so I don't have to hear the sound of my own awful voice begging for—"

Cassie grabbed her around the waist, pulled her in tight, and planted a firm kiss on her mouth that stopped time. When they finally came up for air, they gaped at each other, somewhat dazed, both of them seeming to connect the tattered puzzle pieces of their past.

Deana threw her arms around Cassie's neck, and they kissed again, passionately. She then pressed her forehead against Cassie's and whispered, "I don't want this night to end."

"You want to go out and celebrate?"

She shook her head. "I want to go home, and I want you to come with me."

❖

Cassie followed Deana inside and waited as she keyed in the alarm code. After she finished, Deana wrapped her arms around Cassie and kissed her in a slow, sensual rhythm. Cassie ran her hands down Deana's sides and over her hips, eliciting a slight moan.

Deana wasted no time on ceremony or seduction, grabbing Cassie's hand and hurrying her down the hall to her bedroom.

She'd fantasized about this for years, the chance to make love with Deana once more but in a bed, in private, with no commitments to others and an endless flow of time. She stared into Deana's eyes, full of want, as she slipped her suit jacket off her shoulders and kissed each of them.

Deana groaned. "You have no idea how badly I want you."

Cassie ran her lips around her neck as she unzipped her dress pants. "If it's half as bad as I want you, we have a long night ahead of us." She gently laid Deana on the bed and paused to consume the sight of her lying there in matching seafoam-colored bra and bikini underwear.

"Come here, baby," Deana whispered as she extended her arms.

Cassie stripped herself down to her undergarments, lay on top of Deana, and kissed her with a rush of desire that had been locked away for decades.

After a moment of writhing beneath her, Deana flipped her over and straddled her, pinning her arms above her head. She leaned over her and brushed her lips across Cassie's, whispering, "This night has to be a dream."

"Whatever it is, I don't want it to end," Cassie said.

Deana flicked off their bras and pulled off their undies and flung them all across the room. She grabbed Cassie's hands and placed them on her breasts as she began to grind on Cassie's hip bone.

"I can't stand this ache anymore." She took one of Cassie's hands and slid it into her wetness.

Cassie was almost ready to climax just from touching her. She nudged Deana onto her back and began the slow descent. Starting at her collarbone, she kissed her chest, tantalized her nipples, and then directed her tongue leisurely down her belly. When she finally tasted Deana, she wanted to devour every inch of her.

Deana's cries of pleasure grew louder. She grabbed hold of Cassie's hands and unleashed a powerful orgasm, bucking her hips up and down. She then pulled Cassie up next to her on the pillow and molded her body in hers.

Cassie looked down when she felt tears wetting her cheeks. "Are you okay, baby?"

She began to laugh as she wiped her eyes. "I can't believe I'm sixty-two years old, and this is the first time I've ever truly felt like I'm making love."

Cassie started tearing up, too. "I know what you mean. This night has been more amazing than I'd ever imagined it could be."

"I don't want this to be the end, Cass. I want it to be just the beginning."

"Me, too." She caressed her cheek and then kissed her.

Deana propped herself up on her elbow. "Really? Is this what you truly want?"

"I haven't wanted anything else since I fell in love with you over twenty years ago."

She traced Cassie's bottom lip with her thumb. "What a long time to have to be patient."

"I didn't have a choice. No woman ever came close to you. And I gave a lot of them a chance. Trust me."

Deana giggled. "I believe you did. I feel sorry for all the ones who lost out on you."

"No, you don't." She pulled Deana's hand toward her and kissed her fingertips.

"No. I don't." Deana became animated as she rolled on top of her. "Fuck those women. You're mine now."

Cassie gazed up at Deana's eyes as the moon peered through the parted curtains. "Promise?"

"I'd swear it in blood."

"Impossible. We're both in menopause."

Deana chuckled. "Thank the goddesses."

She brushed Deana's hair behind her ears as they again shared a moment quietly adoring each other. She then kissed her tenderly. "I'll thank them for every second I get to spend with you from here on out."

"You know that this time I'm not letting you go," Deana said as she gently dragged her fingertips across Cassie's collarbone and chest. "You better run now while you can."

"I can't run anywhere with you on top of me," she replied in a playfully strained voice.

Deana buried her face in her neck as she giggled. "That was my plan all along tonight."

Cassie held her chin and kissed her again, her desire for her still not satiated. "Are you sure you want a girlfriend now that you're going to be Connecticut's newest, hottest state senator? You can have your pick."

"I've already made my pick." Deana kissed her forehead.

Cassie gushed at the confidence and commitment in her voice. This was the woman she'd waited an entire lifetime for, and she knew she'd finally found her from the safety she felt lying in her arms. "We're going to do this right this time."

"And nothing's getting in our way."

They made love again until the dawn crept through the curtains, and they fell asleep entwined in each other.

CHAPTER TWENTY-FIVE

One year later

Cassie lay on her stomach, sprawled across the bed in their suite overlooking the breathtaking Elia beach. But for her the real view was watching Deana apply the finishing touches on her makeup. She never understood how such a flawless beauty could be so self-conscious about going anywhere without a full face of makeup. However, tonight, they weren't going just anywhere.

Deana turned from the mirror, playfully suspicious. "What are you staring at?"

"Only the most beautiful woman on the planet." She wasn't kidding. Deana was stunning as she stood there in her bra and underwear, brown shoulder-length hair freshly styled at the resort salon, her face photo-shoot ready.

Deana batted her freshly mascaraed lashes. "Don't you think you should start getting dressed?"

"But I'm so enjoying watching you."

"Babe, we have to leave soon."

"I'm showered. I just have to put on my outfit. That'll take two minutes."

"Oh, right," Deana said, pretending to be envious. "No primping needed for you with your bronze island tan and surfer-girl hair."

Cassie got up and swept Deana into her arms. She looked to the mirror at her left at the image of their naked stomachs pressed against each other. "Do you have any idea how often I've dreamed of this over the years? And how many times I woke in the darkness to the fear that it would never happen?"

Deana cupped her face in her hands and kissed her softly, sensually. "Probably about as often as I have. But I'll tell you one thing: This time I'm never, ever letting you go."

"Ditto," Cassie said. "You'll need a restraining order if you try."

Deana chuckled and playfully pushed her away. "If you don't get dressed right now, you're gonna need one."

"So what you're saying is a quickie's out of the question?"

A naughty smile crept across Deana's face as she took a second to contemplate the suggestion. "Can you manage not to wreck my hair?"

Cassie grinned and backed her against the nearest wall.

Later, as they strolled along the planked walkway from their suite to the beach, they admired the fiery sun lowering itself in the crystal sky. As the turquoise tide rolled into shore, Cassie appreciated this moment of pure paradise. This was what the poets wrote about, what it felt like to crawl inside a Mykonos vacation brochure and delete the existence of reality for a while.

And the absolute best part was walking beside her.

Deana clearly noticed Cassie obsessively staring again. "Are you sure the girls weren't mad about postponing your big birthday trip and having me tag along?"

"Are you kidding? Besides, it wasn't anyone's fault the plans had to change. After everything that's gone on in the past year, the fact that this trip happened at all is nothing short of a miracle."

"True. Still, I feel bad because the three of you planned your fiftieth birthday vacation for so long, and it's turned out to be so not what you planned."

"Sometimes the things you don't plan turn out to be the best experiences of your life."

Deana stopped in front of Cassie and grasped her hands. "I spent so many years of my life wishing things were different, living in a world that I'd had so little agency in. But when I met you, everything changed. And to have this second chance with you?" She glanced around as if needing to remind herself it was real. "I love how my life feels now. I am so empowered to achieve any goal I set for myself and completely content to do nothing but experience sunsets with you forever."

"Oh, babe." Cassie's heart was about to burst from Deana's words and the abundance of love emanating from her. "You're gonna make me start bawling."

"So?" Deana said as she playfully smacked her. "You're not even wearing mascara on those long-ass eyelashes of yours."

Their tender kiss turned passionate as an island breeze blew through Cassie's already wild, sun-bleached hair.

"Speaking of sunsets," Cassie said. "They're waiting."

Maggie and Marybeth were waving them over. After kicking off their sandals, they clasped hands and stepped onto the cool, powdery sand headed toward their gathering near the shore. As they were about to walk into each of their embraces, Jenn, wearing a tuxedo T-shirt and hibiscus board shorts, burst through Maggie and Marybeth, then literally jumped into Cassie's arms.

Amid the laughter, Marybeth tugged at Jenn's T-shirt sleeve. "You're gonna destroy her outfit. Linen wrinkles so damn easily."

"Fine," Jenn said. She jumped down and grabbed Deana in an equally enthusiastic hug.

"Excuse me." An islander with a big camera, bigger boobs, and an enchanting Greek accent stepped in. "We should get going if you want the best sunset lighting in your photos."

The group suddenly dispersed. Jenn scurried on the other side of an archway festooned with colorful peonies, sage, and other greens native to the island.

Holding hands, Maggie and Marybeth stepped to the left side of the archway while Cassie and Deana stepped to the right.

Looking solemn, Jenn took a deep breath and pulled her phone from her shorts pocket. Surprising everyone, she comically flicked down her aviator sunglasses and checked herself in them, picking at her lustrous head of spiky, dyed-black hair.

"Jenn," Cassie said through the laughter. She tapped at an imaginary wristwatch. "The sunset."

"Oh, gotcha." She assumed a professional posture as she cradled her phone in her hands like a prayer book. "Dearly beloved, we are gathered here tonight in this gay-friendly tropical Greek paradise to celebrate, among other things, the love of two thoroughly awesome, extraordinary couples, Cassie and Deana, and Maggie and Marybeth."

Cassie smiled at Deana and leaned forward to glance at Maggie.

"And by the grace of the gods and goddesses of the Pantheon, and an online ordination certificate, I have the honor and privilege of officiating the ceremony that will make these wondrous couples spouses for life."

As Cassie led a round of raucous applause in honor of Jenn's excellent health, Jenn fist-bumped over her heart twice, then shot a peace sign up to the heavens. She paused to give each of her friends a poignant glance before resuming an official tone and demeanor.

"May I have the couples face each other."

Cassie opened her hands, and Deana placed hers on top.

"Cassie...Maggie, repeat after me: 'I, state your name, take you, partner's name, to be my lawfully wedded wife...'"

They repeated in unison: "I, state your name, take you, partner's name, to be my lawfully wedded wife."

Jenn shook her head and joined the giggling at their gag before continuing. "To love, honor, and comfort you in sickness and in health..."

This time, their responses were sincere.

"From this day forward as long as we both shall live."

"Cassie and Maggie, please take out your rings."

Cassie pulled the diamond-chipped platinum band from her pocket.

"Just as a ring is an unbroken circle with ends joined together, so may it represent the joining of your lives, the infinity of your love, and the strength of your commitment to each other. May it always remind you of the love you feel for each other at this moment."

Cassie gazed at Deana in her white spaghetti-strap sundress standing barefoot before her and couldn't imagine her heart being able to hold any more love for her than it did right then.

Jenn continued. "Cassie and Maggie, please place the ring on your partner's finger and repeat after me: 'With this ring, I pledge my love and loyalty to you forever.'"

She repeated the words slowly, drifting off into Deana's loving eyes. She wanted to savor every precious second of marrying the love of her life after they'd had to overcome so much to get here.

When it was Deana's and Marybeth's turn to say their vows and place rings on fingers, Deana's sweet voice quavered with emotion.

"Cassie, this is one of three happiest moments of my life." She glanced down at both of their fingers with their matching bands. "I'm so lucky to have you as my wife, lover, and my best friend. I know that no matter where life takes us from here, I'll be traveling the road with you by my side."

"Now," Jenn said. "Those whom Hera has joined together, let no mortal tear asunder. Cassie and Deana...Maggie and Marybeth, you have given and pledged your faith and undying love to each other in the names of the mighty goddesses and confirmed your pledges with the giving of the rings. So by the power vested in me and Dionysus, god of wine, I now pronounce you wives for life. You may kiss your mutha-fuckin' brides."

The small crowd of resort guests that had stopped to watch the ceremony cheered, whistled, and clapped for them.

Cassie swept Deana into her arms with a flourish and kissed her tenderly. The kiss released a burst of tears from Deana, and she laughed, wiping them away before pulling Cassie in for another.

❖

Their last night on the island, the two newly married couples and Jenn gathered around a fire on the beach for drinks and the best baklava Cassie would ever experience in her lifetime. Actually, ten days in Greece after marrying the love of her life in a double wedding with one best friend, and with her other best friend as officiant, she couldn't imagine anything ever topping it—baklava notwithstanding.

Until she felt Deana's hand gently caress her back. That touch brought on a warm tingle of realization that, with Deana as her wife, the best was yet to come.

She kissed Deana, then frowned. "I can't believe it's already the last night of our honeymoon."

Deana tugged at Cassie's chin. "It's the last night of our trip. Our honeymoon will last as long as we want it to."

Marybeth covered her mouth as though holding back emotion. "Look at all of us, just a bunch of happily married ladies. I'm going to miss you all so much once we're back in the real world."

"What do you mean?" Deana said. "We're still going to see each other. How about we all have dinner next weekend?"

Cassie became distracted from the conversation as the gorgeous, young wedding photographer came into view. She leaned into Jenn. "Hey, did we hire that hottie photographer again for a final night shoot?"

"Demitria," Jenn said as she stood. She opened her arms, and the photographer walked into them and kissed her on the lips. "Everyone, you all remember Demi from the ceremony."

The young woman whipped back her dark hair and waved with a sweet smile before sitting next to Jenn, practically in her lap.

"So, uh, yeah." Cassie tried to reorient herself into the conversation. "How about dinner next weekend? Since we still have some unfinished business, ladies." She looked directly at Maggie and Jenn.

"Ah, yes," Maggie said. "Rescheduling our postponed fiftieth-birthday getaway. I'm still voting for a cottage in P-town."

"I don't know about that," Cassie said. "We need to sit down next weekend and figure it out. I say we just throw our suggestions in a hat."

"Um, I'm going to need to have a proxy vote," Jenn said as Demitria slipped her hand in between hers.

"What does that mean?" Cassie asked.

"It's when you can't make it to a vote, so you appoint someone else to represent you."

Cassie snapped. "I know what a proxy is. I meant why will you need one?"

"I won't be back in the States by then." She looked at Demitria, who returned a googly-eyed smile. "I'll be here. For a while."

Deana beamed. "That's wonderful, Jenn. Carpe diem."

"Exactly, my friend," Jenn replied and extended a fist for her to bump.

Without a word, Cassie got up and walked off toward the restroom. She should've been the first one to say congratulations to Jenn, but the sudden announcement left her feeling waylaid.

"Hey," Jenn said as she rounded the corner.

"Hey," Cassie replied. She was leaning against the wall, one foot pressing against it, as she gazed out at the path of light the moon made out on the water.

Jenn assumed the same posture next to her. "Was it something I said, or did you just need to take a leak at that precise moment?"

"I know, I know. I'm a big baby. You don't have to say it."

"I wasn't going to say that, but since you brought it up…" She playfully elbowed Cassie in the arm.

"Why? Why couldn't you have fallen for someone in Connecticut? Why did you have to pick another continent to meet your next true love?"

"I don't know that she's my next true love. I just know it's worth exploring. Especially while I'm here working."

"Working?"

Jenn nodded. "I'm not staying here because of Demitria. Some Greek tycoon I met at the infinity pool the other day commissioned me for a mural in her manse. Isn't that wild?"

"Very. So what if you fall head over heels for Demitria while you're here working?"

"I don't know. Would you miss me if I didn't come back?"

"Of course, you asshole. You practically died again but didn't. Maggie and I have had the best possible thing in the world happen for us, and now you won't even be around to share our lives and grow old together."

As Jenn stood there smirking, Cassie tried to puzzle out what was funny about any of that.

"Good thing, then," Jenn finally said.

"What is?"

"That Demitria's visit with her family is only for another month. She has to get back to her restaurant in New York City."

Cassie's relief released itself through laughter. "Funny, Jenn. Very funny. You let me think you're moving to Greece and that I'd never see you again. Great fucking gag."

"You're so easy," Jenn said with a few gentle slaps on her cheek. "You totally set yourself up."

As Cassie playfully swatted her hand away, Maggie and Deana came around the corner.

"There you are," Deana said.

"We thought organ traffickers got ahold of you," Maggie said.

Deana placed a patient hand on Maggie's shoulder. "No, we didn't. We just wanted to make sure everything was okay between you two."

Cassie pulled them all into a hug. "Everything is the best it's ever been."

"Then what are we waiting for?" Deana asked. "Let's get back to the party."

About the Author

Jean Copeland is a Goldie-winning lesfic author from Connecticut. While romance is the element that binds all of her lesbian fiction, she enjoys experimenting in various genres. She has published nine novels with Bold Strokes Books as well as several blogs and personal essays in various publications. Jean also enjoys pickleball, murder shows, and a self-care regimen of visiting local breweries and wineries with dear friends.

Books Available From Bold Strokes Books

The Accidental Bride by Jane Walsh. Spinsters Miss Grace Linfield and Miss Thea Martin travel to Gretna Green to prevent a wedding, only to discover a scandalous passion— for each other. (978-1-63679-345-0)

Broken Fences by Jo Hemmingwood. Former army sergeant Seneca Twist has difficulty adjusting to civilian life until she meets psychologist Robyn Mason and has a place to call home. (978-1-63679-414-3)

Never Kiss a Cowgirl by Ali Vali. Asher Evans dreams of winning the National Finals Rodeo in Vegas, and Reagan Wilson wants no part of something that brings back the memory of what killed her father. (978-1-63679-106-7)

Pantheon Girls by Jean Copeland. Cassie Burke never anticipated the detour life is about to take when a meeting with a prospective client reunites her with a past love and reignites the star-crossed passion they shared twenty years earlier. (978-1-63679-337-5)

Roux for Two by Aurora Rey. For TV chef Chelsea Boudreaux and hometown boy Bryce Cormier, love proves as tricky as making a good pot of gumbo. (978-1-63679-376-4)

Starting Over by Nance Sparks. Jennifer has no idea if she can mend Sam's broken soul after the sudden loss of her wife, but it's never too late for starting over. (978-1-63679-409-9)

Three Wishes by Anne Shade. A magic lamp, a beautiful Jinni, and a cursed princess make for one unbelievable story. (978-1-63679-349-8)

Undiscovered Treasures by MJ Williamz. For Cyl and her friends Luna and Martinique, life's best treasures often appear when they're not looking. (978-1-63679-449-5)

Curse of the Gorgon by Tanai Walker. Cass will do anything to ensure Elle's safety, but is she willing to embrace the curse of the Gorgon? (978-1-63679-395-5)

Dance with Me by Georgia Beers. Scottie Templeton mixes it up on and off the dance floor with sexy salsa instructor Marisa Reyes. But can Scottie get past Marisa's connection to her ex? (978-1-63679-359-7)

Gin and Bear It by Joy Argento. Opposites really can attract, and as Kelly and Logan work together to create a loving home for rescue cat Bear, they just might find one for themselves as well. (978-1-63679-351-1)

Harvest Dreams by Jacqueline Fein-Zachary. Planting the vineyard of their dreams, Kate Bauer and Sydney Barrett must resist their attraction while battling nature and their families, who oppose both the venture and their relationship. (978-1-63679-380-1)

The No Kiss Contract by Nan Campbell. Workaholic Davy believes she can get the top spot at her firm if the senior partners think she's settling down and about to start a family, but she needs the delightful yet dubious Anna to help by pretending to be her fiancée. (978-1-63679-372-6)

Outside the Lines by Melissa Sky. If you had the chance to live forever, would you take it? Amara Rodriguez did, and it sets her on a journey to find her missing mother and unravel the mystery of her own heart. (978-1-63679-403-7)

The Value of Sylver and Gold by Michelle Larkin. When word gets out that former Boston homicide detective Reid Sylver can talk to the dead, the FBI solicits her help on a serial murder case, prompting Reid to assemble forces once again with Detective London Gold. (978-1-63679-093-0)

When It Feels Right by Tagan Shepard. Freshly out of the closet Marlene hasn't been lucky in love, but when it comes to her quirky new roommate Abby, everything just feels right. (978-1-63679-367-2)

The Fall Line by Kelly Wacker. When Jordan Burroughs arrives in the Deep South to paint a local endangered aquatic flower, she doesn't expect to become friends with a mischievous gin-drinking ghost who complicates her budding romance and leads her to an awful discovery and danger. (978-1-63679-205-7)

Lucky in Lace by Melissa Brayden. Straitlaced stationery store owner Juliette Jennings's predictable life unravels when a sexy lingerie shop and its alluring owner move in next door. (978-1-63679-434-1)

Made for Her by Carsen Taite. Neal Walsh is a newly made member of the Mancuso crime family, but will her undeniable attraction to Anastasia Petrov, the wife of her boss's sworn enemy, be the ultimate test of her loyalty? (978-1-63679-265-1)

Off the Menu by Alaina Erdell. Reality TV sensation Restaurant Redo and its gorgeous host Erin Rasmussen will arrive to film in chef Taylor Mobley's kitchen. As the cameras roll, will they make the jump from enemies to lovers? (978-1-63679-295-8)

Pack of Her Own by Elena Abbott. When things heat up in a small town, steamy secrets are revealed between Alpha werewolf Wren Carne and her human mate, Natalie Donovan. (978-1-63679-370-2)

Return to McCall by Patricia Evans. Lily isn't looking for romance— not until she meets Alex, the gorgeous Cuban dance instructor at La Haven, a newly opened lesbian retreat. (978-1-63679-386-3)

So It Went Like This by C. Spencer. A candid and deeply personal exploration of fate, chosen family, and the vulnerability intrinsic in life's uncertainties. (978-1-63555-971-2)

Stolen Kiss by Spencer Greene. Anna and Louise share a stolen kiss, only to discover that Louise is dating Anna's brother. Surely, one kiss can't change everything…Can it? (978-1-63679-364-1)

To Meet Again by Kadyan. When the stark reality of WW II separates cabaret singer Evelyn and Australian doctor Joan in Singapore, they must overcome all odds to find one another again. (978-1-63679-398-6)